CHARMED AND DANGEROUS

A WITCH IN WOLF WOOD, BOOK 5

LINDSAY BUROKER

ACKNOWLEDGMENTS

Thank you to my editor, Shelley Holloway, and my beta readers, Cindy Wilkinson and Sarah Engelke. A shout out to Vivienne Leheny for narrating the audiobooks and Jesh Art Studio for the cover design.

Also, many thanks to you, my werewolf-loving reader, for following along with the books. I hope you enjoy the new adventure!

1

"IT'S A LITTLE DRAFTY." AS MORGEN KELLER LOOKED AROUND THE main room in what had been a tannery in the late 1800s and early 1900s, her vegetarian mind tried not to think about the building's shady past. "And not in the core tourist area."

Morgen waved toward a large dirty window with broken panes that faced Main Street. She would have to press her cheek to the grimy glass to see the Roaming Elk Inn, with its Go-Kart track and putt-putt course, which marked the north end of downtown. Even then, with rain pounding the pavement and the cracked sidewalk out front, she might have struggled to glimpse it.

"Your business is making and selling flea-and-tick charms and cat trees for witches' familiars," Phoebe, her mentor and self-appointed commercial-real-estate advisor, said. "You don't need to be in the core tourist area. The people who want such things will know how to find you."

"If not via the internet, then through a Ouija board, I suppose."

"You're thinking of ghost hunters. Witches get information from books."

"I knew there was a reason you were my people." Morgen tapped the e-reader sticking out of her purse.

"Flattery won't get you more than a ten percent discount at the Crystal Palace, I'm afraid," Phoebe said, naming her own business. *Her* shop had a prime location in town.

"Even if I bulk order?" Morgen had never thought she'd be the type to shop in a store full of geodes, crystal points, and stones sorted by how they affected one's chakras, but that had been before she'd started making magical charms, some of which required gems and rare stones.

"I have to make a profit."

"Uh huh. Anyway, *normal* pets can enjoy my charms and Amar's furniture too," Morgen said. "Their owners just won't know there's legitimate magic about them."

"The tannery had quite the stench back when it was used for that purpose." Martha, a mid-fifties coven member who was here today in a real-estate-agent capacity, spread her arms and smiled. "The denizens of Bellrock insisted it be placed away from the market and meeting hall, but today, it's vacant and available for your needs. And the rent is *very* inexpensive."

"For a reason," Phoebe muttered.

"Because nobody wants to take on the task of cleaning it up?" Morgen wrinkled her nose and sneezed three times. Dust floated around the interior of the cavernous brick building like a haboob in the Arizona desert.

"Because it's cursed and possibly haunted." Phoebe pointed toward a loft filled with old tanning vats and furniture cowering under drop cloths. The broken railing and rickety stairs leading up to it would give a building-code inspector a heart attack. Many things about the place would. "Funny that you mentioned Ouija boards, because there's supposed to be a ghost that lurks up there, pushing things to the floor."

Morgen started to scoff, but Phoebe lowered her finger to point out numerous dark stains on the wide pine floorboards. The poor lighting made it hard to tell what *kinds* of stains they were. Perhaps that was a blessing.

She lifted her gaze toward the ceiling. A handful of bare light bulbs dangled on long chains from the rafters, linked by exposed electrical wiring that appeared to be stapled to the beams. They weren't on, and she wondered if they were burned out or if Martha had deemed it too much of a fire hazard to flip the switch.

"Are those meat hooks?" Morgen asked, her gaze snagging on at least a dozen rusty hooks hanging from an equally rusty metal bar running vertically along one of the beams. Her stomach twisted with queasiness. She was fairly certain it would have objected to this place even if she *hadn't* been a vegetarian. "I thought this was a tannery, not a slaughterhouse."

"Maybe they were added later," Phoebe said. "As decor."

"Sure. Nothing says *Welcome to my shop* like giant hooks capable of impaling a rhinoceros." Morgen looked at Martha. "Are there any other spaces available for our business?"

"In your price range?" Martha asked. "No. But look at all that room under the loft. Your hulking werewolf partner could get some real woodworking equipment, like a table saw and a planer. Then he wouldn't be limited by what he can craft with his chainsaw."

Tools to add dust to the air. Great.

"He does good work with his chainsaw. And he's not *hulking*. He's muscular and fit." Morgen always felt protective toward Amar, especially when the witches took digs at him.

As a six-and-a-half-foot-tall werewolf, Amar didn't *need* a protector, but he had feelings, the same as everyone else, and the way he growled when people spoke poorly of him or his work made Morgen want to stand up for him. He was a talented wood-worker. An artist.

"Of course," Martha murmured. "Do you want to see the back

room? There are some counters and built-in cabinets with plenty of storage. I thought it might work for your crafting space."

Morgen wasn't sure she could imagine creating jewelry—technically, magic-infused amulets, talismans, and charms—in an old tannery. Though Grandma's root cellar with the pentagram painted on the packed dirt floor wasn't exactly a Bohemian artist's loft in Manhattan's Upper East Side, it didn't have a spiritual reek of animal death.

More dust crept up Morgen's nose, prompting several additional sneezes. Spiritual reeks weren't the only ones of concern. At least the place no longer smelled of animal hides, lye, and whatever else had been used in the industry. As a former database programmer and current app developer and jeweler, Morgen hadn't spent a lot of time researching it and didn't plan to.

At least Amar wouldn't object to the building, not when he turned into a wolf and hunted prey numerous times a week. Suspicious stains and meat hooks wouldn't faze him. He might even approve of the decor.

"Come, come." Martha waved for them to follow her toward the promised crafting room.

The old floorboards creaked as they walked, and damp air swept in through the broken panes. Morgen counted how many windows they would have to replace in order to make this place serviceable for customers. It might not turn out to be quite the bargain that Martha kept promising.

When they stepped into the back room and turned on a light, a rat or something else dark and furry scurried under a counter.

"Look, a customer." Phoebe smirked and pointed.

"As a fellow entrepreneur," Morgen said, "you should have more sympathy for my predicament."

"Why don't you just sell online? You helped me get the Crystal Parlor into the twenty-first century, and more than half my business is coming through the website now."

"I know, and I'm sure we'll set something up, but if customers can't feel the power of my charms and trinkets, they might not realize what they're worth. Your goods are lovely, but they're not truly magical."

"Some of the powders in the back room are, but it's true that witches looking for potion and crafting ingredients already know the properties of the various herbs and essences. You'll have to establish a reputation before strangers in other states and countries believe they can order your charms and get something genuinely effective."

"Yeah," Morgen said glumly, then frowned at a dusty corner. "Is that the chalk outline of a body on the floor?"

"Ah." Martha pursed her lips as she studied it. "I believe it's another decoration. The last tenant was an artist and rather whimsical from what I remember."

"Are you sure?" Morgen couldn't take her gaze from the outline —or the dark stain in the middle of it. The dark *blood*stain? "That looks like a crime scene."

"I'm sure it's just art. There hasn't been a crime here in decades."

How reassuring.

"And the authorities no longer use chalk outlines." Martha chuckled, though she sounded uneasy. "You can ask Deputy Franklin."

"Oh sure. He loves when I call him."

"Here you go. Lots of counter space." Martha turned her back to the outline and patted a paint-stained wooden counter, though she jerked her hand back when she realized it had come down close to a mouse trap. At least it didn't have an occupant. "There are the built-in cabinets I mentioned, and that doorway leads to the bathroom. I guess you'll have to put a new door on it if you're concerned about privacy."

"I hear customers like it." Against her better judgment, Morgen peered through the doorway. She'd seen outhouses with more modern features.

Sighing, Morgen wondered if she could talk the Lobo pack into helping her clean and remodel this place. She'd already made Talismans of Imperviousness for them, magical jewelry that protected them from werewolf-control spells, but maybe they could use something else? Did werewolves also suffer from fleas and ticks in the summer?

"It looks like some of the previous tenants left tools behind." Martha pointed at pegboards on the wall to either side of the bathroom entrance. "Maybe some would be useful in your work."

Since she'd mentioned an artist, Morgen expected paint brushes, but all manner of axes and fleshing knives hung from the board, collecting dust.

"Those are included, you say?" Phoebe asked. "That's a handy bonus."

"Yes," Morgen said. "I can't tell you how often I've been making jewelry and thought if only I had a good fleshing knife."

"Perhaps your woodworking werewolf can use them," Phoebe offered.

Morgen's doubts about the place increased with every passing minute. It might be better to simply use the barn back at the house, but as an introvert, she hated the idea of having customers driving up to her home to browse the goods or pick up pet furniture. And her sister Sian—an even more hardcore introvert—might never come to visit if she risked running into strangers. Besides, as Martha had pointed out, there *was* a lot more room here. Maybe Amar would like some professional woodworking tools.

Though she doubted she wanted to see whatever had been left in the cabinets, eight-foot-high metal double doors drew her eye. It looked more like the entrance to a swimming pool's mechanical room than a storage locker.

Bracing herself, she tugged open the doors. Whatever she'd expected, a giant metal statue wasn't it. The hulking bipedal... *creation* had a cylindrical tin-can torso and towered almost as tall as the doors. It looked vaguely like a robot from a turn-of-the-century comic book. The turn of the *last* century.

"Which former occupant was responsible for this?" Morgen asked, memories of the original *Wizard of Oz* and the Tin Man coming to mind. This thing was a lot larger than the Tin Man, though, and there was nothing human about its blunt face.

"Hm." Martha peered over her shoulder. "It's before my time, but I've heard that a mechanic who fancied himself a tinkerer owned the place in the forties and fifties and used it as a work-shop. He reputedly came back from the war a little strange in the head, so he didn't have a lot of customers."

"You mean there wasn't a big market for giant robots?" Morgen couldn't imagine the technology of the time had allowed the thing to move or actually do anything, so what was the point? Like having a suit of medieval armor as a wall decoration?

"As a woman about to go into business making pet charms," Phoebe said, "you probably shouldn't mock someone else's niche."

"Ha ha."

Morgen shook her head and closed the doors.

"I can take another two hundred a month off the rent," Martha said, "if you'll sign a two-year lease."

"I should talk to Amar first."

A creak came from the front room, and Morgen peered warily through the doorway. Deputy Franklin walked in with Mayor Ungar, and her stomach sank.

The pot-bellied deputy didn't bother her, but the brawny lumberjack of a man, Ungar, had personally escorted the county tax assessor to her property a couple of months earlier to make *sure* she would be charged her fair share this fall. Worse, he'd been turned into a werewolf by one of the Loups Laflamme long before

Morgen came to Bellrock, and he was presumably loyal to their pack. She believed he had been among those werewolves who'd attacked her home the night she and Amar had battled the *rougarou*.

"Hello, Deputy Franklin." Morgen smiled at him and willed the expression to stick as she nodded at Ungar. "And Mayor. Are you here to see Phoebe?"

She waved to her mentor, aware that they had a relationship of sorts. *Booty calls*, the vet, Dr. Valderas, had called it.

"No," Phoebe said quickly. "He's not."

When confronted, Phoebe had reluctantly admitted to the booty calls, and that Ungar *got her motor running*, but she'd been embarrassed about it.

Ungar smirked at her. He was handsome, in a Paul Bunyan kind of way, but Morgen's mind still boggled at the thought of them together, especially after Phoebe had objected to Morgen having a relationship with Amar because he was a werewolf.

"Phoebe only invites me to visit after dark," Ungar said. "She likes it when I growl for her."

"I most certainly do not." Phoebe lifted her chin, her cheeks growing pink.

"Doesn't this qualify as dark?" Franklin grumbled, shaking water droplets from his raincoat and nodding toward the gray sky beyond the windows. "We were having lunch at the Timber Wolf when a concerned citizen reported that there were cars here and someone poking around inside. I thought hooligans might have broken in." Franklin raised his bushy eyebrows toward Morgen, as if he suspected she had done just that, even though a real-estate agent stood at her side.

"To steal the copious valuables left here?" Morgen waved at the meat hooks.

"Teenagers have graffitied the place in the past," Franklin said. "The owner is out of state and doesn't pay enough attention to it."

"I'm here representing the owner and have permission to do so." Martha jangled a keychain. "Morgen is a prospective tenant."

"Yeah?" Ungar eyed Morgen. "You pay your taxes yet?"

"They're not due yet."

"One month." Ungar smiled at her—it wasn't a friendly and encouraging smile. "It would be a shame if the county had to foreclose on your property."

Morgen clenched her jaw for a long moment before managing to say, "I'll take the place," to Martha.

Amar was handy. They could clean it up together, and once they turned it into an appealing showroom for his furnishings and her charms, the business would flow in. Paying the taxes would be a simple matter then.

"Excellent. I've got the paperwork right here, and these are for you." Martha waved a stack of papers and handed her the keys.

Ungar's smile only turned smug, as if he was certain she would fail to start a successful business and pay her taxes. Maybe he was already envisioning the Loup pack hunting in Wolf Wood and lounging afterward on the deck and in the hot tub at Grandma's house.

That *wasn't* going to happen. Morgen would make her new business work, one way or another.

2

As Morgen stepped out of her car in the parking lot of the vegan bakery, a twinge of nausea came over her. Lucky was in the back seat, so she assumed he wasn't sending her a vision, but maybe something was happening back at the house and Zorro was. She braced herself with a hand to the hood, rain pattering on her head, and waited. But the expected vision didn't come.

Lucky stuck his head out the back window and barked at a dog in another parked car. His whip of a tail smacked the seats with the vigor of a drummer performing a rock solo.

"Put your head back inside and be good," Morgen told him, "or I won't bring you anything."

Lucky tilted his copper short-furred head, long ears cocking, and looked at her. Since she'd inadvertently made him a familiar, he seemed to understand her better. Whether or not he would obey was another matter.

"I know how you feel about scones." She pointed at the steaming mug of coffee and frosted scones painted on the window of the bakery.

Lucky sniffed the air, then looked across the street to a fifties-style drive-in restaurant that served burgers and battered chicken drenched in fryer oil.

"Don't push it," Morgen said. "No self-respecting vegetarian would go to that place. A scone is the best you're going to get, and only if you're good."

Lucky wagged cheerfully.

Willing the nausea to abate, Morgen went inside, telling herself she would only get a couple of scones, make coffee at home, and keep her order to five dollars. Until the business took off, she couldn't afford to make extravagant pastry purchases.

But when she spotted the fall line-up in the display case, complete with a mouth-watering vegan pumpkin cheesecake, she couldn't refrain from getting a couple of pieces. They would be her reward for cleaning up the tannery—the *jewelry and woodworking shop,* she amended. She and Amar would have to brainstorm a name for it, one that didn't bring to mind its unappealing past.

Her phone rang as she was heading out of the bakery.

"Hello, Sian," Morgen answered, always worried when her idle-chit-chat-hating sister called. Usually, little short of an emergency could prompt her to pick up a phone.

"I called to issue a warning," Sian said without preamble.

Monkeys hooted in the background. Presumably she was at work, her new laboratory research job at the university in Seattle.

"Is everything okay?" Morgen asked warily.

"Caden called to pump me for information. Gavin and Rhett were with him."

"Information on what?" Morgen hadn't heard from their brothers since early in the summer and wondered what they'd wanted and why they'd called Sian and not her. Were they still grumpy because Grandma had left the estate to Morgen and nothing to any of them? If they'd had any idea how much trouble inheriting the old farmhouse and Wolf Wood had turned out to be, they wouldn't have wanted anything to do with it.

"They were attempting to be subtle, but I gathered they are worried about your new witch lifestyle."

"How did they hear about it?"

"How much have you been talking to Cousin Zoe lately?"

Morgen's stomach sank. "She came up a few weekends back to scope out the hot men of Bellrock, as she called it, and I... may have mentioned a few things."

"What prompted you to open up to the family gossip?"

"Zoe gave herself a tour of the house and wanted to see the root cellar. The potions, cauldrons, and pentagram tend to require explanations."

"Well, she's your snitch."

Morgen continued to the car, feeling the need to lean against it for support. It wasn't that she was ashamed or embarrassed about the witchcraft she was learning—if anything, she was starting to feel like she fit in somewhere for the first time in her life; many of the witches in the coven were book-loving, quirky, and struggled to connect with normal people. She now considered the nineteen-year-old witch Wendy a good friend, and Phoebe had been invaluable in giving advice on mastering the power Morgen had never known existed within her until that summer.

All that said, she had no desire to *explain* any of that to her extremely normal brothers. Before coming up to Bellrock, Morgen hadn't known magic existed, and she was positive they didn't either. They would never believe her if she spoke of it, nor would they think witches and werewolves were real. They would think she was a kook. Sian was learning witchcraft on the weekends, had seen men turn into furry predators, and was quasi dating the werewolf Dr. Valderas, but even she was skeptical of half the things Morgen told her.

"I thought she was too busy ogling werewolves to pay attention to the witch stuff," Morgen muttered when she realized her sister wouldn't go on without being prompted—or maybe Sian had been distracted by some experiment that required her attention. "As I recall, she hooked up with Juan Martín."

"I have no interest in hook-ups," Sian said. "I merely called to warn you that you can expect a visit."

"From Caden?" Morgen groaned.

"I believe from all of them. Again, they weren't blunt, but I believe they feel the need to show up en masse to stage an intervention."

Morgen groaned again, the nausea returning to her stomach. She slumped against the car and rested a hand on her abdomen, glad for the cool rain moistening her cheeks.

Lucky stuck his head out the window, looked at the bakery bag in her hand, and whined. He peered at the German shepherd he'd been barking at earlier, as if to point out that he'd been a good boy.

She made herself walk over to pet him, but that nausea continued, and she wondered if she would have to run back in to use the restroom. She wasn't getting sick, was she? The flu?

With that thought, inspiration struck.

"Tell them they can't come," Morgen blurted. "I'm sick."

"Sick?" Sian asked.

"I've had some nausea start up. I'd hate to give the flu to all of our brothers."

"Maybe you're pregnant."

"I'm *not* pregnant." At least, Morgen didn't see how she could be. Since she'd never had kids, she wasn't positive what the experience would feel like, but it was far too early to think *that* could be the reason for her illness. So far, this felt similar to the nausea she got from her visions, so she was more inclined to blame the witch world. "Amar and I have only been sleeping together for a month."

Technically, more like six weeks. Hell, when had her period been due? Was she late? She'd been so busy working on the witch database app and charms so she could open her business that she'd lost track of time.

"It only takes once, genius," Sian said.

"I know that, but that's when you're young and fertile. I'm *forty.*"

"True, and you do eat all that soy."

"What does *that* have to do with anything?" Morgen eyed her bakery bag, suspecting the *cheese* in the pumpkin cheesecake was made from soy.

"The isoflavones in it mimic estrogen, and animal studies suggest that eating large amounts of them may reduce fertility in women."

Morgen rolled her eyes but also said, "*See?* I can't possibly be pregnant."

"Perhaps your strapping werewolf lover has virility that overrode your reduced fertility. I trust *he* doesn't eat soy."

"No, he devours wild elk whole and uses the antlers to clean his teeth afterward."

"If he enjoys an organic snout-to-tail diet, he could indeed have substantial virility. Numerous researchers have found that such eating habits have been linked to higher-quality sperm, including overall count, motility, and morphology."

"Have I mentioned how delightful it is to have an encyclopedia for a sister?"

"Not as often as you should, and I'm quoting scientific journals, not encyclopedias."

"So very different."

"They're peer-reviewed, thus superior resources. For your information, such beliefs about the benefits of eating the whole animal predate the modern era. In medieval times, infertile men were advised to consume ground-up pig testicles in wine."

"I'm getting nauseated again," Morgen said.

"Perhaps you should take a pregnancy test."

"Perhaps I should stop talking to my sister about testicles."

"You can do both. Good-bye."

Morgen put her phone away and tore off a piece of scone for Lucky. He chomped it down, his wagging tail hitting the back of the seat again.

"I may need to stop at the pharmacy, buddy," she said.

He cocked his head, as if to ask what she would bring him from there.

"Nothing good," she mumbled, hoping flu medicine was all she needed, but maybe it would be best to pick up a pregnancy test too.

If she somehow *was* pregnant... what would she tell Amar?

3

Morgen stared at the result on the pregnancy test in disbelief. She hadn't expected a positive result, especially since she hadn't waited until the recommended *first-thing-in-the-morning* to take it, but there it was.

Her fingers shook as she pulled up her calendar on her phone to double check the weeks. Had it truly been long enough for this?

"Damn," she whispered, staring at the calendar. She must have gotten pregnant the *first* time they'd slept together.

That had been spur-of-the-moment and in a *cave*, but they'd used condoms. After all, they'd been dating for a while at that point. She'd been prepared.

Chainsaw noises wafted in through the bathroom window. Morgen shook her head. What would she say to Amar? They had spoken about children before, and how she sometimes regretted that she'd never had them with her ex-husband. And Amar had mentioned that knowing the *rougarou* was out there hunting him had kept him from settling down and letting himself get that involved with someone. The *rougarou* was dead and no longer a threat, but did that mean he would be eager to have children now?

They'd only known each other for a few months. Morgen cared about him—no, she *loved* him—but were they ready for this?

"It looks like it doesn't *matter* if you're ready," she mumbled, eyeing the test. "It could be wrong though. I'll have to see my doctor."

Her doctor who was back in Seattle. She hadn't been in Bellrock long enough to think about getting set up with local service providers. She didn't even think the little tourist town *had* a doctor, unless one counted Dr. Valderas. He *did* treat all the werewolves, but she wasn't going to go to the vet for a pregnancy test.

Morgen headed downstairs, intending to go out and talk to Amar. The sooner she told him, the better.

Wendy was in the living room with a tape measure, and Morgen paused. Chittering came from the wood box on the raised hearth, the ferret Napoleon rooting around in the kindling. Lucky was outside, else he would have been in here barking and trying to get Napoleon to play.

"What are you doing?" Morgen asked.

"Seeing how big of a TV could fit in here."

Morgen arched her eyebrows. There wasn't currently a television in the living room or anywhere else in the house. Apparently, Grandma hadn't felt the need to keep up on the latest soaps or sitcoms, and since Morgen preferred books to TV, or used her laptop to stream things, she hadn't bothered hunting one down.

"The monitor in my van isn't very large," Wendy said, "and since you paid me for the graphics work on your app, I have money to spend on important purchases."

"Such as a TV for my living room? You don't even spend that much time in here."

"Well, I would if there was a giant gaming monitor here." Wendy smiled and spread her arms toward the wall. "Or maybe here." She moved to stand in front of the fireplace, waving at the bricks above it.

Napoleon chittered, hopped down from the hearth, and jumped onto the couch. He flopped onto his back and rolled about, little ferret legs in the air. Preparing to make this his new home?

"You have mentioned that we're welcome inside," Wendy said.

"You are, but I thought you were heading off to art school when the new semester starts." Morgen didn't look forward to losing her jewelry instructor—Wendy, who had been crafting charms and trinkets for years, had been sharing her knowledge— but it seemed proper to encourage a young woman to go to school.

"I am, but I can come back on the weekends to visit."

"To visit me or a giant TV?"

Wendy smiled wider, her arms still spread, as if she were hugging that future TV.

Well, at least Morgen would have a babysitter if she needed one. Admittedly, a somewhat distracted babysitter.

The buzz of the chainsaw started up again, reminding Morgen of her mission. After rubbing Napoleon's belly, she headed outside. Lucky was snuffling at a hole he'd dug under one of the garden beds, his tail wagging excitedly as he tried to lure out whatever had made a home down there.

The rain had stopped, and twilight was approaching. The exterior barn lamps shed light on Amar and the stump where he carved his sculptures from logs, but he would have to call it a night soon.

Even though fall had fully come, and the leaves on the deciduous trees in Wolf Wood were turning color, Amar hadn't made any changes to his wardrobe. He still roamed around in boots, jeans, and a black leather vest that left his muscular arms—and a good portion of his chest—on display. This evening, he wasn't even wearing that. The piece he was working on, a bear standing upright among boulders and clumps of grass while holding a mailbox, must have been taxing, for he was vestless, his skin gleaming with sweat.

Morgen couldn't help but pause and admire him, bedroom thoughts encroaching on her mind. Sian's words about Amar's *virility* popped into her head, and she snorted. Still, Morgen couldn't deny that he *was* virile. Oh, she had no idea about sperm counts and the like, but he was the most exciting romantic partner she'd ever had. Her ex-husband had been staid and unimaginative in comparison. Admittedly, she'd always considered herself to have similar tastes in the bedroom... until she'd fallen for a wild werewolf who'd taught her to howl.

Amar must have sensed her watching him, for he turned off the chainsaw and faced her. Morgen attempted to wipe off whatever lustful expression she might have been wearing; they needed to have a serious conversation first.

But Amar, wood-dust clinging to his bare skin, eyed her up and down, a smile curving his lips, as if he also had lustful thoughts in mind. Maybe they could have the conversation *after* a night of lovemaking.

Hoots came from the nesting box in the cedar where Zorro made his home. It must have grown dark enough to stir up his hunting instincts, for he sprang from his perch, wings flapping. Though Zorro could have arrowed off in any direction, he flew directly toward Morgen and Amar.

Aware of how irreverent her owl was, Morgen stepped back. Amar squinted up and also stepped back. Owl droppings splattered to the ground where he'd been standing.

"I made him that nesting box," Amar growled as Zorro continued off toward the woods. "You'd think he would be grateful."

"At least he doesn't go in your barn anymore and defecate on your woodworking projects."

"Only because I keep the windows and doors secured. He sneaked in last week and molted on my blanket." Amar waved toward the loft apartment in the barn, though he usually slept in the house with Morgen now.

"You mean on that dreadful bear hide you *call* a blanket?"

"It's warm, cozy, and perfect for a werewolf."

"It's scratchy, heavy, and used to be perfect for a bear."

"I caught and ate that bear. He was delicious." He smiled at her, showing off his teeth.

Since he appeared normal as a human, if extremely athletic and fit, it was only in her imagination that long fangs leered from his gums. Her wild wolf man.

"I'm glad you weren't forced to consume a poor-tasting bear to get that hide."

"I was not." Amar set down his chainsaw and walked to her, clasping her hands. "It has been some time since you visited my apartment. Perhaps you've forgotten how appealing the hide is."

"It's loathsome, but I haven't forgotten how appealing *you* are."

"Good," he rumbled, gripped her waist with both hands, and kissed her.

Morgen leaned into him, bedroom thoughts returning, and she almost forgot what she'd come out here to talk to him about. In truth, she had a number of things she needed to bring up with him, such as that she'd leased a building without consulting him first. They'd *talked* about getting such a place, but she should have waited until he had a look at it. The smug Ungar walking in and delivering insinuations had prompted her into an impulsive decision.

Though reluctant to do so, Morgen made herself break the kiss and put a hand on his chest.

"I need to, uhm, warn you about a couple of things," she said.

"That dinner will be late because we're going to have hot passionate sex?"

"That would be true." She patted him, appreciating the powerful contours under her palm. "But let me give you my news first."

"Very well."

"First, I've leased an old tannery in town. I should have brought you to see it before signing anything, and I apologize for not doing so. I did, at least, get a good deal on it." Morgen described the building and how much woodworking equipment could fit into it while omitting mention of the chalk outline, the strange metal statue, and the meat hooks. She did feel compelled to admit that cleaning it up would be a lot of work. "Is there any chance your pack would like to help us do a few renovations there?"

Amar lifted his chin. "It is likely I can handle any necessary renovations by myself, but if you make them something useful for their hunts, they may be inclined to help again. They have decided you are one of the pack." He smiled and brushed his fingers along her cheek, always pleased that she had helped out the Lobos, even though she was a witch.

The antagonism between the coven and the Lobos had lessened since they had battled together twice, but Morgen doubted they would ever truly cozy up to each other.

"You'll have to let me know if they need flea-and-tick charms. I'm getting good at those."

He squinted at her. "Werewolves do not get *fleas*."

"Because no flea would dare bite such a mighty creature?"

"Because we bathe." His squint deepened. "But we *are* mighty."

"So I've observed." She smiled and patted his chest again.

He leaned in, kissing clearly on his mind.

"Uhm." She held a finger to his lips, though she was also tempted to let the kissing take over. "That was only the first part of my news. I was just up in the bathroom, and I found out..."

She met his gaze, his blue eyes content as he continued to hold her waist, his smile promising that they would soon spend the evening enjoying each other's company. And why shouldn't he be content? Amar had few worries to concern him now, other than Morgen's looming tax bill. He'd promised to help her with that, since they were partners now. Partners in life and business. And... soon to be parenting?

Would he want that? Or would it come too soon and force them into something they weren't ready for? Force *him* into something he wasn't ready for?

What if he ran off into the woods and didn't come back, and she found herself a single mother at forty—soon to be forty-one? Trying to figure out everything by herself while struggling to start a business because she'd given up her old, steady life in Seattle, her good-paying career as a database programmer.

Panic welled up in her, and she froze, fear keeping her from sharing what she wanted—*needed*—to with Amar.

"What's wrong?" he asked.

"I..." Morgen told herself that he would understand, that he would be supportive. It wasn't as if either of them had made a mistake and been careless. He wouldn't run away. He was loyal. Already, he'd stood at her side countless times in battle. It wasn't fair of her to think he would run off because she might be pregnant. It would be fine. She took a deep breath to continue, but the words that came out were, "My brothers may be coming up to visit."

"Your brothers?" Maybe Amar had read the anxiety in her face, because his brow furrowed, as if he'd expected her to bring up something... bigger.

"Yes. I didn't invite them, but apparently, they heard about my new witch life from Zoe—my cousin, remember her?—and they're concerned."

"Becoming a witch *is* concerning."

"Ha ha." She swatted him on the chest. "Their opinion doesn't technically matter—I don't even see them that often—but I'd prefer they not give me a hard time about the choices I've made these past months. If they show up, will you do me a favor and be on good behavior? I don't want to have to listen to them trying to convince me to go back to Seattle and my old life."

"Good behavior?"

"Like don't growl at them. And maybe wear clothing." Morgen brushed sawdust off his chest and smiled, though she was already starting to doubt her request. She *liked* that Amar was who and what he was. Asking him to try to pass himself off as some normal person, just so her relationship with her brothers would be easier, wasn't right.

At least he didn't seem offended. His eyelids drooped, and he caught her hand before it could go far, pressing it against his pecs. "I believe you *like* it when I don't wear clothing."

"*I* do, though it does concern me that you wield a chainsaw without wearing any safety equipment. What if you cut off an important part?" She glanced down at his crotch before she caught herself, blushed, then waved her free hand toward his fingers. "Like a thumb."

"I am a capable craftsman. My *important parts* are not in danger." Amar pulled her closer to him, all of his parts pressing up against hers. "Your family will appreciate that I am a mighty were-wolf and am protecting you."

Morgen doubted they would, but *she* did, and when Amar's lips found hers again, she couldn't bring herself to pull away. Of their own accord, her hands slid up to grip his shoulders. The rest of what she wanted to discuss could wait until morning. Tonight, they would enjoy each other's company, especially if she could lure him back to her bedroom and her vegan blanket collection.

Amar slid a hand around to grab her butt, then hoisted her into his arms, prepared to carry her inside. Unfortunately, that movement awakened the nausea in her stomach. It came on with alarming intensity, and she swatted his shoulder.

"I need to get down."

"What?" His brow furrowed in puzzlement.

"Please," she panted, the nausea intensifying. "Let me down."

He lowered her to her feet. At first, she took a step toward the house and the bathroom, but her stomach promised she wouldn't make it that far. Instead, she ran around the corner of the barn, stumbled into the shadows, and threw up.

Damn it, wasn't pregnancy supposed to involve *morning* sickness? She was positive she hadn't heard accounts from her friends with kids about breaking off in the middle of lovemaking to vomit.

Hands gripping her knees as she spewed the remains of her lunch into the grass, Morgen was aware of Amar peering around the corner of the barn with concern in his eyes.

When she finished, she wiped her mouth and staggered toward him, though now, going to the bathroom and grabbing her toothbrush was on her mind instead of kissing.

"You are sick?" He rested a gentle hand on her shoulder.

"Sort of." She looked at his chest, struggling to lift her gaze to his eyes. "I mean, I'm not sure yet."

"You're not sure if you're sick?" He looked toward the grass that she'd defiled.

"Not exactly. I'm... going to make an appointment to see my doctor, so I won't be sure until then, but I took a home test, and there's a possibility that... you haven't been eating enough soy."

"What?"

Morgen rolled her eyes at herself. "You could be too virile. And I could be pregnant."

4

———————

Amar blinked a few times. "You are pregnant?"

"I could be. Like I said, I haven't seen my doctor yet, but I'll make an appointment and drive down to Seattle tomorrow." Morgen waved toward the evidence of her sickness, though she watched Amar's face for his reaction.

Would he be horrified? Pleased? Alarmed? At the moment, he mostly looked stunned.

Then he stepped in closer and gripped her hands. "This is good news, yes? With my arch enemy gone, I do not fear having children."

His words sent relief through her, though Morgen couldn't help but think of the mayor and his cadre of Loups. Even if the witches weren't gunning for her anymore, she couldn't say that all of *her* enemies were gone.

Still, the smile slowly blossoming on his face made her smile as well. "I know we talked about it a bit, but... do you want children? With me?" Maybe she shouldn't have asked that, since, unless the test was wrong, it was going to happen. "We haven't been seeing each other that long, and I definitely didn't plan this.

It would have made more sense to wait, but, uhm, do you want to hear my sister's hypothesis about your sperm?"

That got him blinking again. Morgen stifled the urge to roll her eyes at herself once more. Usually, she felt comfortable around him. Why was this so awkward?

"Waiting is not necessary," Amar said. "You are my witch, and I am your wolf."

"That is true." She relaxed into his arms, letting him draw her into a hug. "After my appointment, we'll get things confirmed."

"You could see Dr. Valderas now."

"I'm not going to the *vet* for my pregnancy needs."

"He is very capable. He has many horse breeders for clients and delivers foals regularly."

"And yet, not my first choice." Morgen shuddered.

"Hm." Amar stroked her hair for a few thoughtful minutes before saying, "I must begin preparations."

"Preparations?" She leaned back to look at his face, hoping there wasn't some werewolf ritual that he had in mind. She envisioned the Lobos taking their newborn out into the wilds and Amar holding him or her up to the full moon while the pack howled in the background.

"Baby furniture," Amar said. "There must be a crib. And storage bins for diapers and toys. Dressers for small clothing. I must begin plans immediately."

Relieved that howling wouldn't be involved with his preparations, Morgen allowed him to lead her toward the barn door. Was he going to start tonight?

He paused with his hand on the door. "This will be more complicated than pet furniture. A chainsaw might not be sufficient."

"Well, I signed the lease and got the keys, so you have room for a bandsaw, if you want one." Morgen had vague memories of using a bandsaw in her middle school's mandatory shop class to carve a toy car out of wood, but she had no idea if it was the tool for constructing a diaper bin.

"Large woodworking machinery is expensive. Perhaps later, we can afford such things. For now, I will speak with the pack. They have many tools that I can borrow. You saw the circular saws they used on the deck."

"Uh, yes. Are you... going to tell them about the baby?"

"They will know soon, even if I say nothing. You will smell different."

Morgen decided she didn't want to know what she would smell like, or how she *usually* smelled, and didn't ask for details. "Okay, but can you wait to tell them until I've seen the doctor? Then maybe we can celebrate." She almost mentioned the tradition of baby showers, but the last thing she wanted was to encourage a pack of mostly male construction-worker werewolves to give her gifts. Knowing them, she would end up with four wrenches and a ratchet set.

"We can celebrate tonight." Amar squeezed her hand and smiled at her.

"Now?"

"After I start on the crib."

"We should have nearly eight months," she said, though she was touched that he cared. She felt foolish for even momentarily thinking that he would be horrified and run away. That had been her own fears speaking, nothing to do with Amar and what kind of person he was. "And you work quickly. You made that cat condo for Sakura in days."

"A crib for our baby must be far superior to some *pet* apparatus carpeted with scraps of rug that an owl nested on."

Morgen grimaced, glancing at the stain on the gravel that Zorro had left behind. As she recalled, he'd done more than *nest* on Amar's scraps. "Yes, why don't you leave carpet out of the crib? I'll pick up a mattress and some blankets."

Amar opened his mouth, but Morgen held up a finger.

"No *hides* either," she said.

"I have many to choose from. Some of the pelts are very soft. I have rabbit fur."

"No parts of dead animals go in a child's room. That's a rule. I'm sure it's covered in *American Baby*."

He squinted at her. Her phone rang, saving her from having to further defend her position.

"Zoe," Morgen growled when her cousin's name popped up. She answered with, "Why did you tell my brothers that I'm studying witchcraft?"

"Hi, Morgen. Great to talk to you too."

Amar went into the barn, humming to himself as he flicked on the lights. He headed straight for the workbench in the back where he sketched his pieces before bringing them to life.

"Sian says they're planning to come up here to save me from myself," Morgen said, wandering toward the driveway, "or who knows what craziness." She stepped over the spot where Wendy and the other witches had helped her to install magical wards to keep enemies out of the house. They'd been inactive since the *rougarou* had died, but she wondered if she could turn them on when her brothers showed up, then hide inside and pretend not to be home.

"You should be thankful that I told them," Zoe said. "They were grousing about how *you* got everything when your grandmother died. I told them that from what I'd seen, you'd mostly gotten a lot of trouble."

"That's the truth."

"It's not my fault they think you've joined a cult."

"*Zoe.*"

"I barely mentioned the coven. If it helps, Caden thinks you're not a follower and, if anything, you *started* the cult."

"That *doesn't* help. What am I going to tell them when they come up here?" Morgen fantasized about the wards again—and hiding under her bed and reading books until they went away. Were mothers supposed to do such immature things? She would have to get an actual issue of that parenting magazine and see if there were any tips.

"Perhaps you can distract them with werewolves. That worked for me." Zoe oozed satisfaction and sounded like she was smiling. "That's what I called about."

"Your werewolf fetish?"

"It's not a fetish. I had great sex with Juan Martín, and I'd like to have it again."

"Shouldn't you call him instead of me? I'm not your pimp."

"I didn't get his number or his address. I assumed *your* strapping werewolf lover could point me to him though. It's been ages since I've known such intense pleasure."

"You were here three weekends ago."

"*Ages*. I don't have any client meetings for the next couple of days. Mind if I come up this weekend?"

Morgen was about to say she did mind and that it wasn't a good time, but the filth of the tannery came to mind. "In exchange for free room and board, would you be willing to help me clean the new building I just leased for my business?"

Maybe she could also foist her brothers off on Zoe. Her cousin could be their tour guide and show them around town while Morgen focused on getting the building ready.

"Clean? Morgen, I show houses for a living; I don't clean them."

"This isn't a house. It's a large commercial building."

"So much more appealing."

"It was built in the 1800s. It's historically significant."

"And thus, more desirable to clean?" Zoe asked.

"I should think so."

"Fine, fine, if you let me stay and help me find a werewolf lover to scratch my itch, I'll dust a few shelves for you."

"*A* werewolf lover? You don't care if it's the same one?"

"I'll take him if he's available, but I'm not particular. You know I enjoy broadening my horizons and experiencing new things—and people."

Morgen shook her head at the phone. "How is it possible that we share any blood?"

"You ask that as if *I'm* the weird one who started a cult."

"I didn't start a cult."

Zoe made a kissing sound. "I'll be up later tonight. Thanks."

"*Tonight*?" Morgen asked but Zoe had already hung up. That didn't keep Morgen from muttering, "I'll find a lot more than a couple of shelves for you to clean, cousin."

The phone lit up with a new call.

Morgen frowned, feeling inundated. This was far too much socializing for an introvert, and when Deputy Franklin's name popped up, she groaned, certain she didn't want to hear whatever he had to say.

"Hello, Deputy."

"Ms. Keller, I'm afraid I must report that your building has been broken into. There's fresh graffiti on an inside wall, and the owner of the Roaming Elk Inn reported seeing weird glowing lights through the broken windows."

"Are you kidding me? It's only been two hours since I signed the lease."

"Nonetheless, you might want to come down here."

Morgen stared bleakly at the phone. So much for her romantic evening with Amar.

5

AMAR STARTED THE TRUCK WHILE MORGEN RAN TO GRAB HER PURSE and her staff out of the house. He'd agreed to come with her in case whoever had broken into the tannery was still there.

"Everything okay?" Wendy asked when Morgen jogged inside, waving for Lucky to stay in the house.

"Break-in at the building I leased."

"Didn't you just lease that today?"

"Two hours ago, yes. I had a hunch it would be trouble, but I didn't listen to my gut." Morgen paused once she had her purse and the antler-tipped staff she'd inherited from her grandmother. "Do you want to come along? Deputy Franklin said someone reported seeing glowing lights inside."

Since Wendy had grown up around witches and had been practicing most of her life, she knew a lot more about magic than Morgen. If it turned out to be something otherworldly, maybe she would have some ideas.

"Sure." Wendy waved toward the raised hearth where someone—someone slinky and furry, Morgen had no doubt—had knocked kindling onto the floor. "Come on, Napoleon. We're needed."

The ferret rose up on his hind legs and chittered while looking at the empty fireplace.

"He's been trying to get me to build a fire," Wendy said. "He gets chilled easily this time of year."

"Why don't you get him a sweater?"

Napoleon ran over and launched himself into Wendy's arms. He waved his nose toward Morgen, probably wondering if she had any snacks in her pockets. As if alerted to the possibility, Lucky sat an inch away from her foot and wagged his tail hopefully.

"You stay here," Morgen told him. "I need someone to guard the house and greet Zoe if she shows up while we're gone." She didn't know if her cousin had left right after their call, but it wasn't that long of a drive up from Seattle.

Lucky whined.

Morgen pulled a dog treat out of a pocket, gave it to him, and petted his head. "Good boy."

Napoleon chittered a protest, either at not being called a *good boy* or at not getting a goodie.

"Does he like dehydrated chicken strips?" Morgen offered one of the treats to Wendy.

"Probably." She accepted it and tore off a piece for the ferret as they closed the door on Lucky and headed to the driveway. "He's a carnivore and likes anything meaty."

As Morgen recalled, Napoleon also liked pistachios and avocado crisps. Some carnivore.

Wendy started toward Morgen's car, but Morgen pointed at Amar's sixty-year-old blue truck, which was already turned on and idling like a double-decker freeway in an earthquake.

"We're taking backup," Morgen said.

"Oh." Wendy hesitated. She and Amar got along all right these days—Amar had even learned her name—but Napoleon still hadn't warmed up to any of the werewolves, even the one he shared the property with.

"I'll sit in the middle." Morgen slid into the truck first, making room on the single bench for Wendy, something that was difficult while maneuvering a long staff with antlers on the top. At least Amar's beater of a vehicle didn't have upholstery on the ceiling to rip. There was barely upholstery on the seat, and the duct tape that covered large swaths of it offered further protection.

"You anticipate a battle?" Amar eyed the staff as it almost whacked him in the head.

"I don't know, but I'm taking this and my app along in case any enemies show themselves." Physical *or* spectral. None of Morgen's life experiences had given her a reason to believe in ghosts, but before she'd moved up here, she hadn't had a reason to believe in witches or werewolves either. Now, she felt obligated to keep an open mind.

When Wendy slid in beside her, Napoleon spotted Amar and squeaked dramatically before falling limply into her lap. It wasn't that convincing an act of *playing dead*, because he was still working on the dehydrated chicken strip, a treat meant for dog-sized jaws, not ferret chompers.

"You will bring that useless rodent instead of your hound?" Amar put the truck into drive.

"Napoleon *isn't* useless." Wendy glowered over at him, inasmuch as someone with freckles and blonde pigtails could glower. "If you're ever trapped in a jail cell and need someone to slink through the bars and steal the keys from a hook, you'll see how useful he is."

"Do you spend a lot of time in jail cells?" Morgen asked as they rolled down the long winding driveway, the potholes attempting to launch her into the ceiling.

"Well," Wendy said, "I'm going somewhere with you, so it seems possible they could be in my future."

"Hilarious. Lucky is staying home to greet Zoe if she shows up at the house while we're gone."

"Your cousin would be aggrieved if your hound weren't there to jump on her as she opens the door?" Amar asked.

"Wouldn't you be?" Morgen smiled at him.

He slanted her a sidelong look.

"Don't pretend you haven't cozied up to and bonded with him. Half the time, when he sleeps in bed with us, you're the one he uses as a pillow."

"The dog sleeps with you?" Wendy asked. "When you're having, uhm, relations?"

"We keep the door closed until *after* the relations." Morgen braced her hand on the dash as they hit one last pothole before rolling out onto the paved street. "After that, I let him in, and Amar firmly tells him that he must sleep on the rug, which he does until we fall asleep. At some point, I wake up with paws in my back, and Lucky's head slung across Amar's chest."

"I'm glad ferrets don't take up much space." Wendy stroked Napoleon's still-limp form.

"I'm just glad Zorro doesn't want to sleep in the bed too." Morgen pulled out her phone and tapped open her app to look for incantations that could create glowing lights.

Until she saw for herself what Franklin had reported, she would assume there was a mundane explanation—maybe some teenagers with flashlights had broken in, and the dust filming the windows had made the beams *seem* to be eerily glowing—but given the number of peculiarities that occurred in and near Wolf Wood, it was possible they were some magical phenomena. She hoped not. She didn't need any paranormal wackiness taking place in the building she'd just leased.

"Have you heard anything about the tannery outside of town, Wendy?" Morgen asked, realizing she had with her a resource who'd lived in Bellrock her whole life.

"Just that it's haunted. Kids like to ride by on their bikes and throw rocks through the windows to stir up the ghost."

Morgen started to scoff, but the chalk outline popped into her mind. "Whose ghost is supposed to be in there?"

"Nobody knows, but people have reported moaning sounds emanating from the building in the middle of the night."

Maybe Morgen should have brought Wendy with her for the tour with the agent. Though there weren't a lot of buildings for lease in Bellrock, so it wasn't as if they'd had an abundance of choices. Especially, as Martha had pointed out, in Morgen's price range.

"I'm hoping that a good cleaning and some window repairs will make it respectable," Morgen said.

"I don't think those things get rid of ghosts," Wendy said.

Not commenting on the subject, Amar turned the truck onto Main Street. Did he believe in ghosts?

"Do you know anything that does?" Morgen asked.

"Ecto-goggles and a proton pack?" Wendy suggested.

Morgen sighed at her.

When Amar parked in the street in front of the tannery, a sheriff's department SUV was already there, though the lights weren't on inside the building. Morgen expected to find Deputy Franklin investigating the premises. Instead, he was in the driver's seat of his SUV with his phone out, playing a word game.

"This is how you investigate suspicious activity that people report?" Morgen asked when Franklin rolled down the window.

"I looked around outside and didn't see anything except some recently broken glass. I wanted to wait until the owner—the renter —arrived before presuming to go in."

"Because you need a warrant otherwise?" Morgen asked.

"Because the place is haunted."

Apparently, that was common knowledge to the residents. Morgen definitely should have asked around more before leasing the place. She hoped a ghost wouldn't deter tourists from coming to shop once they got the place up and running.

"Besides—" Franklin held up his phone, "—I need a five-letter word with a U in the middle."

"Crumb?"

"Hm."

Morgen left him to finish the game and headed toward the side of the building, where the cracked parking lot and the front door were. She glanced in the windows as she passed them. Whatever glowing lights had been there earlier, they were gone now.

Amar and Wendy were waiting for her at the front door, Wendy holding her limp ferret and Amar sniffing the air.

"Mayor Ungar was here," Amar grumbled. "I recognize his scent."

"Do you think *he* would throw rocks at the windows?" Wendy asked. "That seems really immature for a grumpy adult."

"You're nineteen. I believe in the eyes of the law *you're* an adult now too." Morgen didn't bring up the fact that Wendy had been taking measurements for a TV for video gaming earlier.

"Yeah, but I mean like *old* and grumpy."

"I think Ungar is in his forties." Morgen didn't point out that she was that age and *definitely* not old. "Maybe forty-five. He's got some gray in his hair. Amar, he was here earlier when I was leasing the place. That might be what you're smelling."

Amar squinted at her. "Did he threaten you?"

"He asked if I'd paid my taxes yet."

"That is all? He was at the battle at your house last month, letting himself be commanded by the *rougarou*."

"I figured. A lot of the Loups were." Morgen shrugged, though the thought had crossed her mind too. Had the mayor tried to keep himself from being controlled? Or had he been happy to go along with a command to attack Morgen's home and her witch allies?

"The Loups do not like that the Lobos are getting along better with the coven now," Amar said. "They've been puffing out their chests and threatening us again lately."

"Maybe we were premature in assuming all of our enemies are gone." Morgen smiled sadly at him, leaned her staff next to the door, and fished out the key.

"If they cause trouble, I will deal with them."

As Morgen pushed open the door with a creak loud enough to wake the dead—or the ghost—Napoleon lifted his head and sniffed. Once they stepped inside, he squirmed until Wendy set him down. He took off across the floor and scampered up the steps to the loft.

"He probably smells mice," Wendy said.

"Tell him to help himself but to watch out. There are some old traps lying around."

Wendy closed her eyes, as if she was communicating the message telepathically.

Graffiti on the wall opposite the bank of windows overlooking the street caught Morgen's eye. Words in green paint that almost glowed read: *Freedom isn't given. It must be taken.*

Morgen couldn't tell if the message had been painted in the past couple of hours or if it was only that it had grown more visible with the fall of night. When she turned the lights on, the words faded and were barely noticeable.

Amar strode inside and looked and sniffed around the front room. Floorboards creaked under his boots.

A twinge of nausea came over Morgen, and she gripped the doorjamb and cursed. Her earlier brief look at the bathroom had revealed that the water wasn't turned on—among other deficiencies. She might have to run outside to throw up behind the building.

But a vision came over her, Main Street from high above, the focus on the downtown area. Zorro was nearby, sharing his flight with her. Did he see something threatening?

The owl flew past trees and over a block to the Back Alley Pub, a place Morgen had visited only once, to extract Wendy when she'd been drunk and playing video games there after her sister's death. Several dark figures stood or lounged against the wall in the alley. One looked up when Zorro flew overhead, and Morgen recognized him as one of the Loups. She couldn't remember his name, but she'd once cut his belt and bootstrings when he'd attacked Amar.

One of his buddies also saw Zorro, snarled, and grabbed a broken bottle to throw at him.

"Bastard," Morgen whispered.

Fortunately, Zorro easily evaded the clunky projectile. He flapped off toward the beach beyond town and turned north, perhaps looking for mice now that he'd reported on the goings on in town.

I think there are rats in the loft here, if you want to visit later, she thought to him.

A squeak came from the loft, not a rat but a ferret. A moment later, Napoleon ran down the stairs at top speed, cobwebs and dust coating his head.

"What's wrong, Nappy?" Wendy bent, offering her arms.

But Napoleon squeaked again, darted past her, and ran out the door.

Wendy swore. "I have to get him."

She rushed outside, almost crashing into Deputy Franklin, who was walking up.

"Everything all right?" Franklin asked, frowning after her as Wendy kept going, chasing the ferret down the street.

"He found something in the loft that scared him," Morgen said.

"I don't hear or smell anyone up there," Amar said. "He may have brushed against a trap and startled himself."

"Did you hear one go off?"

"No, but its mere presence may have alarmed him," Amar said. "I haven't noticed that *bravery* is one of his qualities."

"True." Even so, Morgen couldn't help but eye the loft uneasily. Maybe coming down here after dark hadn't been the best idea.

Her gaze caught on one of the meat hooks, and she shivered.

"I will look in the loft." Amar took a step, but Morgen stopped him.

"Wait. Zorro just shared a vision with me. A bunch of the Loups are at the Back Alley Pub. They looked like they were loitering, but it's possible they were doing something more threatening. Or *planning* something more threatening. Could they have known we would come down here?"

"If they threw the rocks, they might have intentionally drawn us down here," Amar said. "The pub is only a few blocks away. They could be planning to attack us."

Morgen tightened her grip around her staff, glad she'd brought it, but if that many Loups came after them, would it be enough? She'd successfully used the werewolf-control spell on a couple of them before, but it was difficult to control more than one person at a time, and as strong a fighter as Amar was, even he couldn't take on half a pack at once.

A new fear came to her as she imagined him dying before their baby was born, of him never getting to meet his son or daughter, and of her having to raise the kid alone.

She shook her head, reminded that she hadn't yet confirmed with her doctor that there *was* a baby. It was too early to worry about such things—and Amar had often proven himself capable of dealing with the Loups. Besides, they weren't alone.

"Let's hope they won't do anything with a law officer here." Morgen waved to Franklin, who stood in the doorway.

Amar looked Franklin up and down, his gaze lingering on the pot belly that slumped over the deputy's belt, but he didn't say anything disparaging.

Still, Franklin straightened his back and patted his sidearm. "They had better *not* do anything with me here."

Movement outside a back window caught Morgen's eye.

"Someone's out there." She pointed.

Amar and Franklin stepped outside. Morgen debated whether to follow them or stay inside and look around—with her staff in hand. She opened her app and searched for ghosts as well as glowing lights in her *database of witchdom*, as she thought of it, hoping to find something useful.

A number of incantations could produce lights of various sorts to guide a witch in the dark. There was also one to extinguish someone else's light. Fewer entries about ghosts appeared. That surprised her, as she would have thought witches had experience interacting with otherworldly beings. After all, she'd experienced Calista summoning a demon—unfortunately. She hoped to spot an incantation with instructions for banishing a ghost, but all that came up was one for forcing a ghost to show itself.

Did she *want* that? She wrinkled her nose.

"Arturo," Amar barked from around the corner of the building. "*¿Qué estás haciendo?*"

Morgen stepped into the doorway as Arturo and Amar walked into view, speaking in Spanish. Franklin had moved out to the street and was looking up and down it. Wendy had disappeared from view, and Morgen frowned with worry. What if she crossed paths with the Loups?

"*Está bien, tío, está bien.*" Arturo waved placating hands toward Amar, then walked up to Morgen. He smiled proudly and held out a paper. "I'm glad to have found you, Ms. Keller. I have a big order for you."

"An order?"

"From Dr. Valderas. He has a bunch of clients who need flea-and-tick charms, and the word is getting out that you're the lady for those."

Crafting charms wasn't at the forefront of Morgen's mind at the moment, but with the mayor reminding her about her impending tax bill, she would take any work she could get. She accepted the paper with a nod. "Yes, I am."

"Have him look at the graffiti," Amar suggested, squinting at Arturo. "He should be an expert on such matters."

Morgen raised her eyebrows, wondering if Amar suspected Arturo of having painted the message. He was known to smash the mailboxes of witches, after all. She didn't think Arturo had a reason to pester her—she'd even helped heal him when he'd been half-eviscerated by the *rougarou*—but it was possible he hadn't known she'd leased this place. He might have been engaged in a random act of hooliganism.

"How did you know I was here, Arturo?" Morgen asked casually, not wanting to openly accuse him of anything.

Arturo shrugged. "Dr. Valderas knew. I was getting a check-up so he could make sure my wounds are all healed up. The scars are super epic. Look." He lifted his shirt, showing the lines of pink scar tissue that remained from his encounter. "He said women love scars. Is that right?" He beamed a smile at her, apparently having reached the age at which one develops an interest in the opposite sex. "I thought about showing them to Wendy."

"Wendy is too old for you—and your scars."

"She's a teenager."

"She's nineteen. That's a big age difference in teen years." Morgen didn't think he'd told her his age, but she was fairly certain he was only about thirteen.

"I'm almost a man. Look, I have abs and pecs." He turned left and right to better display his torso.

"Yes, they're very nice." Morgen pushed his shirt down. "Come give me your opinion on this graffiti and how fresh it is, please."

"Amar," Franklin called from the street, waving and pointing.

A Land Rover was rolling slowly in their direction, the windows down. This late at night in the off-season, Main Street wasn't busy, so it stood out.

"That's one of the Loups' cars." Amar held up a finger to Morgen. "If they stop, I'll take care of it."

"Yell if you need any help." Morgen waved her staff and touched the amulet hanging around her neck.

Amar issued what sounded like an I-can-handle-them-without-help grunt and strode toward Franklin.

Arturo headed inside and peered at the walls. Though Morgen didn't want to wander around the place in the dark, she turned off the lights so the message would be easier to see.

"Huh." Arturo headed over and touched the glowing green words. "This was painted a long time ago. Look at the cracks. Yeah, this is really old."

"Are you sure?"

"Yup. I'm a connoisseur."

"Of graffiti?"

"Yup." Arturo grinned at her.

"I guess it's a relief that someone new isn't vandalizing the building I leased. Other than throwing rocks at the windows." Morgen eyed a round river stone lying on the floor amid shattered glass. "Which seems to have been a pastime of the town for generations and probably has nothing to do with me."

But if not a graffiti artist, who had been wandering around inside the building causing lights to glow? The ghost? Or had the hotel owner imagined seeing such a thing?

Outside, car doors slammed.

"I'd better go help." Arturo jogged out the front door.

Morgen was inclined to do the same. Even if there hadn't been potential trouble outside, she wouldn't have wanted to be alone in the building at night.

Staff in hand, she headed for the door, but a gust of wind blew through the broken windows, and it shut.

"Lovely." She refused to feel creeped out, intimidated, or take that as a sign.

But her courage wavered when she reached the door, tried to turn the knob, and found it locked. The old lockset required a key to unlock from both sides. She slid hers in but couldn't turn it. Scowling, she rattled the key and the knob, but nothing worked.

What the hell? She'd unlocked the door to come in, and Arturo couldn't have locked it without the key.

She twisted again and tugged, certain the old door was simply stuck. But it didn't budge.

Outside, more car doors slammed, and someone shouted something in French. Amar called back in Spanish. Morgen had no idea what they were saying but hoped it was something along the lines of, *Let's agree to share the town and leave each other alone,* not, *I'm challenging you to a duel to the death.*

Once more, Morgen tugged at the door, but nothing had changed. It didn't budge. She thought about giving it a solid kick, but any damage she did she would have to pay for later. She eyed the windows, but they consisted of dozens of small panes. Even though many were broken, she couldn't climb out without breaking the frame first.

"Oh." She snapped her fingers and opened her app to refresh her memory for an incantation she'd used before. Gripping her amulet, she said, "Under the moon's magic, coerce this door to unlock, so that forward I may walk."

The star-shaped amulet warmed in her hand, and she sensed power flowing toward the door. When she'd voiced the incantation before, it had instantly unlocked the library door in her house. This time, the result was different. The doorknob glowed green—a green eerily similar to the color of the graffiti paint.

When she glanced toward the words on the wall, they seemed to glow brighter, matching the glow of the doorknob.

Though she wasn't sure about *touching* something glowing—the word *radioactive* floated through her mind—Morgen grabbed it and tried to open the door again. A zap of energy stung her palm, and she jerked her hand back.

An ominous creak came from the loft, as if someone was walking around up there.

Morgen shook her head. Either someone was playing an elaborate hoax on her, or the townspeople were right. The tannery was haunted.

6

Morgen thought about yelling for help, but the insults being thrown back and forth outside, French mingling with Spanish and English, promised Amar was busy. She didn't want to distract him, and unless ghosts packed heat and could start shooting at her, she doubted she was in any immediate danger.

"Let's hope."

She was more worried about Amar and Wendy.

Another creak came from the loft. What had Napoleon seen up there that had scared him?

A thud and a clunk and a yelp of pain came from the street, followed by the sound of another vehicle driving up. Loup reinforcements?

Worried that Amar and Franklin would need her help, Morgen jogged toward the back room. She remembered seeing another door in there.

As she passed the graffiti, the words grew even brighter, almost pulsing with light.

"Yeah, yeah," she muttered, refusing to be scared. "A decent self-respecting witch ought to be able to handle a mere ghost."

And she would. Later.

She ran into the back room but halted. The chalk outline was also glowing faintly in the dark.

"Admittedly creepy," she whispered and gave it a wide berth.

The back door was locked.

"Damn it."

It *should* have been locked, as she hadn't opened that door to come inside, but when she applied the key, nothing happened. Again, she tried her incantation. Again, the knob glowed green and did not unlock.

Morgen blew out a slow breath, struggling for calm. If she had to, she could use her staff to break a window and escape.

But dealing with whatever was haunting the place would be a better solution. Could she communicate with it somehow and ask it to unlock the doors? She had found that incantation that was supposed to force a ghost to show itself.

As she pulled it up on her phone, she headed back to the main room and the stairs to the loft. Before she started chanting ghost-summoning incantations, she wanted to make sure someone wasn't hiding up there, sniggering at the door-locking tricks. She didn't know who would play such pranks on her, but it was possible Arturo had a contemporary among the Loups.

Before starting up, she flipped the light switch. Earlier, it had worked, the bulbs not so much as flickering, but now, they didn't come on.

"Of course not," she grumbled.

Morgen thought about calling Wendy to check on her, but she started up the stairs first. She wanted to make sure nobody was spying on her from above. A *ghost* might not be packing heat, but a human could be.

The floorboards creaked riotously with each step. If someone *was* in the loft, she would never sneak up on them.

After memorizing the ghost incantation, she stuck her phone in her pocket so she could put both hands on her staff, leveling the antlers at the gloom ahead of her. She might need her flashlight app to search, but she wanted to be prepared in case someone jumped out at her.

Her heart thudded in her chest as she drew close to the top. A part of her wished she'd brought Lucky along, if only so she wouldn't be alone here, but he might have run off with Napoleon. He wasn't that brave either.

The last stair wobbled under her foot, and she flailed, catching herself on the railing. The old board gave way, clattering to the floor. Off-balance, Morgen lurched toward the wall. The step wobbled again, and she backed to the one below it. Now, her heart had a legitimate reason to hammer.

From her perch, she could see into the loft, but so much old machinery, furniture, vats, and who knew what else cluttered the space that she couldn't see far. Drop cloths covered many of the items, leaving them a mystery. There wasn't a clear aisle through the mess, and something hazy made it hard to see to the back of the loft. Smoke? No, she didn't smell anything like that. *Fog?*

Special *loft* fog?

Morgen shook her head.

The creaks that she'd heard earlier had fallen silent. Outside, the werewolves were still shouting at each other, but their voices sounded farther away than they should have, as if Morgen had traveled to some other dimension only partially anchored in reality.

Avoiding the wobbly step, she stepped into the loft. Once again, the floorboards creaked under her weight. Were they thinner than the pine planks below? That would be surprising, given that there were thousands of pounds of junk up here.

She didn't go far, instead peering and leaning around objects.

She risked one-handing her staff so she could pull out her phone and turn on the flashlight. Dust assailed her nose as she shined the beam around, the hazy fog muting its power.

She spotted tiny ferret prints on the dusty floor and realized there would have been human-sized prints if someone had been in the loft recently. There weren't any. So, the only thing up here was her ghost.

"Or my imagination," she muttered, then raised her voice to try the incantation to force a ghost to reveal itself. "Under the moon's magic, deceased soul stuck on this mortal plane, come forth and your presence explain."

Long seconds passed. Morgen was about to try again when the board under her foot gave way with an abrupt snap.

Her foot plunged through, and she cursed as she flung herself to the side, staff clattering against a crate. She caught herself on the wall, banging her knuckles, and barely managed to keep ahold of the weapon. With shaking hands, she pointed it at the spot that had betrayed her.

A ragged hole was visible, one of the floorboards snapped in half, no hint of the support beams that held up the loft visible. Morgen swallowed, decided she'd explored as much as she would dare, and eased back toward the steps. If nothing else, she'd convinced herself that nobody was up here playing a prank on her. Whoever—*whatever*—was responsible for this wasn't a Loup.

"Well," she breathed, carefully navigating down the creaky stairs, "you're a witch now, and you know magic exists. You can't be that surprised when you find it."

It would have been nice if she hadn't found it in the building she'd signed a two-year lease for. Grimacing, she crept toward the front door, intending to try it again.

Before she reached it, a breeze whispered through the broken panes, stirring fog that had descended from the loft to create a haze in the main room. A glowing white figure hovered in the middle, a hint of arms and legs and a head, though Morgen couldn't tell if it was male or female or even supposed to represent a human.

"What do you want?" She pointed her staff at it, though she reminded herself that she might have called the ghost with her spell and probably shouldn't threaten it. It might be wondering what *she* wanted. "Is there any chance you can open the door?"

It didn't speak or move, simply continuing to hover in the air.

Morgen eased toward the door and tried the knob again. It was still locked.

"Can I help you with something?" Morgen figured it would be wise to be polite to a ghost. "I don't suppose you're in need of a flea-and-tick charm? Or maybe something to keep hoodlums from throwing rocks through your windows?"

The ghost reacted by drawing back. The legs didn't move, but the entire body floated toward the rear room.

Help me, a female voice said—or did that sound only in Morgen's mind? *Please, help me.*

The voice sounded older, and was that a Russian accent?

"How? How can I help you?"

The ghost paused in the doorway to the back room.

Once again, Morgen thought of the chalk outline. Had it been made of the ghost when she died? Had she been murdered?

With little else that she could do as long as she was locked in, Morgen walked after the ghost. It floated through the doorway and hovered in the back room. Waiting.

Before Morgen reached the doorway, a faint clink came from above. Her instincts shouted at her to get out of the way.

Morgen threw herself to the side as something thudded down, then clanked. Her foot slipped, and she fell, hitting her shoulder on the floor. Gasping in pain, she rolled away and scrambled to come up to her knees so she could defend herself. As she got one foot under her, she leveled the staff toward the place where she'd been standing.

One of the giant meat hooks lay on the floor.

Her mouth drooped open with the realization that if she hadn't moved in time, the sharp tip might have gone through her head and killed her.

7

THE FRONT DOOR OPENED, STARTLING MORGEN ALMOST AS MUCH AS the falling hook had.

Amar stepped inside, saw her on one foot and one knee, pointing her staff, and frowned around the room. "What happened?"

"There was—" Morgen pointed toward the back room where the ghost had been hovering, but it had vanished.

Amar flipped the switch by the door, and the lights came on, as if they'd been working all along. He frowned at the hook. At least *that* was there, evidence of something disturbing going on.

"Did that *fall?*" Amar strode toward her. "Are you all right?"

"Yeah," Morgen said, her voice squeaky. She cleared her throat, looked up at the ceiling beam and the long bar that supported a dozen more meat hooks, and stepped well away from them. "It did fall, yes. I'm all right, but..."

She looked around. With the lights back on, the graffiti was barely visible, and she debated how much to explain. As a were-wolf, Amar was familiar with magic, but... did he believe in ghosts? Would he think she was going crazy from studying too much kooky witch stuff?

"Let's just say I'm starting to think there's some truth to the stories that this place might be haunted." Morgen crept over to peer in the back room, making sure the ghost wasn't lurking in a corner, but it was empty, and the chalk outline had stopped glowing. She waved at the front door. "Did you force that open?"

Amar shook his head. "No. It was unlocked."

"Of course it was." Morgen rubbed her face. "What happened outside? Is everything okay with the Loups?"

"I sent Arturo to get more of the pack. The Loups were challenging me, saying they know I was the reason the *rougarou* came and that it's *my* fault that some of them were killed." Amar hesitated, his expression growing uncharacteristically conflicted. "As much as I dislike them after all of the run-ins we've had, they're... not wrong. The *rougarou* followed the Lobos here and had it out for me, in particular."

"It's not your fault, and it's been over a month since the *rougarou* died. Have they been stewing about it all this time?"

"I think they might have just put all the pieces together. The Loups aren't that bright." Amar smiled faintly, but the humor didn't reach his eyes. "Now they're saying there have been too many werewolves in this town for too long and that they're going to do something about it. If Franklin hadn't been there, I think they would have tried something tonight. They seemed to be considering it even though he *was* there."

Morgen's phone rang. Still worried about Wendy, she answered right away, but it was her cousin.

"Hey, Zoe." Morgen thought about saying this wasn't the best time for her to come after all. Between the ghost problem and the Loups, this weekend might be nothing but trouble, and she winced as she remembered her brothers were also planning to show up.

"I've made it to town," Zoe said before Morgen could voice her concerns, "and I was wondering if you have food—*real* food—at the house, or if I should get some groceries."

"You're already here?" Morgen glanced at the time.

"Obviously."

"If by real food, you mean steaks carved off poor defenseless animals, then no, but I have peanut butter, plant-based breakfast patties, and a new box of strawberry-spinach-cashew protein bars."

"That's disgusting," Zoe said as Amar also curled his lip.

"You also have a haunch of elk in the freezer in the laundry room," Amar said.

"I have a *what?*" Morgen hadn't checked that freezer for a while, and, as she envisioned a huge slab of meat on the bone, she was glad.

"I stashed it there for the winter," he said. "In case we're snowed in."

"And need to gnaw on a frozen elk haunch together for sustenance?" This time, Morgen curled *her* lip.

"While getting cozy on the couch in front of a fire. It'll be romantic." Amar grinned.

"As haunch-gnawing often is."

His grin widened.

"Did you hear that, Zoe?" Morgen asked. "There's also an elk haunch."

How did one even prepare such a thing?

"You people are damaged. I'll get groceries."

Since the grocery store was only a few blocks away, Morgen felt compelled to say, "We're at the tannery building on Main Street just north of town if you want to stop in and see what you promised to help clean." After glancing toward the back room to make sure the ghost hadn't returned, she shared the address. Hopefully, the haunting portion of the night was over. "The first thing we're going to do tomorrow is get a bunch of meat hooks down from their precarious and deadly perch in the rafters. I hear customers don't like to be impaled when they visit shops."

"Cleaning. You really know how to entice me. Are there any hot werewolves there? Juan Martín, perhaps?"

"Amar and Arturo are around," Morgen said, though she didn't know if Arturo had returned from his errand.

"Arturo?"

"He's thirteen and has scars that women dig." Not sure how long the conversation would last, Morgen started a text to Wendy to check on her.

"Ew, Morgen. I meant hot werewolves of legal age."

"What's going on here?" a gruff voice said from the doorway.

Morgen jumped as Mayor Ungar walked in. She groaned. Wasn't once a day frequently enough for him to show up and harass her?

"The Loups were threatening me," Amar said coolly, looking him in the eye.

"They have reason to," Ungar said, having no trouble holding his gaze for a long moment before looking to Morgen. "I suppose now that you're leasing this place, there'll be non-stop trouble here."

"I don't think *I'm* the reason for any trouble."

"You were why the church was damaged and the graveyard decimated."

"I was the *target* of the witch who called a demon who damaged the church and graveyard." Morgen lifted her chin. "You can't blame me for that."

"I can, and I do," Ungar said.

Amar growled at him. It sounded *very* lupine.

Morgen hurried to put a hand on his bare forearm, hoping to keep him from shifting forms and seriously threatening the mayor. As if being a Loup wasn't bad enough, Ungar probably had the power to kick them out of town. He was *already* eyeing Wolf Wood and no doubt scheming about how much his pack would enjoy it if the property went back to the county.

A text came in from Wendy: *I'm fine, and I caught up with Napoleon, but he's still shaking, so I'm taking him to the vet to make sure he wasn't injured. Don't worry about me. I can get a ride back to the house later.*

Let me know if you need anything, and tell him he was wise to flee the loft.

Morgen lifted her foot and rotated it, aware of soreness now that her adrenaline levels had dropped.

"Hello?" came a familiar call from the parking lot. "Morgen? Is this the right place?"

Amar and Ungar turned around as Zoe sauntered up in heels, a high-low maxi skirt, and a blouse that managed to show off her cleavage *and* her belly button. She was dressed for a night out in Seattle, not a visit to a sleepy tourist town whose most exciting form of entertainment was the mini golf course.

"It could be," Ungar rumbled, eyeing Zoe's chest.

Horrified, Morgen lunged between Ungar and Amar, grabbed her cousin, and pulled her inside. That didn't keep Zoe from fluffing up her wavy brown hair and winking at Ungar on the way by. Amar opened his mouth to say something, but as soon as Morgen had her cousin inside, she pushed the men outside and shut the door.

"Private girl talk," she blurted by way of explanation. The last thing she wanted was for Zoe to hook up with *Ungar*.

"Yes, this is the old tannery I mentioned." Morgen smiled and spread an arm, standing to block the view of the meat hook on the floor. "Thanks for coming to play maid with me and help tidy it up."

"*Tidy it up?*" Zoe mouthed. "Morgen, you need a demolitions crew, not a maid. Never mind." She pointed to the board that

Morgen had stepped on earlier, the broken remains on the floor under the stairs. "I see you've already started on that."

"I'm the renter, not the owner. I can't demolish it."

"Are you sure? I'd double-check the contract."

"Ha ha."

"Maybe there's insurance money that could be collected if it burned down." Zoe eyed the ceiling, her gaze lingering on the meat hooks.

Alas, there was nowhere that Morgen could stand to block her view of the ones up there. "The owner would get the insurance money, not me. Please don't torch the building."

"You can get renter's insurance, you know."

"*Zoe.*"

"How long is the lease? You're not paying a lot, are you?"

"Two years, and no. As soon as I get the place cleaned up, fix the windows, and banish the ghost, it'll be fine."

"Banish the *ghost*?" Zoe gaped at her. "Maybe your brothers are right, and they *do* need to stage an intervention."

"We discussed this last time you came up. Magic is real." Morgen squinted at her. "You *said* you believed me."

"I do. Sort of. I became a believer after Juan Martín shifted into a wolf in front of my eyes. And then back into a man. He prowled into bed like a *wild thang.*" Her brown eyes gleamed with appreciation. "It was pretty titillating. Is he here?" Zoe peered under the stairs, as if hot werewolves might be hiding in the shadows, prepared to leap out and ravage her.

"No, but you can ask Amar if he's around and is available for a booty call."

Morgen reached for the door, hoping Ungar had wandered off so she could let Amar in. But it opened before she touched it, and Ungar and Franklin walked in.

"I need to get back to the station," Franklin said, waving his tablet. "Was there fresh graffiti or anything else you'd like me to put in my report before I go, Ms. Keller?"

"I was hoping you would catch the rock-throwing delinquent before you went." Morgen watched, horrified anew when Ungar stood next to Zoe, scant inches separating their shoulders. "Amar?" she called. "Are you still out there?"

Amar leaned through the doorway, his eyebrows raised. Maybe he'd planned to stay outside and keep an eye on any Loups lingering in the area. Too bad. This was more important.

Morgen gripped his hand, drew him in, and positioned him between Ungar and Zoe. "You remember my cousin, don't you? She struck up an acquaintance with Juan Martín last time she was here but failed to get his address and number. She's wondering if you could put her in touch with him."

"Juan Martín?" Ungar grunted. "That's the pool boy, isn't it?"

"Juan Martín designs and installs pools and hot tubs," Amar said. "He's good at his job."

"Every time I see him, he's got a shovel, and he's digging a hole like an undertaker."

"Hole digging is part of installing a pool." Amar looked at Zoe. "He's staying with the woman who owns the bakery."

Zoe's jaw drooped. "He has a girlfriend?"

"It's recent." Amar shrugged. "She gives him free bear claws."

"The pastry kind or body parts gnawed off bears?" Zoe asked.

"The former, I trust," Morgen said. "She runs a *vegan* bakery. I go there often."

"To pick up your spinach protein bars?" Zoe wrinkled her nose.

"No, I get those delivered by the box. Anne Marie—the baker —has berry scones that Lucky and I adore, and she's recently added a pumpkin cheesecake for the fall."

Amar's expression grew troubled as he regarded Morgen. "Those foods aren't good for you. Now that things have changed

—" he glanced toward her abdomen, "—shouldn't you purchase some healthy staples?"

"I've got plenty of healthy food."

"I meant meat. And organs." Amar started to say more but must have remembered that Morgen didn't want the word to get out about the baby until she'd confirmed it, for he drew her aside to whisper, "My grandmother insisted that riñones al jerez, menudo, and her famous fish-egg spread were ideal foods for the pregnant women in our family."

"That's nice, Amar, but you know I'm not eating animal products. Especially *organ* products."

"They are very healthy."

"So is high-fiber, low-carb granola."

Amar shook his head. "That's not real food. I'll talk to José Antonio, and we will bring you some quality food."

"I'm not eating organs."

"He's a good chef. He will make them so you like them."

"Amar." She planted a hand on his chest. "I appreciate that you care and want a healthy son or daughter, but I'm not eating kidneys or liver. *Ever*."

He squinted at her, and she imagined him mulling over ways to sneak pieces of the ghastly stuff into her smoothies.

"Look, let's just wait until we know for sure and not worry about things yet. We have other problems." Morgen eyed the meat hook.

Amar nodded, though he wore a mulish expression that looked like it might stick around. "Once you are certain, you will realize how important proper nutrition is. For the baby. The doctor will tell you so." His expression lightened. What, was he positive the doctor would side with him and give Morgen a long list of organ meats to consume?

If that happened, she would get a new doctor.

Not wanting to argue further, Morgen patted Amar on the chest and headed back to the others.

And none too soon. Franklin was wandering around, tapping notes into his tablet and snapping pictures—he'd taken one of the *freedom* message—but Ungar and Zoe were chatting with their heads tilted alarmingly close together. He said something, and she chuckled and swatted his arm.

What was Zoe doing? Ungar was neither witty nor charming.

As Morgen approached, Ungar smiled at her. It was a smug— maybe even *scheming*—smile, not a friendly one.

"This is your cousin, Keller?" he asked. "You didn't properly introduce her."

"She's pretty good at introducing herself." Morgen frowned at Zoe. Was her blouse unbuttoned farther than it had been when she'd walked in?

"Are you also a witch?" Ungar frowned at Zoe, as if he'd just realized that could be a possibility. "Another of Gwen's grand-children?"

Morgen wished Zoe *were* a witch so she could put a hex on the man.

"Nope." Zoe shook her head, managing to fluff her hair and toss a lock over her shoulder as she did so. "Morgen and I are related through our fathers, which means I didn't get anything from Gwen except an invitation to come for the weekend now and then. Sadly, I don't have any witch blood. I have to make do with my other attributes." Zoe let her hand trail from her hair down to her chest, fingering one of the unbuttoned buttons next to her cleavage and winked at him.

"Good," Ungar said, growling like the werewolf he was as he watched her fingering that button.

"Zoe, I need to tell you something," Morgen blurted, grabbing her cousin's wrist and pulling her away. It wasn't easy. Zoe appeared far more interested in latching herself to Ungar's side than hearing what Morgen had to say.

Ungar chuckled, watching Zoe's butt with appreciation, then looking at Morgen with that smug, scheming smile again. What was he thinking? That he could use Zoe to hurt Morgen somehow? The ass.

"What is it?" Zoe asked, glancing over her shoulder.

"You can't flirt with him," Morgen whispered. "He's the enemy."

"Enemy? Like a heinous criminal?" Leave it to Zoe to sound more intrigued than horrified.

"No, the mayor."

"You seem confused about how the law works and which side you're supposed to be on."

"He's also a werewolf from a rival pack."

Zoe's eyes brightened. "I *knew* he was a werewolf. They've all got that sexy animal magnetism about them."

"I know, but you can't date him. Or *sleep* with him. He's enemies with Amar. And Juan Martín." Morgen realized mentioning the man—werewolf—Zoe had slept with might do more to convince her. She barely knew Amar.

"If Juan Martín is shagging the baker, I don't care much about his enemies." Zoe looked over her shoulder at Ungar again— thankfully, he'd joined Franklin to discuss vandalism and wasn't smirking at Morgen anymore. "He fills out that plaid shirt like a quarterback."

"Just... avoid him, Zoe. Please. Amar and I will find you another werewolf. A *younger* one. Haven't you mentioned that you prefer hot young studs? Ungar's older than I am."

"Maybe, but he's very fit. I squeezed his arm, and it was like there were boulders under his shirt."

"Nothing sexier than rocks."

Zoe smiled. "That's right."

Franklin and Ungar walked over, Franklin tucking his tablet under his arm.

"As I mentioned, this has been a popular place for hooligans to target," he said. "If you're planning to move inventory and machinery in here, you may want to invest in a security system."

"She *has* a security system." Amar folded his arms over his chest.

"Are you going to start sleeping here?" Morgen asked him.

"I'll speak with the pack. We have some young men who might be willing to keep an eye on the place for less than the cost of a security system."

Morgen imagined Arturo lounging out front, attempting to look surly and dangerous to anyone checking out the building at night.

"I'll check with the local security outfit," she told Franklin.

"Do you want me to show you around town?" Ungar offered Zoe with a lazy smile. "We could grab a steak at the Timber Wolf."

Zoe opened her mouth, but Morgen rushed to sling an arm around her shoulders and speak first. "I'm making a special dinner for my cousin, so she can't go out tonight."

"Special dinner?" Zoe asked skeptically.

"Swedish meatballs. I've got a new recipe. You'll love them."

"Is there actual *meat* in the meatballs?"

"I make a meat version for Amar, and a meatless version for me. You're welcome to sample from either pan, though you may be surprised at what I can do with minced mushrooms."

Zoe looked wistfully toward Ungar, but Morgen used her arm to guide her outside before she could accept his dinner offer.

"The rival pack owns that restaurant," Morgen whispered as they stepped out into night air damp with the promise of rain. "Eating there is a bad idea."

After the others followed her out, Morgen locked the door, glancing once more toward the loft and the spot where the ghostly specter had hovered. Hopefully, it only came out at night, and if they did their cleaning during daylight hours, it wouldn't disturb them. Nonetheless, removing the meat hooks and anything else dangerous would be her first order of business. Maybe removing that whole death trap of a loft.

As for the ghost... she didn't know. Maybe Phoebe would have some ideas about how to banish it.

"You remember how to get to the house?" Morgen stopped beside Zoe's car, wanting to see her into it so she wouldn't wander off to join Ungar as soon as Morgen left.

"Yup. Go straight up the mountain, hit eighty-three potholes, and you're there."

"It's eighty-six, but close enough."

Zoe snorted and opened the door to her car.

The mayor was leaning against the door of his black SUV, watching them. No, watching Zoe's butt as she climbed in. As she took her *time* climbing in. Was she deliberately sticking her butt out?

Morgen ground her teeth and shifted to block Ungar's view. That man was going to be trouble. She was sure of it.

8

THE NEXT MORNING, MORGEN woke to the smell of something awful cooking. Her stomach protested mightily, and she lurched out of bed and to the bathroom. Fortunately, Amar and Lucky had already gotten up, so she didn't have to crawl over either of them, and she made it to the toilet in time.

"Morning sickness," she mumbled, growing more and more sure that her doctor's appointment would confirm that she was pregnant.

She threw on the bathroom fan, hoping it would suck up the stench coming from the kitchen. Whatever Amar—or might Zoe be responsible?—was cooking, it couldn't possibly be for human consumption. Maybe Lucky had begged until Amar had agreed to make something for him.

Once she brushed her teeth and suitably braced herself, Morgen went downstairs, but the odor only increased, making her want to run outside and gasp in fresh air.

"What are you *cooking*?" she asked as she staggered into the kitchen, her shirt pulled up over her nose.

Amar stood in front of the cooktop in nothing but his underwear and an apron, with a spatula in his hand as he browned sausages. Whatever was inside their casings, it wasn't anything *normal*. There was no way maple-pork sausages could smell that bad.

Lucky sat obediently beside Amar, snout pointed toward the frying pan as his tail swished on the floor. Apparently, he disagreed that the contents smelled awful, but Morgen knew well what kinds of things he enjoyed putting in his mouth, so his tastes were highly suspect. And so were Amar's.

"Good morning, Morgen." It wasn't yet dawn outside, but Amar launched a brilliant smile at her, as if the sun were beaming in the window and it was the perfect start to a perfect day.

Had the kitchen not been filled with such a dreadful scent, Morgen might have ogled Amar's near nudity, but all she could do was hurry to the cooktop to turn the fan from low to high—*very* high—then beeline to the coffee maker in the hope of overriding the foul scent with the delicious aroma of brewing arabica beans.

"I'm making you sausage," Amar said.

"Unless those are tofu sausages, which I'm *positive* they aren't, I'm not interested."

"I've also set out your favorite almond milk and granola." Amar gestured to the kitchen table with its checkered cloth. "But I want you to try one of these. You'll thank me for it. The *baby* will thank you for it." He gazed imploringly at her with an earnest I'm-doing-this-for-you expression. "José Antonio managed to snag the last of these from the butcher."

"The *last?* As if to imply that other people purchased them first? I don't believe you." Morgen started the coffee maker, eyed the table—he'd set out bowls, spoons, and plates already—and looked wistfully toward the outdoors. Too bad the sun *wasn't* streaming in, or she would have taken her coffee outside, but the thermometer on the porch read forty-three. A bit nippy for dining al fresco.

"They're favorites of the Loups. Normally, my pack would sneer at anything they like, but when something is delicious, sometimes it's all right that it comes from another country. They're called andouillette sausages," he said.

"I've heard of andouille sausage," Morgen said.

"Those are good if you can get authentic ones. The American versions just seem to be made from pork meat."

"And what are *those* made from?" She filled a coffee mug and pointed it at the frying pan.

He dished the brown sausages onto a plate, and Lucky's tail swished more vigorously.

"The pig's entire gastrointestinal system. As I told you, organ meats are very healthy. When we hunt, we consume all of our prey, everything except the fur." Amar took the plate to the table and waved for her to join him.

"I knew I was right to throw up." Morgen wrapped her hands around her coffee mug and backed away from the table. Since the fan wasn't sufficiently clearing the air, she opened the window, the brisk forty-three-degree air sweeping in. The scent of autumn leaves and dew rode the breeze, and she inhaled it deeply.

"I know you do not wish to eat such foods, but I want you to make an exception while you're pregnant. Just a few times a week."

He not only wanted her to eat those sausages, but he wanted her to eat them more than *once*? Torture. Even a non-vegetarian would find them dreadful. Nobody but a werewolf could get excited by the idea of eating pig intestines.

"Amar." Morgen made herself turn away from the window to meet his eyes. "I'm not going to eat meat just because I'm pregnant. My doctor assured me this is a healthy diet—much healthier than the way I used to eat."

He frowned at her. "I do not believe this is true. I have done research, and you must take vitamins to get all the nutrients you need. Your strange foods—" he gestured toward the pantry, "—are fortified with them, because they lack substance on their own. But vitamins are not good enough for a mother creating *life*." His finger shifted toward her abdomen.

"Amar..." Morgen rubbed her face.

He pronged a sausage on a fork and held it up toward her. "Just try one."

Lucky stood up and whined hopefully at the sausage being thrust into the air.

"No. I'll talk to my doctor about what he recommends, but I'm *positive* that won't be it." She pointed at the sausage dripping grease onto the floor and shuddered.

Lucky surged forward to lick up the spatters.

"I need to get ready for the drive to Seattle. Will you keep an eye on Zoe while I'm gone? I'm worried that she might try to hook up with Mayor Ungar."

"Do you wish me to go with you to your appointment?"

Morgen imagined him running into the office to show Dr. Brightman the sausage and explain his theories about nutrition. "No, thank you. Maybe when things are further along, but I don't want to leave Zoe here alone. Or Lucky. You know how needy he is."

Amar eyed the dog who'd polished the floor to a sheen. Morgen made a note to mop later.

"Your hound *is* needy."

"Thank you," Morgen repeated, kissing Amar on the cheek and fleeing the kitchen before he could wave the sausage at her again. As much as she appreciated that he cared, she worried this wouldn't be the first argument over food, and a part of her was already starting to dread the next eight months.

9

Morgen drove back from Seattle, her electric car on autopilot in the slow lane on the freeway. Dr. Brightman had confirmed what she had believed: she was pregnant. They'd *briefly* discussed nutrition, but all the doctor had recommended was taking a multi-vitamin with folate in it. Intestine sausages hadn't come up. Morgen hoped Amar wouldn't be cooking anything else when she returned home.

She'd already checked in on Wendy—fortunately, Napoleon had recovered from his harrowing experience—so she called Phoebe. The pregnancy wouldn't change anything for a while. The haunted building, however, needed to be taken care of immediately.

"Crystal Parlor, your source for the best healing crystals and rare powders in the Pacific Northwest," Phoebe answered, her voice coming over the car's speakers.

"Don't you have caller ID?"

"Of course. Despite spending all that time here, organizing the goods and getting the shop online, you've failed to purchase even a single crystal. I thought it might be time."

Morgen started to snort but caught herself. "Actually, the formula I found for making tracking charms for dogs calls for agates. If you can give me a bulk deal on those, I'll take some."

"Excellent. I'll put together a package of a hundred."

"A *hundred?* I was thinking more like twelve."

"That hardly constitutes bulk. I've put more agates on a keychain."

Morgen imagined someone falling into a pond and being dragged down to the bottom by such a keychain. "I don't need to make a hundred tracking charms. I've only got orders for three."

Remembering the list Arturo had given her, she vowed to get to work on the flea-and-tick charms as well. Until they got the new shop up and running, she could perform the rituals in Grandma's root cellar.

"For now," Phoebe said. "Once the word gets out that you're making them, they'll be popular. Should I put you down for two hundred agates?"

"This isn't what I called to talk to you about."

"Two hundred, it is. What else can I help you with?"

"What do you know about the ghost in the old tannery building?" Morgen wished she'd asked for more information during the tour—and hadn't signed the lease until she'd gotten it.

"Ghost?"

"You mentioned it yesterday."

"Oh, yes, but that's just a story that the townspeople have told for decades. I've not seen conclusive evidence that ghosts exist." Phoebe paused. "Have you?"

"Last night was somewhat conclusive." Morgen thought of the meat hook and shuddered.

"Interesting. About half of the members of the coven believe they exist, and some claim to have seen them—Theodora often goes to the graveyard, seeking advice from her dead ancestors—but the rest of us are skeptical."

"The witches believe in magic and cast incantations and hexes, but they're skeptical of ghosts?"

"*Magic* is not synonymous with the supposed existence of paranormal apparitions."

Morgen sighed. "Does that mean you don't have any ideas about how to banish one from one's newly leased property?"

Phoebe's second pause was longer. "What exactly did you see?"

"A floating white shape with vague arms, legs, and a head."

"That sounds like the Hollywood rendition. Are you sure someone wasn't pranking you? That Lobo boy who favors mailbox baseball to more legitimate activities, perhaps?"

This time, Morgen hesitated. Arturo *had* been in the area, but the Lobos called her part of the pack and acted respectfully toward her these days. Why would Arturo or any of them have played a prank on her? If anything, the Loups would be the ones she would suspect, but they tended to be blunt and direct. Pranks didn't seem like something in their repertoire.

"I'm not sure, but if the ghost shows up again, I'll be sure to mention how Hollywood she is."

"Did, uh, *she* talk to you?"

"She asked for help, then tried to drop a meat hook on my head and kill me."

"Seriously?"

"Well, the meat hook dropped at the same time as the ghost was in the building. I suppose it could have just *happened* and been a coincidence, but..." As Morgen took the exit for Bellrock, rain started up, pattering on the windshield.

"You're aware that there are incantations for moving objects?" Phoebe asked.

"I inputted some into my database, yes."

Morgen twitched as she thought of the incantation that allowed a witch to turn invisible. She'd used it herself a couple of times. Why hadn't she considered that the night before? Maybe it hadn't been a werewolf pranking her but a *witch*. As far as she knew, Wendy's sister Olivia was still out there—and she might be holding a grudge. In fact, Morgen would be shocked if she *wasn't* holding a grudge. However inadvertently, Morgen had caused their sister Nora's death.

"Do you know if there are any incantations for seeing *through* an invisibility illusion?" Morgen tried to recall if she'd inputted anything like that, but she'd scanned and hand-copied thousands and thousands of pages of information when she'd been building her database, so it was just luck when she remembered something specific.

"Yes. Look up *detect invisibility*. I'll poke around in some of my old books to see if there's anything mentioned about ghosts, but you may learn more by researching the specific history of that building."

"That's a good point. Like I should find out how many people have died there, for starters." Maybe she could visit the town library. Despite her love of books, she hadn't checked out the little building behind the Grocery Expedition yet. Ever since she'd taken her reading digital, she'd been a less faithful patron of physical libraries.

"I imagine that would be useful. Is there anything else I can help you with?" Phoebe's voice turned smug as she added, "I have an order of agates to pack up."

"No hurry on that. Oh, there is one more thing I was wondering about." Morgen hesitated, seeking a delicate way to bring up a relationship that seemed to embarrass her mentor. "Are you and Mayor Ungar... monogamous with each other?"

"Goodness, no. As I told you, I don't want to see him at all. It's just..."

"The animal magnetism, I know."

"When he shows up, it's hard to say no. Since my husband died, I haven't had that many steady relationships."

"I'm sorry. I didn't know you'd been married."

"He was older than I and passed nearly eight years ago. And since then... Well, this may surprise you, but the townsfolk tend to think I'm a touch quirky."

"I've heard that selling geodes isn't the most typical business that people start." Not that Morgen, who was getting into the magical-charms business, could talk. She'd had to quash three people's smirking suggestions that she name her establishment *Lucky Charms*. As if she could use something that was trademarked.

"Those of us in the coven aren't always the most normal people in general," Phoebe admitted. "On top of that, there are a lot more single women in town than men. So, when a hunky virile young stud shows up at your door..."

Morgen made a heroic effort not to gag at that description of the mayor. She supposed to fifty-something Phoebe, forty-some-thing Ungar counted as young, but her brain refused to accept that the other adjectives fit him.

"I understand," she made herself say. "I just brought it up because..." Should she mention that Ungar had been flirting with Zoe, or would that hurt Phoebe's feelings? Just because she said they weren't monogamous with each other didn't mean Phoebe wanted to hear about Ungar panting over another woman. Still, Morgen worried about that scheming look he'd worn, as if he wanted to hurt Morgen through her cousin. She had to know if he was someone who would do that. "He strikes me as kind of a jerk, Phoebe. I know I'm predisposed to not like the Loups much—the interactions I've had with them haven't exactly been joyful—but am I reading him wrong? Is he... okay to someone he's dating?"

"He's not abusive or anything like that, if that's what you're getting at. I mean, he's a little rough, but..."

"Sometimes, a girl likes that?" Morgen asked, quoting words Phoebe had used before.

Phoebe cleared her throat. "Sometimes. Why are you asking? Is everything okay with you and *your* young hunk?"

"Yes, everything's fine with Amar." Morgen didn't bring up the sausage fiasco. "I'm definitely not interested in Ungar. Trust me. But, uhm, someone who's visiting me might be. I'm trying to steer her away from him, but..."

"Not your sister?"

"No, no." Morgen almost choked on the idea of Sian having a physical relationship with Ungar—or anyone. "But my cousin is here, and she's more of a flirt. She met Ungar last night."

"I see." Damn, Phoebe's voice had gone stiff. Maybe she *did* want to keep Ungar for herself.

Morgen shook her head as she took the turn up to the house and wished she hadn't brought this up, but she had to know. "Like I said, I'm trying to deter her interest..." Morgen couldn't believe that odious man had multiple women interested in him. Couldn't they see his *personality* through his bouldery muscles? "But in case I'm not able to, I wanted to make sure he wouldn't hurt her."

"I don't think so. Not *physically* anyway."

"What does that mean?"

"Well, he's not the type to develop strong feelings for a woman. Or anyone except his mother, as far as I can tell. I'm a little surprised he takes care of her. He's quite aloof. The love 'em and leave 'em type. If you profess that you have feelings for him, he'll pat you on the cheek and say he doesn't get attached. Then off he goes. Which is fine." Stung emotion laced Phoebe's words. "As if any self-respecting witch would want to be involved with a furry werewolf."

"Sorry, Phoebe. I didn't mean to upset you." Morgen grimaced, wishing she hadn't brought this up and also wishing she knew what to say to make Phoebe feel better. Like her sister, Morgen was horrible at understanding people's emotions and saying the right thing. Their mother hadn't been good at it either. "And thanks for the warning."

She almost said that she would let her cousin know, but she doubted Zoe would be deterred by such information. Since Zoe would head back to Seattle after she'd satisfied her urges, she might *prefer* a man like that.

Unfortunately, the description of Ungar only worried Morgen more, making her certain that he was the kind of man who might try to manipulate Zoe to get at Morgen. She shook her head. What had she done to earn all these enemies?

She resolved to put Phoebe's two hundred agates to use, craft as many charms as she could, and sell the heck out of them so she could pay the taxes on Wolf Wood and ensure Ungar had no reason to interact with her again or think of her at all.

10

When Morgen parked in the driveway, the barn door was open wide, the whir of power tools emanating from within. Wendy's van was gone, but Zoe's car was there, and Morgen blew out a relieved breath, glad she hadn't gone on a sightseeing adventure with Ungar.

Although, she realized with a start, he could have come to pick her up. The car being there didn't mean she was home.

Wanting to check, Morgen strode toward the house, but she paused to peer into the barn. The framework of a half-constructed crib rested on the cement floor next to several completed dog beds, cat condos, and a fancy six-foot-tall parrot—or maybe crow? —perch.

At the workbench, Amar was bent over a project with his electric sander—thankfully, he was wearing more than his underwear and an apron now. He spotted her, glanced over, and turned it off. "What did the doctor say? You are pregnant? Everything is well?"

Though still nervous about the whole thing, Morgen smiled and nodded at him. "I am, and things are good. It's still very early, but there's nothing awry so far."

"I am glad." Amar set down the sander and strode toward her, waving at his projects along the way. "I am working hard to build up an inventory and fill orders. We must have enough money to pay for all the things a baby needs that I can't build."

"I agree. As soon as I check on Zoe, I'll get to work crafting charms. I want to get those taxes paid so Ungar doesn't have any reason to harass me." Morgen thought about mentioning the possibility that an invisible witch had been responsible for the ghostly incidents in the tannery, but that sounded almost as silly as the notion of ghosts themselves. Once she found an incantation that would help her detect people through invisibility magic, she would drag Amar down there, and they could see for themselves if a tangible being was behind the trouble.

"He has been harassing you?" Amar reached her and clasped her hands, his eyes narrowing.

"Not physically. Not even verbally, I guess. He just smirks and makes snide comments about the county taking back the house and his Loups cavorting unimpeded through Wolf Wood."

"That will *not* happen," Amar growled.

"Good."

Amar looked toward the house, as if he'd heard a sound. Hopefully, that meant Zoe was inside. "He was lusting after your cousin."

"I noticed."

"I thought about challenging him and telling him to knock it off, but she..." His lip curled.

"Encouraged it. I know."

"A Loup would be an inferior lover."

"I have no doubt. I'll let her know." Morgen threaded her fingers through his and kissed him. "It should be obvious that *Lobos* are the best lovers."

"Yes." Amar slid his arm around her as he returned the kiss.

All thoughts of getting right to work tumbled out of her mind as she leaned into him.

But Amar pulled back sooner than she expected and frowned toward the driveway. "Someone is coming."

Morgen groaned. It wouldn't be Ungar, would it? She was positive she hadn't given Zoe enough time to get his number, but Morgen *had* mentioned he was the mayor. If Zoe was determined enough to hook up with him, she might have called his office.

Amar's nostrils twitched. "It's Dr. Valderas," he said before the vet's truck rolled into view.

Morgen sagged in relief, but only for a moment before a thought occurred to her. "You didn't call him, did you? About my pregnancy?"

No, he shouldn't have. Amar had known she was going to see her own doctor. Still, his words about Valderas's expertise with delivering *foals* popped into her mind.

"I did not call him," Amar said.

"Huh. He knows Sian is back in Seattle for her new job. I wonder what brought him up." Morgen slipped out of Amar's grip as the truck parked in the driveway.

Valderas stepped out, wearing a suit, vest, and loafers, and nodded toward them. His face was grave, and Morgen tried to tell if he appeared worried about something, but he was never very ebullient.

"Hi, Doc." Morgen waved. "What's up?"

Valderas smiled briefly. "Don't you mean, *What's up, Doc*?"

"Sure, though I'm not waving a carrot or dressed like a cartoon rabbit today."

"This morning, one of the Loups came in to see me, one of their younger members. He's known to be a bit of a delinquent."

"Aren't they *all* known to be delinquents?" Morgen asked before remembering that Valderas was technically one of them. At the least, a Loup had bitten him during a full moon and turned him into a werewolf. He'd said he hadn't had a choice, and she believed him, but he did treat both packs, so he might not have as much antipathy toward the Loups as she did.

"Not all," Valderas said. "The one this morning is young, not much older than Arturo. You know how youths tend to find trouble."

"I've heard that."

"He also found what I believe is a *meat hook*."

Dread swam into Morgen's stomach. "From the tannery? Did he hurt someone with it?"

Valderas leaned into his vehicle and pulled out a rusty meat hook identical to the one that had fallen—it might *be* the one that had fallen. Since Morgen had been in a hurry to get Zoe out of the tannery—and away from Ungar—she'd left it on the floor.

"Actually, he himself was hurt with it." Valderas held it up to the sun and grimaced at blood staining its tip. "It was lodged in his lower back when he hobbled into my office. Fortunately, he was smart enough not to yank it out on his own. The curved tip makes it quite wicked, and it barely missed one of his kidneys."

"Who lodged it in his back?"

Had a fight broken out behind the tannery? Or *inside* it? She'd locked the door, but after her experience the night before, she was skeptical of those locks.

"He doesn't know. He said someone threw it from behind as he was wandering through the parking lot beside the tannery." Valderas raised his eyebrows. "I got the feeling he wasn't telling me the whole truth and that he might have been skulking around inside. He seemed sincerely confused about who threw the hook though."

"Why is that place catnip to all the delinquents in town?"

Valderas spread his hand. "It's been abandoned since before I came to Bellrock, so I don't know much about it."

"You mean you haven't heard the stories about it being haunted?"

"I hear a lot of stories about this town." Valderas shrugged dismissively.

"Do you think someone did throw it at him? Was the angle right, or might it have fallen from above? I had one drop off and almost impale *me* last night."

"That's odd, especially considering they've presumably been up there for decades. Or at least years. I suppose some previous renter might have installed them for atmosphere or some such."

"The enticing atmosphere evoked by meat hooks, yes." Morgen shook her head, wondering if it was too late to back out of that lease. She and Amar might have been better off pitching a tent on the Main Street sidewalk and selling their wares in the open air.

Valderas closed his eyes, perhaps envisioning the wound. "It *might* have come from above, especially if he was bending over for some reason, and his back was toward the ceiling, but it also might have been thrown. *He* thought it was thrown."

"He didn't say what he was doing there?"

"Just hanging out, he said." Valderas lifted a shoulder. "The Loups don't confide in me as much as they used to. I believe they know that I've... made friends with your sister. And they have strong feelings about *you*."

"So I've gathered."

Amar had come over, so Morgen leaned against him for support.

"I stitched him up, and he'll recover," Valderas said, "but I thought you should know it was possible he'd been skulking in your new building."

Her new old haunted building, yes.

"Thank you. I appreciate that, and I'm about to start working on the order you gave to Arturo."

"Excellent." Valderas turned toward his truck but paused with his hand on the door and looked back. He cleared his throat diffidently. "I was thinking of sending a gift to Sian to let her know... I've appreciated her conversation and hope she'll return to Bellrock for a visit soon. Do you have any suggestions about what she might like? I've picked up a first-edition Jane Goodall for her but wonder if she has a favorite sweet that might be an appropriate accompaniment."

"Uhm, she likes lots of sweets. Chocolate caramels are a particular favorite. When she was working out of the country, she made me send some from the factory store in Seattle that we like. I'm sure they melted as soon as they arrived in Borneo, but she didn't seem to care."

"Good. I'll look into that."

"Ah, Doc?" Morgen stepped away from Amar and lowered her voice. "I'm glad you guys are becoming friends, but you know Sian isn't very *physical*, right? I don't think she's that interested in that."

She hoped Sian had already made that clear to Valderas, but if she hadn't, Morgen hated the idea of the good vet being disappointed when the chocolate-covered caramels didn't lead to a passionate night of amore.

"Oh, I know," Valderas said. "She made that clear, and I find it quite refreshing."

"Oh?" Morgen had hoped that might be the case, but she hadn't been sure. In her experience, most guys were interested in sex.

"Indeed. As I mentioned before, some of the less morally upright members of the coven used their magic to coerce me into —" his lips twisted, "—satisfying their desires. The authorities either refused to believe it or said I should consider myself lucky, since they were *hot*." His lips twisted further into a full-on feral snarl. "I did *not* consider myself lucky. Perhaps it is wrong of me, but I'm not displeased that Nora did not survive her last encounter with you. It's a shame that Olivia wasn't in the wreck too."

Morgen couldn't bring herself to nod in agreement, not when they were talking about the deaths of people, but she was glad to have someone on her side, someone who seemed to believe she'd done the town a service. With all the enemies she'd managed to acquire, she needed as many allies as she could get.

"In the aftermath of that," Valderas said, smoothing his vest and recovering his equanimity, "I'm quite content not to have to *perform* for a woman. And I find Sian to be a stimulating conversationalist."

"Does that mean you like her lectures?" Morgen smiled.

"As she likes mine. And argues the points and demands I produce evidence to back them up." He found his smile again.

"Who doesn't love someone who argues with them?"

"Who *challenges* them. We should all find someone like that." Valderas bowed to her, tossed the meat hook onto the passenger seat, and climbed into his truck.

"I challenge you." Amar wrapped an arm around her shoulders as Valderas drove away.

"I'd be content if you simply supported me, especially when it comes to food choices."

"Mm," he said neutrally. "Didn't you once say your diet allows you to eat fish?"

"Yes." She eyed him, afraid he would show up with fish-intestine sausage next. Hopefully, that wasn't actually a thing. People usually threw *away* fish guts, didn't they?

"I told you about my grandmother's fish-egg dish. She believed the eggs were highly nutritious."

"Oh, Amar." She thunked her forehead against his chest.

"Perhaps if you consumed such eggs, it would overcome the other deficiencies in your diet. Also, they are salty and briny and delicious."

"I'm having the urge to throw up again."

"I am reading about morning sickness. Once you pass the first trimester, it should go away."

She doubted it would ever go away if he kept bringing up his favorite foods.

11

"Who was that sexy man with the goatee and mustache who came to visit you earlier?" Zoe asked as she and Morgen scrubbed the floor in the back room of the tannery.

After spending two hours making charms in the root cellar, Morgen had been interrupted by her cousin wanting to see the town and do something fun. Morgen had taken her to the fudge shop and the bath-and-body store before swinging into the tannery to start cleaning. Though Zoe had said that didn't qualify as *fun,* she was willing to do it. At least for a while.

It probably helped that Amar and several of the handy Lobos had come down and were replacing the broken windows and reinforcing the loft. Zoe had her butt toward the door as she scrubbed on her hands and knees, and more than one Lobo had peered in, checking her out. She wasn't wearing a skirt today, but her leggings left little to the imagination.

"Dr. Valderas is the town vet, and he's taken." Morgen shook her head, bemused that she and Zoe were related, and shifted from scrubbing one of the stains—she might have to bring in a sander—to the chalk outline.

"Not by another baker, I hope."

"No."

"I guess that means I should keep my focus on the mayor."

"There are plenty of available werewolves out there." Morgen waved toward the door, but Arturo happened to be walking by, and she shooed him along. He was too young to ogle Zoe's backside.

"Hm." Zoe glanced back and smiled at Fernando as he wandered past carrying panes of glass. "There are some decent possibilities, but a lot of them could stand to wash their armpits more often. The yellow stains on their tank tops aren't that sexy."

"I thought you liked the rugged, hard-working types." Since Morgen had also observed that the pit-stained wife-beater tank tops that many of the Lobos favored weren't sexy, she couldn't blame Zoe for curling a lip at that. Still, they were honest, hard-working guys, and Morgen would recommend them over the mayor, who didn't seem to have anything better to do than pester her.

"I do, but not if they're overly fragrant. Love enters through the nose, you know."

"I actually did not know that. You could always ignore the werewolves, and we could hang out and talk about ways to lower one's property taxes."

Zoe smiled sadly at her. "I looked up your record when you mentioned it had been updated. There's not much that can be done. Grandma owned a lot of land, and you don't qualify for any of the exemptions she had. You're neither a veteran, married to a veteran, nor a senior citizen. And what were you thinking when you added that fancy deck and hot tub? It looks like something from those multi-million-dollar houses that overlook Puget Sound."

"I didn't ask for that deck. It just appeared one day, thanks to the hard-working Lobos. Since it only overlooks a forest and an owl nesting box, that ought to make it less valuable." Morgen scrubbed harder at the chalk outline. She could understand a bloodstain that had been sitting for decades being hard to get up, but why couldn't she rub out these white lines?

"The appraiser who valued the house didn't think so."

"No kidding." Morgen wagered Ungar had made *sure* the appraiser didn't miss anything. "Do you think their estimate of the land value is too high? Would it be worth talking to a real-estate lawyer?"

"Maybe, but in the meantime, you better plan to pay the taxes this year. Do you have enough?"

"I'm working on it. I could move some more money out of my 401K, but, Zoe, I have to pay that much every *year*." Not to mention that, with a child now on the way, she hated the idea of taking anything out of her savings; dear God, she would one day have to send the kid to college. "What I really need is for my new business to take off. And maybe to start charging for my app, though that doesn't seem right. I'd hate to charge witches just to access the information they need for their potions and spells. Maybe Wendy and I could work on another app with the idea of monetizing it from the beginning."

Morgen took a deep breath and told herself that things would turn out fine. She had a knack for making magical talismans and charms, and she had already received a lot of orders. She just needed to be patient.

"Either that, or you could put a tip jar by the hot tub. Sian mentioned it was popular with the werewolves." Zoe smiled out the doorway at someone. "Mind if I invite a few of them up?"

"Just not the mayor."

"Are you sure? I could tell from patting his arm that he'll look *great* naked."

"You were groping his arm, not patting it, and my hot tub is a nudity-free zone."

"What a prudish thing to say. Are you forty or eighty?"

"I'm the person who has to clean the tub. I don't want naked body parts rubbed on the benches or pubic hair in the filters." Morgen shuddered.

A creak came from the corner, startling her. She spun, hefting her scrub brush like a weapon.

One of the metal doors to the oversized closet that held the dusty metal statue had swung outward. Nobody stood next to the door, and there was no reason for it to have opened.

"What kind of hideous decor is that?" Zoe asked.

"It came with the place."

Morgen eyed the statue from its bulbous metal head to flat feet, expecting a raccoon or rodent to dart out. Something had to have bumped the door and caused it to open. There hadn't been wind or a draft—Amar and Fernando had already replaced the windowpanes in this room.

"Like the meat hooks," Morgen added, though she'd talked a couple of the Lobos into climbing up and taking those down. That had been the first order of business.

"Uh," Zoe repeated.

Morgen set down the brush—she still hadn't managed to get the outline up—and climbed to her feet. She grabbed her staff, pointed it at the open door, and gripped her amulet.

"Under the moon's magic, enemy who lurks forbidden, reveal to this witch where you're hidden," she said, whispering the incantation she'd found, thanks to Phoebe's direction, that was supposed to let her detect invisible people.

"Reveal the what to who?" Zoe asked.

"I'm saying an incantation to detect invisible enemies." Morgen felt sheepish, especially since nothing happened, but she willed more power into her words and repeated them.

The gauzy mesh of something like a wedding veil came over

her vision. Did that mean she'd successfully cast the spell and was peering around for invisible people?

"Did it work?" Zoe asked skeptically.

Morgen peeked into the closet behind the metal sculpture, didn't see so much as a rat, then looked all around the room. They could hear the Lobos working out front, but she and Zoe were alone back here.

She closed the door on the statue, then stepped out into the main room, searching for an intruder among the working men. Nothing. She peered toward the loft but couldn't make out much from her position. Besides, if someone had opened that door, they couldn't have run out of the area that quickly. If they'd tried, the keen-eared and keen-nosed werewolves would have detected them.

As Morgen turned toward the back room again, she spotted a rust-brown stain on the wall beside the door and almost shrieked. A gasp must have escaped, for Amar rushed over to stand next to her.

"What's wrong?" He rested a hand on her shoulder and looked where she was looking.

Morgen pointed, though she doubted he would be able to see the stain. She'd walked past that wall a dozen times and hadn't, not until she'd cast the spell.

"That old wood paneling needs paint," Amar said, "but I doubt that's what startled you. You look like you've seen a ghost."

She wished she could laugh at the familiar saying, but it was too relevant—too *true*—right now. "Not a ghost. Another blood-stain. A very prominent one. You can't see anything there?" She outlined the large stain on the wall—a *lot* of blood had splashed against it, if what she saw was an indication of something that had once happened.

"No." Amar stepped toward the wall and ran his hand over it, eyeing it closely. "Actually, I think there was something here once.

Something dark. It seeped into the wood, but it's long since been cleaned." He sniffed, though Morgen doubted decades-old blood smelled like much. "Interesting," he said, sniffing again. "Fernando, come smell this wall."

Morgen raised her eyebrows. Maybe she was wrong, and some vestige of the scent remained.

Fernando joined them, and she might have laughed at seeing the big men sniffing a wall, but she knew better.

"Blood," Fernando said. "Very old blood, but it was human."

"The same as with the other stains." Amar waved toward faded dark spots on the floor.

Morgen hadn't seen him sniffing those, but she trusted his nose.

"It's hard to see this one." Fernando turned toward Morgen. "How did you know?"

"She is powerful." Amar smiled proudly at her. "She knows many things."

"You were wise to make her your mate," Fernando said.

"Yes." Amar stepped closer and wrapped his arm around Morgen's waist.

She didn't feel that powerful, and something about the garish bloodstain disturbed her more than the old ones on the floor— maybe because it appeared so vibrant in the vision she was having. It was as if the violence had *just* happened.

It wasn't a vision, she reminded herself. She'd cast a spell to see that which was invisible. Or... had been deliberately obscured? With some magic?

Since she hadn't found an invisible witch sneaking around, she released her amulet and willed the power of the incantation to leave her. The gauziness that had fallen over her eyes disappeared, and the bloodstain faded until, once more, all she could see was the wood paneling.

"More than animals were slain in this place." Amar was watching her.

"Yeah," she whispered, willing the rattled expression on her face to smooth over. "When there's time, I'm going to the library to see if I can find old records on the building. I already tried to check online, but there's not much about anything in Bellrock. Our little town doesn't even rate a Wikipedia entry. One wonders how the tourists find it."

With orders to fill and the building to get cleaned up, Morgen didn't know *when* she could visit the library. Too bad she couldn't outsource that work to an assistant. Wendy might be willing to do it, but Morgen didn't know how much time she spent in libraries —especially *old* libraries that probably still relied on card catalogs and microfiche.

Too bad Sian had gone back to Seattle. She *loved* research. Research about animal socialization and psychology, not ghosts, admittedly, but Morgen might be able to talk her into stretching her boundaries. Or maybe the opportunity to socialize with a man currently shopping for a gift for her would entice her.

"Hm."

"Your expression has gone from troubled to scheming," Amar observed.

"Has it? You're getting to know me well."

"Wolves are observant. It helps with hunting."

"You need to know when your prey is scheming?"

"Indeed. I once had an antelope try to lead me off a cliff."

Morgen looked at his face, wondering if he was teasing her or if that was true. "Are you saying that the local woodland creatures are like the roadrunner, and you're Wile E. Coyote?"

"I didn't *fall* off the cliff, so I'm nothing like a cartoon coyote." He lifted his chin. "Or *any* type of coyote. They are weasely scavengers. Wolves are mighty hunters."

"Who have to look out for scheming antelope." She smiled and rested her hand on his chest.

"Better than a scheming mayor."

Morgen lowered her hand. "Do you think he is? That the Loups might be behind the trouble here?"

Amar eyed the wood paneling. "It's unlikely they had anything to do with a decades-old stain, but Ungar has been here a long time, possibly his whole life."

"He could be a resource about this place if he wasn't such a prick."

"I would avoid him if I were you."

"I hope I'll be able to," Morgen murmured.

"I didn't know I'd have to scrub this place down by myself," Zoe called from the back room.

"I'd better get back to cleaning." Morgen eyed the wall one last time, grabbed her scrub brush, and returned to the chalk outline.

12

RAIN FORMED PUDDLES ON THE SIDEWALK OUTSIDE AS MORGEN straightened and rubbed her back. Three flea-and-tick charms lay on the counter, glowing a slight blue, proof that she could work in the old tannery, at least for the rituals that didn't require nudity. The Lobos were cleaning in the other room, and the windows lacked curtains, so that would have been a no-go.

After an hour of helping with cleaning, Zoe had headed into town to shop. That was what she'd claimed. It was possible she'd gone to visit the mayor's office, but she did enjoy browsing for knickknacks to fill the shelves in her apartment. Morgen had promised to pick her up on the way home.

Amar leaned his head into the back room. "Do you have any problem with some of the Lobos working on projects here from time to time? Pedro and I are talking about going in together on a table saw and sharing it. He said they'd chip in a couple hundred a month to contribute to the rent."

"Then I have no problem whatsoever." Morgen already had plans to section off the woodworking area from what would be the showroom for the clients, so it wouldn't matter if there were extra werewolves in there.

"Good. We're going to head out for a snack at Angus before gathering to hunt later. Do you want to come?"

Morgen was about to say *yes*, since the last thing she wanted was to be left here alone after dark again, but Pedro and Fernando ambled up to stand behind Amar in the doorway.

"Congratulations on your future offspring," Pedro told Morgen, sticking out a hand.

Fernando gave a thumbs-up.

"Uh, thanks." Morgen accepted the handclasp, though she looked at Amar. Hadn't they agreed not to tell people yet?

"I didn't say anything about it," Amar said. "They figured it out based on some questions I was asking the men who are fathers."

Morgen's mind boggled as she tried to imagine *any* of the Lobos as fathers, but she supposed some of them were in their thirties and forties. Maybe it made sense that they had women stashed away somewhere. Not in caves, forced to tan hides and cook elk bones into soup stock, she trusted.

Amar lifted his shoulders. "It's all new to me. I... want to make sure it goes well and that I do all the things I should."

"It's fine," Morgen said, "and I appreciate it."

"We will celebrate," Pedro said, "with a party. José Antonio will make excellent dishes for a pregnant woman."

Morgen couldn't stifle a groan, but the Lobos didn't notice.

Pedro elbowed Amar in the ribs. "You know what to bring her back from the hunts, yes? Female reproductive organs. You know what they say: like supports like. She must eat the best foods to ensure a healthy baby."

Morgen groaned again. Did *all* werewolves have these beliefs?

"I'm trying to encourage that," Amar said, a now-familiar aggrieved expression entering his eyes, "but she insists on eating junk food."

Pedro and Fernando gasped and murmured softly in Spanish as they crossed themselves. Were they *praying* for her? She hadn't thought any of them were religious.

"High-fiber, high-protein vegan granola isn't junk food," Morgen assured them, though she couldn't say the same about the pumpkin cheesecake that kept calling to her.

All three men shook their heads with concern. They might have said more, but someone called out from the entrance of the building.

Amar glanced over his shoulder. "Your mentor is here."

"Phoebe?" Morgen asked, glad for an excuse to drop the subject.

"Yes."

"I'll see what she wants."

"You will join us to dine?" Pedro asked.

"As long as you don't have the chef at the restaurant prepare any special meals for me." Angus was a competitor to the carnivore-favored Timber Wolf, and, from what Morgen had seen of the menu, offered dishes along the same lines.

Pedro opened his mouth, closed it again, and shook his head woefully at Amar. He and Fernando wandered off, leaving only Amar in the doorway. Morgen waited warily, afraid organs would come up again.

He glanced toward the wood paneling where she'd seen the stain. "I can wait with you until you're ready to leave, if you wish."

Morgen took a deep breath, almost thankful to have his attention focused back on the building. "It'll be fine. It's not fully dark yet."

"You think the Loups will only harass you at night?"

"I think a *ghost* will only harass me at night."

His eyebrows rose.

Morgen smiled and shrugged, not sure yet what she believed was responsible for the trouble. Since her invisibility spell hadn't revealed anyone skulking about, and since the things she'd experienced the night before would have been difficult for someone to orchestrate without magic, she wasn't that inclined to suspect the Loups.

"Very well." Amar inclined his head and walked toward the door.

Phoebe's voice floated in, something about the building already looking better, as Morgen's phone rang. They had managed to clean the dust, sand the bloodstains, and repair some of the questionable posts and beams supporting the loft, but the chalk outline still taunted Morgen from the floor. After scrubbing it had failed, Fernando had run his electric sander over it, but three seconds into his efforts, the outlet had died, shorting out something in the tool in the process.

"Hello, Sian," she answered, holding up a finger when Phoebe appeared in the doorway. "What delightful circumstance has resulted in you calling me twice in the same week?"

"Our brothers are heading up tomorrow." There weren't any monkeys hooting in the background, so maybe Sian had gone home early. "I thought you should know."

"Thanks. Any chance you'd like to come up for the weekend?"

"For what purpose?"

"You mentioned your eagerness to continue learning about your witch heritage and how to access the magic in your blood, but you've only been up once since you took the new job."

"I've been busy, and I believe I mentioned a *willingness* to learn those things, not an eagerness."

"Please excuse my lack of precision."

"You're not an uneducated woman. You should have a better command of your vocabulary."

"Yes, I'll strive to do better," Morgen said. "As to the rest, I thought you might like to learn a few new things, maybe see your vet friend who's been pining in your absence, and I'm starting a new research project that might intrigue you."

"Dr. Valderas is not pining, and what research are you doing? As far as I know, you don't publish any papers in your field. You aren't even *working* in your field." Amazing how someone with such a deadpan voice could so effectively insert condemnation in her words.

"I'm working in a new field, and I don't think there's a publication accepting articles on magical-charm enchantment."

Sian snorted. "I can't believe you're selling tchotchkes for a living now."

"Don't forget my app. I'm still working on databases."

Never mind that it was a database that held spell ingredients and incantations rather than something Sian would deem respectable, like medical information for patients or maintenance records for a transportation company.

"The app that you give away for free and get two dollars a month in tips for?" Sian asked.

"Keep taunting me, and I won't tell you about my research." Morgen's cheeks had warmed, mostly because Phoebe was close enough to hear everything rather than out of genuine embarrassment of her new projects. Maybe they weren't what she'd gone to school for, but she enjoyed learning new things, setting her own schedule, and spending time in Grandma's quaint old house with Amar, who was a lot more fun and stimulating than her ex-husband had been. She *liked* her new life. Maybe not the part where it was haunted by a ghost or intruded upon by enemy were-wolves, but overall, things were more stimulating than they had been in years.

"Go ahead," Sian said, perhaps curious.

"There's a century-plus-old building in town that I've rented for my business. It has a mysterious past including artists, tinkers, and tanners, an eighty-year-old robot-statue in the closet, and bloodstains on the floors and walls. Someone may have been murdered here, and I'm trying to get to the bottom of it." Morgen left out the part about the ghost, knowing Sian would scoff. "I'm concerned that I won't be able to entice the locals in to shop until I do so."

"This sounds like research you should have done *before* you signed a lease."

No kidding.

"Well, the commercial real-estate market is hot," Morgen said, "and I didn't want someone else to snap it up."

Phoebe snorted softly but kindly did not point out that the building had been vacant for years.

"Researching real estate sounds like a project for Zoe. Or is she too busy wooing chunks?"

"You mean *hunks*, and I believe that *is* why she came up. But perhaps you two could go to the library here together."

"Bellrock has a library?"

"Oh, yes. It's old and quirky and full of history." Morgen looked at Phoebe, hoping that description was accurate.

Phoebe nodded.

"You'd love poking around in it," Morgen added.

Sian sighed. "Very well. I'll see if I can come up tomorrow."

"Excellent. Thank you. I'll make you cookies."

"Get some bacon too. And make sure there aren't werewolves loitering all over the property. Or witches. Your brothers will be quicker to condemn you if they see your cult mates."

"Sian, you're exasperating."

"And yet, you're still willing to implore me to come up to do research for you."

"Well, obviously. I have *tchotchkes* to make."

As was typical, Sian considered the call over and hung up without saying goodbye.

"I thought your sister had seen enough to believe in magic," Phoebe said.

"Oh, she believes in it. She just doesn't think it's worth changing careers to study."

Phoebe looked toward the glowing charms. "But you've got Gwen's blood, and you're good at it."

"Thank you for that. Tell Sian, will you? And my brothers, if you meet them." Maybe Morgen shouldn't have added that. They might find the eccentric witch owner of a shop that sold crystals, gems, and mysterious powders a less than suitable friend and mentor.

"You have brothers?"

"Three. They're not much like me. They're coming to visit because they've heard about my new, ah, career and think... Oh, I don't know what they think. So far, they've gossiped to Sian and Zoe, not me."

"It's difficult when the rest of your family doesn't support your dreams and goals." Phoebe smiled wistfully.

"My main goal right now is to pay my taxes."

"Is that all?" Phoebe asked.

"I wouldn't mind getting to the point where I make more as an entrepreneur than I did as a database programmer. To prove to myself... Well, I don't think leaving Seattle was a *mistake*, not exactly, but I don't want to have to worry about my finances, especially going forward." Morgen rested a hand on her abdomen.

Phoebe watched the movement. "Is it true, then? You're expecting?"

Morgen dropped her hand. "Someone told you?"

One of the Lobos? She couldn't believe how quickly the word was getting out.

"I ran into Amar at the grocery store earlier, and he was buying the entire shelf of jars of fish eggs. I thought he might have bait in mind for a fishing trip, but they were human grade, and when I asked, he said it was vitally important for his mate to improve her eating habits."

Morgen dropped her face in her hand.

"I read between the lines that you might be pregnant," Phoebe added.

"Not only did his overly virile sperm slip through the bastions of my defenses, but now he's appointed himself my nutrition counselor."

"Do you eat fish eggs?"

"Does anyone?"

"Well, some people like caviar. Though I don't think that's quite what he picked up at Grocery Expedition."

Morgen's stomach writhed. "The ones there probably *are* for bait."

"I'm sure he means well, but I brought you this and some instructions." Phoebe drew out a silver chain with a half-moon pendant, and Morgen's burgeoning senses told her that it didn't have any magical qualities, at least not yet. Phoebe also handed over something written on a lined piece of paper pulled from a spiral notebook. It looked like a cookie recipe, but the heading at the top read *Child Charm*. "I checked your database and didn't see it in there. I don't think this one was in Gwen's collection."

"Child charm?" Morgen skimmed the recipe—the formula.

"Witches enchant them and give them to expecting mothers. The magic is both protective and enhancing. It's said that a baby born to a mother wearing such a charm will not only be healthy but will also inherit more of the witch power in the mother's blood and be able to learn magic at a young age. I don't know if the latter is true, but over the years, I *have* observed that the mothers all tend to deliver healthy babies."

"You mean I can wear a magical charm instead of eating nasty food?" Morgen went from skimming the recipe to devouring every word and committing them to memory. "It's a dream come true."

Phoebe snorted. "I should think so."

"It requires some rare herbs and powders." Morgen ran a finger down the ingredient list, trying to remember if Grandma's root cellar held them. "And it recommends nudity for the ritual." The only reason Morgen had been willing to make the flea-and-tick charms in the shop with all the Lobos around had been because the formulas for those hadn't mentioned that requirement. They also hadn't called for any special ingredients.

"As all good rituals do," Phoebe said. "At least those for making truly valuable talismans, amulets, and charms."

"My flea-and-tick charms are highly valuable to those who need them."

"Yes, I'm certain your cat and dog clients are grateful."

Morgen shot her a dirty look and might have chastised her for mocking the new business, but Phoebe smiled apologetically and extended a hand toward the exit.

"I have the ingredients in my shop, and you're welcome to use the privacy of my back room if you'd like to make the charm this evening," Phoebe offered. "My understanding is that the earlier in the pregnancy the mother dons it, the more effective it'll be."

"Oh." The urge to get to work right away swept over Morgen. Maybe she could even finish in time to join Amar and the Lobos for their dinner. If she assured him that the charm worked, he might return the jars of fish eggs before asking her to eat them. "I accept your offer."

A hint of nausea came over her, and she wondered if there was a charm to help with morning sickness—that was something she would look up as soon as she finished this one. She imagined herself walking around Wolf Wood, a dozen charms jangling around her neck. If it helped her future baby, it would be worth it.

13

As Morgen and Phoebe headed toward the Crystal Parlor, a *hoo hoo* came from above them. Zorro glided into view, flapped his wings a couple of times, and alighted on the rooftop over the door.

Morgen stopped and looked up at him. "Do you have a message to deliver, or are you just being sociable?"

Zorro gagged up an owl pellet and spat it out. It splatted on the sidewalk in front of Morgen.

"My goodness." Phoebe gripped Morgen's arm. "That owl is as uncouth as your dog."

"He may be more so. Lucky doesn't try to poop on or throw up on me."

"The last time I was there, he urinated on the tire of my car." Phoebe grimaced.

"If that's true, it was because he was overriding someone else's territorial mark."

Phoebe looked at her, taking a moment to parse that. "Are you saying something *else* urinated on my tire first?"

"It might be the trendy thing to do. Maybe you should stop

parking your vehicle outside at night. Werewolves roam the neighborhood, after all."

"My house was built in the thirties. It doesn't have a garage." Phoebe waved toward the side of town where the original lumberjacks' cabins and cottages had been updated and modernized.

"Maybe it's time to get one. Or at least toss some caltrops around your car at night for protection."

"Caltrops?" Phoebe mouthed, then squinted at her. "Sometimes, I'm amazed that Belinda backed your application to the coven."

"Oh? I thought all of the witches were a tad quirky."

"You're more than quirky."

"And yet you're teaching me." Morgen patted her on the shoulder.

"Because you helped increase my prosperity by setting up an online store and an organizational paradigm for my shop."

"I've found the best way to gain the affection of others is through gifts."

"Is that how you won your werewolf? With that talisman?"

"I also let him growl at me in bed. He likes that." Morgen didn't mention that she sometimes growled back.

"They all do," Phoebe grumbled.

Morgen didn't know if she meant all men or all werewolves. Maybe both.

Zorro hooted a few times, his head turned toward the nearby Timber Wolf restaurant. The lights were on inside, with numerous diners visible in the booths. Morgen couldn't tell if some of the Loups were among them, but she wouldn't be surprised.

"Is there a threat he's warning you about?" Phoebe squinted toward the restaurant.

"It's possible."

Morgen glimpsed a familiar brunette in one of the window booths and winced. That was Wendy's older sister, Olivia. Morgen couldn't see the face of her dining companion but hoped it wasn't one of the Loups. The idea of them conspiring made her curse, especially since the coven and the Loups didn't get along.

But Olivia wasn't *in* the coven anymore. She'd been kicked out.

Morgen took a deep breath and told herself not to panic. Maybe Oliva was there on a date and simply appreciated a good steak now and then.

As Morgen looked away, her gaze snagged on a car parked near the restaurant. *Zoe's* car.

"Damn it, I told her to stay away from them. Or at least *him*." She didn't see Mayor Ungar's black SUV, but there was a parking lot in the back, so it might have been there. Or Zoe could have found some *other* werewolf to spend time with.

Morgen groaned. Why couldn't she stick to the Lobos?

"Who?" Phoebe asked.

Morgen almost answered, then remembered that Phoebe had sounded hurt when she'd suggested Ungar might be interested in someone else.

"Never mind," Morgen said. "I'm not her babysitter. If she wants to have sex with any werewolf who checks out her boobs, it's none of my business."

"Your cousin? She's only in her twenties, isn't she? Young people do tend to be driven by their hormones."

Morgen kept herself from pointing out that Phoebe continued to see Ungar because she couldn't resist his animal magnetism. Feelings like that *had* to be driven by hormones. Or some primitive part of the body that was as active in the fifty-something witch as in Zoe.

"Yes," was all Morgen said and pointed her staff toward the Crystal Parlor. "I'll check on her later."

When Phoebe stuck her keys in the lock, caws came from within the building. Zorro hooted in response. As soon as Phoebe opened the door, her raven Zeke flew out.

"It's past his bedtime," she said. "I wonder where he's going."

Zeke flew up to the rooftop, perched a few feet away from Zorro, and cawed at him, which prompted Zorro to hoot back.

"Poker night, maybe. Male bonding." Before heading inside, Morgen looked at Zorro and said, "Let me know if you see Zoe, will you? Or any trouble heads this way?"

Zorro lifted a wing and preened his armpit—his *wing*pit. After one more caw, Zeke stuck his head fully under his wing.

"I trust your owl will keep you apprised of trouble," Phoebe said. "I believe Zeke only flew out because he knew I was going to turn on the lights, and that interrupts his sleep."

"How does he feel about naked women chanting in the back?"

"Oh, he doesn't mind that. Witches do that all the time."

"After hours, I hope." Morgen tried not to envision a nude Phoebe wandering out of the back room to help a customer pick out an agate on a keychain and some nice hexing powder. She wasn't quite successful. Maybe it was good that much of the Crystal Parlor's business came via the internet now.

Phoebe led her to the back room, measured ingredients from jars on shelves, then pulled out a cauldron and Bunsen burner. "I think that's all that the ritual requires. I'll tidy up out front while you work. Let me know if you need anything."

"Thanks."

After double-checking the ingredients, Morgen pulled the door shut, not wanting a draft blowing it open while she worked sans clothing, but a broken latch kept it from securing fully. Oh, well. It wasn't as if Phoebe would barge in, and with the tourist season past, and full darkness outside, Morgen doubted many potential customers would wander in either.

After laying everything out, Morgen removed her shoes and hoodie and was about to pull her T-shirt over her head when nausea came over her. More pregnancy sickness? Or was Zorro or Lucky going to share a vision?

She'd no sooner had the thought than imagery of the street outside floated before her eyes, the street from the rooftop view of the building. Zorro had finished preening but hadn't left the area. He was looking at two people walking arm-in-arm on the opposite side of the street.

Morgen clenched her jaw. Zoe and Ungar.

Well, at least she wasn't inside the Timber Wolf, wining and dining with the whole Loup pack. Unless she'd done that earlier.

Their heads were bent together until Zoe stopped and pointed into a boutique clothing shop. It was a couple of buildings down the street from the Crystal Parlor but in full view, at least to an owl perched on the roof. Zoe admired a dress on a mannequin in the window, then leaned against Ungar and rested her hand on his chest, laughing at something witty he'd said.

"Wit. Yeah, right." Morgen had yet to observe wit from any of the Loups. "You can let the vision go," she murmured, willing Zorro to hear the words.

Even though she agreed that it was good to keep tabs on Ungar, and appreciated that Zorro had sent the vision, she didn't want to spy on her cousin. Besides, Zoe was doing what she'd said she would do, shopping.

While Zoe admired the dress, Ungar stood close and looked up and down the street, as if he were a law enforcer watching for trouble. Or a Loup looking for Lobos to pick on?

A normal human wouldn't have noticed the owl perched in the shadows several buildings away, but Ungar had the same werewolf senses that Amar did, and he spotted Zorro. Spotted Zorro and stared at him.

Did Ungar recognize the owl? Or somehow know he was a witch's familiar? Maybe he knew about Zeke and expected witches —and their familiars—at the Crystal Parlor.

Either way, he eyed the owl for a long time, then pulled Zoe into his arms, kissed her, and grabbed her ass. Morgen gawked, certain the mayor was deliberately putting on a show for Zorro. He had to know Zorro was Morgen's owl. Unless he was doing that for *Zeke*. Was he still on the roof too? If he was, Morgen detested Ungar all the more for a move that might be designed to hurt Phoebe.

"I don't want to see any more," Morgen rasped. "Unless he hurts her, you can stop the vision, Zorro."

Judging from the way Zoe leaned into Ungar, he wasn't hurting her—if anything he was enticing her to join him in bed later that night—or in an alley in the next few minutes.

Thankfully, the vision faded. Zorro had either heard her entreaty or decided on his own that this wasn't worth sharing with his witch.

Morgen hoped Zeke had been sleeping and hadn't shared it with Phoebe. She'd been quiet out in the front room, reading, the last Morgen had seen.

Wishing she could make a talisman to repel werewolves, then secretly tuck it into Zoe's pocket, Morgen made herself focus on the child-charm formula. The sooner she finished, the sooner she could round up Amar and head home for the night. Too bad he'd mentioned going hunting with the pack later. The last couple of days' events had disturbed her, and she wouldn't have minded snuggling into his arms that night. Hopefully, he would finish early and come home.

After Morgen took off the rest of her clothes, she started on the ritual, pouring the ingredients into the cauldron, per the instructions. Once she chanted over them, mixed them with water, and boiled everything together, she doused the moon pendant in the mixture to finish. She repeated the chant, willing her power to infuse it and create a charm that would do all that Phoebe had promised. She didn't care that much about a child of hers inheriting all of her witch abilities—Amar might prefer that *not* happen —but she dearly hoped their baby would be healthy.

Surprisingly, the pendant didn't glow or do anything to indicate she'd succeeded in infusing it with magic. Maybe she hadn't focused enough?

As she started to chant the words again, the tinkle of the door chime sounded. Morgen flinched, almost lunging for her clothing. But even if customers came in, it wasn't as if Phoebe would lead them back there. This was her workshop and storeroom, and she usually had a chain across the doorway with a sign that read *Employees Only*.

Besides, Morgen had to finish before the mixture she'd doused the amulet in dried up. Willing her body to conjure up the power within it, she gripped the workbench, stared at the moon pendant, and chanted the spell once more, though she kept her voice down so that whoever had come in wouldn't hear her through the door. In case it helped, she also held her amulet as she chanted.

This time, the charm hummed with power—*she* hummed with power. In her mind's eye, she saw magical energy flow from her chest toward the moon pendant to enrobe it. The charm glowed a soft silver as the power took effect.

"There's nothing in here but trinkets and overpriced junk for tourists," a male voice rumbled.

Morgen froze. That was Ungar again. Had he brought Zoe over here to flaunt her in front of Phoebe? Showing off that he'd snagged a younger woman? That jerk.

"I *am* a tourist," Zoe said with a chuckle. "And I like decorative things. Oh, look at that purple crystal. It says here it has mystical power and will bring good luck."

"To the owner who takes your money."

Was Phoebe out there? Listening to him disparage her goods?

If Morgen hadn't been naked, she might have barged out to put a stop to it.

"Really, Ungar," Phoebe's voice sounded from the other side of the room. She must have been in her reading chair and out of their view. With all of the carousels and display cases, it was impossible to see from one side of the room to the other without standing on something. "You know I have my own luck charms and don't need to fleece my customers."

"Yeah, yeah, I know you believe in this stuff." Ungar didn't sound contrite in the least.

"I have good reason to," Phoebe said stiffly.

Was she irked at having her wares insulted? Or because Ungar had brought Zoe in with him? Maybe some of both.

Furious at the thought of her mentor being hurt, Morgen grabbed her underwear and started dressing. She would drag Zoe back home and leave Ungar to explain himself to Phoebe—if he could.

"Zoe, this is Phoebe," Ungar said, "one of the resident witches here in Bellrock. Phoebe, Zoe, a visiting real-estate agent."

"With an irresistible butt and lips, I gather."

Silence followed that statement. Morgen tugged on her jeans, almost falling over. Her hip bumped the workbench, and jars rattled.

"Is someone back there?" Ungar asked.

"Yes," Phoebe said. "A warlock lover who satisfies my urges in a way that no mere werewolf ever has."

Ugh. Morgen pulled on her T-shirt, now thinking of fleeing out the back door instead of going out front to grab Zoe.

"If that's true," Ungar said, "I'm happy for you. I just ask because I want to make sure you're not being robbed or molested."

Morgen put her shoes on.

"Only by you," Phoebe said, "and the *date* you were groping outside my window."

"Hell, Phoebe. I didn't think you were in here. And it wasn't outside *your* window. You had to have had your nose pressed to it to see us."

"Uhm," Zoe said, "should I leave? I just thought this shop looked interesting. I didn't want to, ah, get in the way of anything."

"It *is* interesting," Phoebe said.

Morgen put the new charm over her head, the pendant warm to the touch, and it clinked softly against her amulet.

"You're not in the way," Ungar said. "Phoebe and I have hooked up in the past, but we're not a couple."

"We hooked up two weeks ago," Phoebe snapped.

"Because *you* were randy."

"I didn't have to coax you hard to perform."

"I wasn't seeing anyone then. You know I don't mind *performing* for you when I'm not."

Did that mean Ungar thought he was *seeing* Zoe?

Morgen grabbed her staff and took a deep breath—if her own cousin hadn't been involved in this, she *definitely* would have fled out the back—and eased the door open. With his sharp eyes, Ungar spotted her right away.

Surprisingly, he wasn't standing arm-in-arm with Zoe. She was next to a carousel of keychains in the middle while he leaned against the wall by the door, his arms folded over his chest. Phoebe had her hands on her hips and was frowning at him. Morgen expected him to look smug, but shockingly, he appeared a little chagrined, maybe even apologetic as he met her gaze.

So, the kissing show outside had only been for Morgen, not Phoebe?

"You're the virile warlock satisfying Phoebe?" Ungar looked at Morgen's chest.

She scowled, tugging her hoodie closed, then realized she hadn't been paying enough attention when dressing and had managed to put her T-shirt on both backward and inside out. Her tag was sticking out at him.

"Does your Lobo know you swing both ways?" Ungar asked, his eyes lighting with amusement.

Zoe leaned around the carousel so she could see Morgen.

"I was doing a ritual," Morgen said. "It required nudity."

"I'll bet," Ungar said.

"Zoe, do you need a ride home?" Morgen knew her cousin's car was parked down the street, but it seemed a good excuse for both of them to flee the premises.

"Uhm." Zoe looked at Phoebe, her face still frosty. "Maybe that's a good idea."

Ungar dropped his arms and frowned. "You don't need to go. We'll shop somewhere else."

"Like in your bedroom?" Phoebe asked. "So you can perform for her too?"

"We're not *dating,* Phoebe. You don't get to lecture me on who I sleep with."

"Actually, yes, Morgen." Zoe waved for her to come and turned toward the door. "Thanks for shopping with me, Ungar. I need to go."

Ungar lifted a hand, his frown turning on her. The humor had left his eyes, and he looked like he would stop them instead of letting them out.

Morgen strode forward to stand beside Zoe, her staff in hand, the antlers pointed at Ungar. The werewolf-control incantation came to mind, and she glared at him, ready to use it if he didn't move. A part of her contemplated using it even if he did—maybe making him drop to his knees to apologize to Phoebe for being a dick. But that was the kind of abuse of power that Amar and the werewolves resented, and as much as Ungar *deserved* it, Morgen couldn't do it. All she would do was make sure she and Zoe could leave.

Ungar's hard gaze shifted to her, as if he could tell what she was thinking. Maybe he could guess.

For a long moment, he stood there, blocking the way, and Morgen grew more and more convinced that she would have to use the incantation. Then he stepped aside, extending a hand toward the doorway.

"I'll talk to you later, Zoe," he said, his voice softening.

Morgen wished Zoe would have brushed him off, saying nothing and walking out with her chin up. But she nodded and touched his arm before stepping through the doorway, and Morgen feared her cousin wasn't done with him.

As Morgen started after her, Ungar growled, "If you ever use your witch magic on me, you'll regret it."

Morgen should have said nothing, merely walking out with *her* chin up, but she couldn't stop herself from snapping back. "If you hurt my cousin, *you'll* regret it."

He glared after her but didn't say anything else. Morgen, conscious of his hard gaze upon her, had to resist the urge to break into a run as she guided Zoe toward their parked cars.

14

As Morgen led Zoe toward the cars, streetlamps shedding pools of illumination on the sidewalk, Zoe kept glancing back toward the Crystal Palace.

"I'm sorry you're not going to get the night you were envisioning," Morgen said, though she was more relieved than apologetic and wished she could convey to her cousin what a bad idea Ungar was.

"*I* was envisioning some shopping. *He* was the one envisioning it ending in his apartment."

"Really?" Morgen glanced at her.

"Well, maybe not entirely." Zoe flashed a grin. "That growly rumble he does when he talks to you is pretty sexy."

"Maybe when he talks to *you.* He glares at me and asks if I've paid my taxes yet. It's *not* sexy."

"That's okay. You've already got a werewolf. I trust that Amar growls and rumbles for you."

"A little." Morgen managed a smile, but it faltered when she spotted two big men in expensive ski jackets standing on the sidewalk next to her car.

She was about to suggest they take Zoe's car, and that she return for hers in the morning, when warning hoots came from above. Zorro flew past overhead. The men—the *Loups*—looked up at him, then turned to face Morgen and Zoe.

One smirked and leaned against the car.

Morgen tightened her grip on her staff and kept walking. "I can convince them to leave if they try to make trouble," she whispered. The werewolf-control incantation might work better on one foe, but she was fairly certain she could convince both of them to get out of the way, at least for long enough to drive away.

Then two more Loups walked out of an alley to join the first pair.

"How are you going to do that?" Zoe gripped Morgen's arm and slowed down.

"With magic."

Zoe eyed her. She hadn't yet seen Morgen use her power on werewolves. Morgen had been a lot more confident about that power before the second pair of them had shown up.

"Are you sure we wouldn't be better off flirting with them?" Zoe asked.

"I'm positive *I* wouldn't." Morgen waved to her unsexy hoodie and inside-out T-shirt, though it wasn't as if she would have been willing to flirt even if she'd been in more appropriate attire.

"Are you guys looking for someone?" Morgen stopped about twenty feet away to give herself time to use the incantation if needed.

"Heard the Lobos were in town tonight," one drawled, checking out the skin Zoe had on display.

The Loup next to him swayed slightly. Were they drunk?

Zoe lifted her fingers to button her blouse up higher. Maybe the Loups didn't make the cut as far as guys she wanted ogling her went. Or maybe it was the dangerous vibe floating off them.

"Well, they're not in my car." Morgen waved for them to leave, hoping the one leaning against her passenger-side door would take the hint.

The Loup peered through the window, fogging it with his breath. "Guess not." He eyed them. "We've got some beef to settle with them. We've decided this town isn't big enough for two packs."

"I've heard that. Maybe it's time for the Loups to go back to Canada. Or check out another town. Spokane has a lot of nice forests, I hear."

"We like *this* town. And we were here first." He smiled at her. "Maybe the Lobos would come out if we kidnapped their witch and took her back to our lair."

"Your lair? You mean the oversized log house with the tennis court out front?" Morgen hadn't been to the Loups' *lodge*, but she'd gotten the description from Amar.

"It's got a dungeon."

"In the real-estate biz, they call those basements. Right?" Morgen glanced at Zoe.

Zoe shifted uneasily. "Depends on how many shackles are hanging from the walls."

"We've got all *kinds* of toys down there," the Loup said. "Your sweet friend there is invited along. She looks fun."

"I'm not," Zoe said.

"We'll see." His eyes narrowed, and he prowled forward. All four did.

Morgen gripped her amulet. "Under the moon's magic, turn the snarling hound from angry foe to witch bound." As she spoke the words, she willed all the power she could summon into them.

All four Loups halted mid-step.

"Go back to the bar and finish your drinks," Morgen ordered.

Two lurched, turned around, and walked stiffly away. One

remained rooted to the sidewalk, grimaces spasming across his face. The tendons on his neck stood out as he fought the magic. The other growled and walked *toward* Morgen and Zoe.

As Morgen repeated the incantation, focusing on the two who'd been least affected, she waved for her cousin to get back. The closest Loup crouched and sprang for Morgen. He was still in his human form, but he snarled like a wolf.

She swung her staff at him. He ducked and grabbed it, trying to wrench it free. With his strength, he almost managed, but Morgen clamped down tight and kicked him in the knee.

She connected hard enough to make him swear and loosen his grip. She yanked her staff free and chanted another incantation as she pointed the antlers at him. "Under the moon's magic, bad behavior correct and this witch protect!"

Magical green energy gathered among the tips, then coalesced into a beam that slammed into his chest. The Loup stumbled back, yowling in pain, the noise echoing from the buildings.

"You bitch," he snarled as the energy faded.

"Back off, you drunken bastard." Morgen kept the staff leveled at him, prepared to chant the words again. "I'm armed and dangerous."

The Loup crouched but eyed the staff and didn't spring for her again. She was about to chant the control spell once more, focusing all her effort on him, but he glanced past her shoulder and smiled.

"What's going on here?" came Ungar's voice from behind Morgen.

Not wanting to turn her back on her attacker, she resisted the urge to swing her staff toward Ungar, but she turned sideways so she could see both of them.

"We're kidnapping the witch to piss off the Lobos," the Loup said, "and so we can have a little fun back at the lair tonight." He glanced not at Morgen but at Zoe—at Zoe's chest.

"You idiots need to grow up," Ungar said. "Go home, and quit harassing people."

Surprise flashed in the Loup's eyes. "You're one of the pack. You're supposed to be on *our* side."

"I'm still the mayor of this town."

"We'll tell the alpha. He'll teach you a lesson for going against the pack."

"He's welcome to try," Ungar growled.

"If you wanted to piss off the Lobos…" a new voice spoke from across the street. Pedro. "You've succeeded, *amigo.*"

He wasn't alone. Amar and several other Lobos strode across the street, past the parked cars, and inserted themselves on the sidewalk between Morgen and Zoe and the remaining Loup. Amar came to stand next to Morgen, shoulder to shoulder with her, though he looked over her head toward Ungar instead of focusing on the man she'd zapped.

"You Lobos need to control your witch." Her would-be assailant rubbed his chest. "She's a menace."

"We like her that way," Pedro said.

Ungar strode forward, and Amar tensed.

"Get off the street," Ungar ordered. "*All* of you. This is a civilized town, and I aim to keep it that way."

The mouthy Loup glared at him but only for a second. He looked at Morgen and her staff for longer. "Come to our lair when you get bored with your Lobo boys. You make *us* some talismans, and we'll take good care of you."

"A delightful offer considering you wanted to lock us in your sex dungeon a minute ago," Morgen said.

Amar's eyebrows shot up. He crouched and growled, looking like he meant to spring at the Loup and start a fight right there. Even though Morgen wouldn't have minded seeing the guy pummeled, she rested her hand on Amar's chest, feeling she should keep things from escalating if she could. She didn't know if the Loups had anything to do with the trouble at the tannery, but she didn't want to give them a reason to keep targeting it—or her.

"It's fine," she said. "They're leaving."

Amar growled again, his eyes locked on the Loup. His hard chest reverberated under her palm.

Ungar walked past them, gave the mouthy Loup a shove, and escorted him and the other one who'd stuck around out of the area. Morgen wondered if he'd come out to help because he cared about anyone's welfare, or if he'd seen the Lobos approaching and had simply wanted to put a stop to things before a huge fight broke out. She doubted he cared if the werewolves tore each other limb from limb, but as the mayor, he might feel responsible for broken storefronts and damaged cars.

Once Ungar and the Loups were out of view, Pedro turned toward Morgen and Amar.

"I like your female more and more," Pedro said, "except she needs to aim lower. I wanted to see that bastard get zapped in the balls."

That comment resulted in numerous zealous agreements in Spanish accompanied by more than a few crude gestures. Morgen shook her head and pointed Zoe across the street to where she'd parked.

"We're going to head home, Amar," Morgen said. "Thanks for coming over, and enjoy your hunt."

Amar wrapped an arm around her. "Are you all right?" He looked at her with concern. "We didn't hear them and get out here in time to see everything." His eyes narrowed. "He didn't hurt you before you whacked him, did he?" His intense expression promised he would show up at the Loups' lair ready to murder them if they had.

Even though she was getting better at taking care of herself, Morgen couldn't help but shiver a little at Amar's intensity—and feel warmed by the fact that he cared and wanted to protect her.

"No," she said, "I whacked him first. It's fine."

"That's good." Amar looked a little wishfully toward the corner the Loups had disappeared around and lowered his arm and flexed his muscles. "Though I wouldn't have minded an excuse for a fight."

"Yeah, I was ready to pound them." Pedro thumped his chest and lifted his nose to the sky. "A good hunt is what we need to unleash our energy."

Murmurs of agreement came from the other Lobos.

"I want to check on the house," Amar said. "I don't trust the Loups not to skulk up there and make trouble." Amar looked at Morgen again. "Are your protective wards set?"

"No, but I'll engage them as soon as we get back. You can go hunt with the others."

"We'll check on the house first. Then hunt in Wolf Wood. I'll stay close in case you need me." His eyelids drooped. "Though I know you can take care of yourself now." His lips curved and he kissed her.

She leaned into him, enjoying his respect and appreciation— and the little nip that left her breathless and had her wanting to ask him to keep his hunt short.

Had the other men not snickered and elbowed each other, she might have kissed Amar for a lot longer, but their comments embarrassed her—even if *he* didn't seem to notice them—and she stepped back.

"I'll make you boys some cookies while you're hunting." Morgen had put in an order for pumpkin scones from the bakery—perhaps sweet pastries would make her family more amenable during their visit—but they wouldn't be ready until the next day.

"We are strong, virile, and powerful *men*, not boys," Amar rumbled.

"So... you don't want cookies?"

"Of *course* we want cookies. With frosting and sprinkles." Amar swatted her on the butt, then strode off with the others.

15

WHEN AMAR HAD PROMISED TO CHECK ON THE HOUSE, MORGEN hadn't realized that meant six Lobo trucks would drive up and park and that the pack would start their hunt there. She immediately quadrupled the ingredients she'd pulled out for the cookie recipe.

While mixing the dough, she hoped the werewolves would finish the hunt early, certainly well before morning, since Sian was coming up. Her introvert sister would complain if the house was overrun with visitors. She also hoped they would be long gone before her brothers arrived. They might not be introverts... but she didn't want to give them any more reasons to believe she was in a cult or anything else overly odd.

To people who lived in Bellrock, cavorting with witches and werewolves was perfectly normal. But she well remembered her old life and that such things *weren't* normal in Seattle.

Once the cookies were out of the oven and cooling, Morgen found Zoe sitting on the swinging bench on the covered porch out front. October had arrived, and it wasn't that warm out, but it was a pleasant evening with a clear sky full of stars and a bright three-quarters moon. No wonder the Lobos had wanted to go hunting.

"Everything okay?" Morgen offered her a warm cookie with pink sugar sprinkles on top. The frosted versions would have to wait until the rest of the cookies cooled; she trusted they would before her manly werewolf with a sweet tooth returned from his hunt.

"Yeah." Zoe had her phone out and her contacts open, though she didn't look like she'd been calling or texting anyone. "I just thought I would be doing something more stimulating than sitting alone on a porch swing tonight."

"Almost getting mauled, kidnapped, and toted off to a sex dungeon wasn't suitably stimulating for you?"

"Maybe pleasurable is the word I should have used." Zoe glanced at her. "Don't take this the wrong way, Morgen, as I'm happy to come and visit you, but I've been on such a dry spell when it comes to dating back home. I came up here hoping..."

"Yeah, I caught the gist. Maybe one of the single Lobos will be interested when their hunt is over."

"Oh man, did you see them all getting naked?" Zoe waved toward the trucks where the Lobos had left their jeans, shirts, and jackets draped on hoods and mirrors. Some had even tossed their clothing on the porch and back deck railing.

As usual, they'd thought nothing of shapeshifting out in the open in front of Morgen and Zoe. Morgen could have done without the show, but Zoe had been enthralled.

"I try to give them their privacy when they do that," Morgen said.

Except with Amar. He was *her* wolf, as he always reminded her, and she knew he liked it when she ogled him. And she liked it too.

"You're kidding." Zoe cast her an incredulous look. "I had no idea they were up here getting naked all the time."

"Not *all* the time. It's just when they hunt in Wolf Wood.

Admittedly, that's one of their favorite spots. There are magical mushrooms out there that spit out spores that seem to be the equivalent of catnip for wolves."

"Amazing. I know you and Amar are lovers, but do you ever..." Zoe smirked and waved her hand in the air.

"What? Invite the rest into the bedroom? Good grief, Zoe. What do you think is going on up here? You know I'm not into anything... outré."

"Yeah, I guess you're too prudish to consider such things."

"Not considering *that* isn't prudish. It's *normal*."

"I'm not sure *normal* is a word I've generally applied to you, though admittedly, you did always strike me as someone who doesn't rustle the sheets much."

Heat warmed Morgen's cheeks.

"And Jun was the same. Did you two even have to make the bed in the morning?"

"I can't believe I brought you a cookie," Morgen said. "You're awful."

Zoe grinned. "I bet I'm not wrong though. And I bet things are a little different now." Her eyes twinkled, but only for a moment before she looked at her phone again. "I'm thinking of calling him."

"Who?" Morgen asked, though she was afraid she already knew.

"Ungar. What's the deal with him and that woman? Phoebe? I don't want to get in the middle of anyone's relationship, but I thought he was single."

"I don't know, but can't you hook up with one of the young randy ones? Preferably one who doesn't think of me as an enemy?"

"Ungar—his first name is Brad, by the way—didn't say anything about you or hating you."

Brad? *Bradley?* Morgen mouthed it, but it didn't fit. At all.

"Good," she said, "but that doesn't mean he doesn't want to hurt me."

Zoe frowned at her.

"Look, I'm sure he's genuinely into you because you're pretty and sexy and stuff, but I also got the vibe, from the way he kept glancing at me, that he maybe thought dating you would be a way to screw with me."

"Full of yourself much?"

"You don't know this town—*or* him. You just got here." Morgen thought about telling her how Ungar had arranged to kiss her in front of Zorro, but she hadn't explained her familiars or the visions she received from them yet and didn't know if that would sound far-fetched. Just because Zoe had seen her zap a werewolf with magic earlier didn't mean she was ready to believe everything.

"I don't see how us having sex could screw with *you*," Zoe said.

"I think he might be planning to... I don't know, love you and leave you. Or do something to hurt you. Phoebe didn't think he would do anything *physically*." Morgen certainly hoped not, since the werewolves were all big, strong, and powerful, and Ungar was no exception. "But emotionally."

Zoe rolled her eyes. "I'm not a teenager with her first crush. What do you think *I* was planning?"

"To have your way with him, then depart abruptly in the night and leave him a demolished husk of a man?" Morgen decided it would be immature to fantasize about that—much.

And Zoe rolled her eyes again. "Listen, Morgen. I know you're bookish and introverted and appalled by the idea of recreational sex, but it's a thing. Mature consenting adults do it."

"With werewolves?"

"Given the creaking and groaning coming from your bedroom last night, I *know* you don't object to werewolves."

Morgen blushed. She'd given Zoe the guest room farthest from hers. Maybe she should have put her cousin in the barn.

"Just the troublesome ones," she murmured.

Barking started up in the living room, and Lucky's head appeared in the window. Before Morgen could wonder what he'd heard, headlights shone through the trees—someone coming up the driveway.

More of the Lobos?

A familiar vehicle rolled up, finding a free parking spot near the barn, and Morgen groaned. She'd seen far too much of that black SUV lately.

"Oh." Zoe surged to her feet. "Is that Brad?"

"Probably here to remind me to pay my taxes."

"Don't take this the wrong way, cousin," Zoe said, fluffing her hair, "but I doubt he's here for you."

The car door thudded shut, and Ungar walked into view, eyeing the Lobo trucks and their clothes draped everywhere. At least knowing they were in the area ought to keep him on good behavior.

A faint crackle of energy emanated from the magical wards around the house, and Ungar halted in front of them. His lip curled as he glanced down. They were invisible, and Morgen knew he couldn't see them, but he probably felt the energy—the warning that he would be zapped if he came closer without being invited.

Lucky, perhaps realizing a werewolf had arrived, stopped barking, though Morgen could hear the clack of his nails on the wood floors on the other side of the door.

"Hi, Brad. What brings you up here?" Zoe propped a hand on her hip and turned so that her profile—her *chest*—would be outlined by the porch light.

"I want to talk to you." Ungar eyed her profile. Sure, *talking* was what had brought him out here. "I had to straighten some stuff out with Phoebe, but we've reached an understanding."

"That you're more interested in having sex with a young stranger than an old lover?" Morgen asked.

Ungar squinted at her. "It's a mystery as to why the Loups don't like you."

She bared her teeth at him, though it was interesting that he didn't call them *my pack*. Was he, like Dr. Valderas, someone who'd been turned into a werewolf but didn't feel any loyalty to them? From what Morgen had heard, he *did* go on hunts with them. He'd certainly been at the house attacking the witches alongside the rest of the Loups... Yes, the *rougarou* had magically compelled them to obey his wishes, but Morgen couldn't help but wonder how hard the Loups—and Ungar—had tried to buck those commands.

"Is it also a mystery as to why they're picking fights with the Lobos and messing with my new building?" Morgen asked.

"I don't think they've done anything to that wreck of a building," Ungar said.

"Someone threw rocks through the window."

Ungar snorted. "That happens a *lot*. Why don't you talk to the Lobo kid who crushes mailboxes with a baseball bat?"

Zoe cleared her throat and lifted a hand to cut off Morgen's reply. "Brad is here to see *me*, Morgen. Don't you have cookies to frost?"

"You'll have to come join me." Ungar extended a hand toward his truck. "There's a magical protection that I can't get through."

Zoe turned a questioning look on Morgen.

"Wards," Morgen explained. "They keep out those who don't live here or aren't formally invited in."

"Can't you invite him in?"

Morgen grimaced.

"It's either that or we'll be steaming the windows in his truck," Zoe said.

Ungar arched his eyebrows but didn't object. A smile crept across his craggy face.

"I thought you were going to talk," Morgen said.

"It might be breathy talking."

Zoe started for the stairs.

"Fine, fine. Mayor Ungar," Morgen said, willing the wards to hear her words, "you are formally invited to come up to the porch. Until midnight. Zoe has a curfew."

"I'm twenty-eight, Morgen," Zoe said.

"Make it eleven." Morgen backed toward the door as Ungar climbed the steps. She *did* have cookies to frost. And she vowed to put on music so she wouldn't hear any breathy talking coming from the porch. "I feel like a chaperone," she muttered as she pushed open the door.

As Ungar settled next to Zoe on the swing, Lucky surged outside. Morgen started to grab him, not wanting him to irk Ungar and get growled at—or worse—but he'd been inside for a few hours, and she realized he might need to water a bush. Or, more likely, the beautiful pumpkins and spaghetti squash that hadn't yet been picked in the garden.

But Lucky turned an immediate right and planted himself in front of Zoe and Ungar. He wagged at them, his tail thwacking the porch railing.

"What does this dog want?" Ungar asked.

"Adoration, affection, and someone's hands to rub his ears," Morgen said.

Zoe obliged, petting him on the head and telling him he was a good boy. That might have been too much attention, for Lucky proceeded to climb up on the bench as he tried to get in her lap. His tail whacked Ungar in the face, eliciting a grunt. Zoe lowered her hand, perhaps realizing her mistake, but Lucky sat on the bench, squeezing in between them. He seemed to have gotten over some of his meekness around werewolves.

"Morgen," Zoe complained as Lucky licked her cheek.

Ungar didn't look delighted—especially since Lucky's tail was now attempting to excavate his nostrils—but he gave the dog a grudging pat and didn't make any motion to hurl him over the railing. Maybe the mayor wasn't *completely* loathsome.

Deciding Lucky was an even better chaperone than she, Morgen said, "You can let him inside when he's ready," and closed the door on them.

As she headed to the kitchen, Morgen looked out the window, hoping Amar would return soon. She also hoped Zoe was right and that she could handle Ungar and any emotional manipulation he might try.

16

MORGEN HADN'T RECEIVED A VISION FROM GRANDMA'S AMULET IN over a month, and she didn't expect to have one after she dozed off for the night, but when she woke to a glow in the corner of the bedroom, she knew right away what was happening. Shapes appeared in the light, soon turning into a view of a cabin in the woods, moonlight reflecting off a window next to the plank door.

Not recognizing it, Morgen propped herself up on an elbow for a better look. In the past, these visions had often contained clues. They'd led her to powerful ancient books hidden in the house and shown her how Grandma and Amar first met. What could this one intend to convey?

Something heavy lay on one of her legs—Lucky. Zoe had either come in for the night or she'd let *Lucky* in for the night and wandered off who knew where with Ungar.

A tall slim woman with a long white braid stepped into view, her back to Morgen. Grandma.

What would she have been doing wandering a trail in the woods at night? And was this Wolf Wood or someplace else?

There were still parts of the woods that Morgen hadn't explored, but she hadn't heard from Amar about a cabin on the property.

Grandma carried the antler staff, and, since this had to be at least a year in the past, all of the tips were still intact. Maybe it was the moonlight reflecting off them, but they seemed to glow a faint silver. Either way, it was a reminder that Grandma had been able to take care of herself. Only someone's sabotage to her motorcycle had taken her down.

As it had before, that sense of longing came over Morgen, regret that she hadn't come up to visit when Grandma had still been alive and hadn't gotten to know her better. Hadn't been able to learn from her. Hadn't been here to keep her from being lonely, with only a surly werewolf for occasional company.

Surprisingly, a familiar gray-and-black wolf loped out of the trees and came to stand at Grandma's side. Amar. They looked at the cabin together.

The door swung inward with a creak, as if inviting entrance, and Morgen waited for someone to come out. Nobody did. The door merely swayed, as if in the breeze, but none of the branches on the nearby trees were moving.

Grandma looked at Amar. "You dragged me out here to see a creaky door on a dilapidated cabin? Don't you know how old I am? My bedtime is nine, and I'm crabby in the morning if I don't get my sleep."

Amar shifted into his human form, his nude butt toward Morgen. Not surprisingly, Grandma didn't appear worried by his muscular bulk looming beside her.

"You're crabby whether you get sleep or not, witch. Your lips would wither and fall off if you smiled."

"I know you're not talking, wolf. I saw a butterfly land on your chainsaw art, and you growled at it. Who growls at butterflies?"

"I'd just varnished that piece, and it was wet. I didn't want wing marks on it."

"Yes, much art has been ruined by the hideousness of butterfly marks."

"Are you going to help me with my problem or not?" Amar extended an arm toward the cabin.

"Since you asked so nicely, how could I resist?"

A keening wail emanated from the cabin, raising the hair on Morgen's arms. Grandma and Amar stopped their arguing and looked at it.

"The place is haunted. Ever since that bounty hunter died here, it's been like this." Amar waved toward the swaying door.

Bounty hunter? That brought to mind a story Amar had told her of a hunter who'd settled into a cabin in the woods, hiding out until he got an opportunity to kill werewolves. One of the witches had hired him for the job. He'd brought a bunch of silver to create silver bullets, and they'd been effective until the Lobos and Loups had teamed up to kill the man. Had this been the hunter's cabin?

"When you say died," Grandma said, "you mean he was ripped to pieces by werewolves, right?"

"As I said this morning. But he deserved it." Amar growled toward the dwelling.

"Then why do you care if his spirit is haunting an abandoned cabin in the woods? This isn't even in Wolf Wood."

"Because something I value is in there, and I can't get it back until he's gone." Amar touched his chest, and Morgen realized he wasn't wearing the tooth thong that had occupied that spot as long as she'd known him. He didn't take it off even to bathe.

"You can't walk in and get it during the day when the ghost isn't haunting things?" Grandma asked.

"It's not visible during the day. I've looked." Amar waved toward a window. "It only shows up at night. It's some foul magic I don't understand."

"You don't understand *much*, wolf. You should read books instead of throwing them at butterflies."

"That was the manual for a tool, not a *book*. And I read plenty. In *two* languages. How many can *you* read in?"

"If you count Latin, four. *Carpe lupum*." She looked down at his crotch. "Though not, I suggest, when he's naked."

"Hilarious."

"I'll take a look." Grandma headed toward the door.

Amar shifted back into a wolf and prowled after her, his nostrils twitching as he tested the air. His hackles were up, as if he expected to be attacked by an enemy pack at any moment.

Another keening wail came from the cabin, and Morgen shifted uneasily, wishing she were there and able to help, not watching this play out from her bed. She reminded herself that this had happened long ago and that whatever threat they'd faced, Amar and Grandma had survived it.

When they drew within five feet of the door, Amar sat on his haunches.

"Going to stand guard while the old lady goes in, huh?" Grandma asked. "People who die horribly and aren't able to pass to the spirit world tend to be even grumpier than wolves."

Amar merely pointed his snout toward the door.

She stepped closer and peered inside. "That your fang in the corner back there? Looks like the thong broke."

Amar growled what might have been assent. Unlike Lucky, he didn't wag or bark. None of the wolves did. He merely watched intently, his hackles remaining up.

Grandma pushed the door open wider and stepped across the threshold, but she halted. The silver light around the antler tips flared brighter, and she leveled the staff toward the empty room.

Morgen leaned forward, wishing she could see what was inside. A ghost? Like the one she might be dealing with in the tannery?

Whispering under her breath, Grandma crept in farther. The words were too soft for Morgen to hear. Had it been an incantation? The one Morgen had used to make the ghost show itself? Or something more effective? Like something that could *banish* a ghost?

No breeze rustled Amar's fur, but the door slammed shut, shutting Grandma inside. Amar surged to his feet.

A startled curse—or cry of fear?—came from the cabin. Silver light flared behind the window. From the magic of Grandma's staff? Or something else?

Amar snarled as he ran at the door and threw his shoulder against it. It didn't budge. He raced to the window and sprang at it. The glass should have shattered under his weight—and the power of his jump—but it flared silver and also didn't budge. As if he'd hit a brick wall, he bounced off, barely managing to land on his feet.

Light flashed inside, as if Grandma were in a battle with something. Amar ran around the corner of the cabin to another window. Once again, he sprang at it, trying to force his way inside, but once again, some magic repelled him.

When he landed, he shifted back into his human form. He ran back to the door and tried the knob with his hand. It didn't turn.

"Gwen!" he shouted. "Are you all right? Let me in!"

He rammed his shoulder against the door. The thick planks shuddered under his weight, but the hinges held. Inside, the silver light faded.

Amar backed up and launched a side kick at the door. Finally, wood splintered, the hinges breaking loose, and the door flew inward. Amar halted short of lunging inside, for Grandma stood there, her staff held at the ready. She was facing him, not some enemy inside, and his thong necklace dangled from her fingers.

"You overly muscled wolf, you almost hit me in the face with the door."

"I thought you were in trouble."

"Well, I wasn't on the rides at Disneyland; that's a certainty."

Sweat gleamed on Grandma's forehead, and locks of white hair had fallen out of her braid. Her clothing was rumpled, as if she'd been in a wrestling match. "But I believe I've set the ghost's spirit to rest, so he'll haunt this world no more. You ought to be able to visit the cabin now without getting the creepy-crawlies."

Amar stared at her. "More than *creepy-crawlies* attacked you when you walked in."

"Yes." Grandma stepped outside, holding the tooth necklace out to him. "It's a good thing you know a witch who can deal with such things and doesn't mind putting up with grumpy, book-throwing werewolves."

Amar accepted the thong and offered her his arm. "It is a good thing. And it was a manual, not a book."

"Still terribly uncouth." Looking weary after her ordeal, Grandma accepted his arm, and they headed toward the trail together.

The vision started to fade.

"No." Morgen stretched out a hand. "I need to know how she got rid of the ghost. What did she do in there?"

But the vision faded completely, leaving her in the dark bedroom, a snoring dog across her legs. Morgen slumped back. Unless Amar had seen more than she believed he had, and could tell her where to look for a ghost-banishing incantation, that vision hadn't helped her with her problem at all.

17

MORGEN WOKE TO THE SOUND OF VOICES OUTSIDE. AMAR AND THE Lobos?

Foggy daylight shone gray against her window, and she pushed her hair out of her eyes and glanced at the time. It was past eight. She and Lucky had both slept in. Was Amar just now returning from the hunt? That was surprising.

Her stomach writhed, forcing her to detour to the bathroom before looking outside. And gaping at who was out there. Not the Lobos—their trucks were still there, but she didn't see any sign of them. Her brothers had arrived in two cars, and they were standing in the driveway and looking around, pointing in confusion at all the trucks—and the clothes draped over them.

"What the hell?" Morgen lunged for her jeans and hoodie and hurried to change. "They got up at *dawn* to drive up here? How worried *are* they?"

She nearly fell over as she jammed her legs into her jeans, then almost fell a second time as Lucky woke up, hopped out of bed, and bumped her on his way to the window. He rose onto his hind legs with his front paws on the sill and barked uproariously at the strangers in the driveway. No, not strangers. He'd met her brothers numerous times, and he was wagging while he barked.

The noise drew their eyes, and Morgen felt compelled to open the window. "I'll be right down. I didn't expect you to arrive so early."

Big bluff Caden in one of his typical UW Huskies gray-and-purple sweatshirts waved, but his broad face held uncertainty, and his gaze drifted to a pair of overalls draped over the railing. Morgen groaned, wishing she'd thought to pluck up the Lobos' clothes and put them in the barn. Or better yet, in their trucks.

But what kind of crazy family members arrived for an out-of-town visit at *eight*? She'd assumed they would show up in the afternoon—and had hoped Sian would arrive first to help Morgen deflect questions. Or at least offer moral support before heading to the library for research.

Morgen rushed downstairs, sadly not catching a whiff of coffee. She could have used a bracing cup, but Wendy must not have been up yet, either, and Zoe... Morgen grimaced, imagining her in Ungar's embrace, their butts plastered to the upholstery in his truck.

Figuring everyone would want coffee, she started a pot before heading outside. Lucky bounded ahead of her.

Morgen glanced at the staff leaning by the door, half-tempted to grab it, but she didn't know an incantation that could make her family believe she was neither unhealthily odd or in a cult. She would only look strange waving the antler-tipped staff around.

Morgen stepped outside, forcing a smile for Caden, Gavin, and Rhett, and they'd brought their wives... Suze, Minh, and Erica. More people to judge Morgen. Wasn't that nice?

And who was that sitting in the back of one of the cars, the door still closed? It opened, and the person who stepped out made Morgen gape and almost trip.

"Jun?" she croaked.

Why had her family brought her ex-husband up here? Didn't her brothers *know* they were divorced? And that it had been Jun's idea? That Morgen hadn't even known it was coming until the lawyer brought the papers over?

The urge to flee back into the house and lock the door assaulted her like a grade-school bully.

Oblivious to her feelings, Lucky raced around, wagging and trying to get everyone to pet him. When Morgen met Jun's concerned eyes, she tried to wave and say hi, but she couldn't move. Her smile, such as it was, froze on her face.

"Are you... having a party, Morgen?" Caden waved at the trucks, his finger lingering as it pointed at a pair of jeans hanging from a side mirror.

"Or an *orgy?*" his wife, Suze, asked.

"Thank God we didn't bring the children," Erica whispered, clasping Rhett's hand with a vise-like grip.

"No, no." Morgen forced a laugh and lifted her hands as she groped for an explanation.

The truth was the only thing that came to mind that made sense, but would it make sense to *them*? Not until they, like Sian had, saw proof of one of the werewolves shifting form in front of them. But since it was daylight, that might not be possible. And the werewolves weren't even *here*.

In the aftermath of the orgy comment, silence fell across the driveway until the barn door clattered open.

Morgen turned, hoping for Amar. What he could do, she didn't know, but she desperately wanted his support.

Unfortunately, Zoe and Ungar walked out, Zoe holding a bear hide around her nude body, and Ungar... not holding anything around his. Morgen dropped her face in her hand.

"Hey, guys." Zoe smirked, not sounding as mortified as she *should* have, given the circumstances. "You're early," she added as she headed to Ungar's truck, opening the door to pull her clothes out. Thanks to the angle, everyone got a good look as she removed her panties from his rearview mirror.

"Dear God, Zoe," Suze said. "You weren't a part of this... this... *orgy*, were you?"

Gavin peered into the barn. "How many people are in there?"

Ungar, damn the bastard, looked amused at all this.

"Just us," Zoe said. "The orgies take place in the main house."

"*Zoe!*" Horror—or maybe that was sheer panic—swelled in Morgen's chest.

What was she supposed to say? She had no idea. Would Caden report this back to their father? He lived on the other side of the world and barely called, but that didn't mean he wouldn't make an exception to lecture Morgen on her depravities. Or try to get her admitted to a psych ward. Could parents have such things done to children who were forty?

"There wasn't an orgy," Morgen said. "I just have some friends who came over to go hunting."

"Without their clothes?" Caden asked.

Jun shook his head slowly as he stared at Morgen. Abruptly, she was glad they'd never had kids, or he would have been vying to take custody of them from her. Hell, what would he think when he found out she was pregnant? Or when he met Amar?

She clenched her jaw and reminded herself that Jun's opinion shouldn't matter to her anymore. It *didn't* matter. Why had her brothers brought him?

"They have to take their clothes off before they turn into werewolves," Morgen said, attempting to make her voice sound reasonable, though she heard an annoying squeak in it. "Uhm, Mayor Ungar. I don't suppose you could demonstrate your wolfishness to my family? They're... not from Bellrock."

What a ludicrous thing to say. Of course they weren't.

Ungar only smirked. "I believe the stories say that werewolves only come out at night."

"I've *seen* Amar change on stormy days *and* in fog." Morgen waved her arm to indicate the gray sky overhead and the haze blanketing the hilltop.

"Well, isn't he an overachiever?" Ungar's smirk widened. He slapped Zoe on the butt and headed for the driver's seat. "It's Saturday morning. I have to visit my mother for breakfast and make sure her cat horde hasn't taken over the house yet."

"Don't forget to order a deluxe cat condo from Morgen." Zoe winked at Morgen, as if she were doing her a great favor.

A great favor would be for her to dress and stop wandering around in a *bear hide*.

"Uh huh," was all Ungar said before driving off.

Morgen slumped. He was the only one present who could have changed into a wolf and proved to her family that she was telling the truth. That she wasn't crazy.

Movement in the trees drew her eyes. Amar, Pedro, and more than a dozen other Lobos walked out of the woods and onto the dew-kissed lawn. For a few seconds, Morgen felt relief. Then she realized they were all naked and her family was gaping at them with even more horror.

If the light level was too great for them to shift forms, Morgen wouldn't be able to prove anything to her brothers and their judgmental wives until twilight. If they stayed that long. They might have plans to kidnap her and drop her off at a mental hospital before lunch.

Amar, a puzzled tilt to his head, walked toward Morgen as the others went toward their vehicles and the porch railing for their clothes. She drew a breath and wrapped a hand around her amulet, struggling for calm. Nobody was going to kidnap her, not with Amar here and not when she had dozens of incantations memorized and thousands more on her phone app. She just had to figure out a way to explain things, and if they didn't believe her now, they would eventually. Sooner or later, Bellrock gave up its secrets to visitors.

"We didn't come soon enough," Minh murmured to Gavin.

"I didn't realize how bad it was," Jun whispered. "This is my fault. I... shouldn't have gone so long without checking on her."

"Who *are* those men?" Caden balled his fingers into fists and crouched as Amar walked closer to Morgen.

"This is Amar." Morgen held a hand up toward her brother, aware that Caden had boxed in college—and aware that Amar would flatten him if they fought. "He's a friend."

"A friend?" Amar stopped beside her, his eyebrows raised.

She swallowed, embarrassed to have called him that, especially now. He was the father of her future child and her partner in life and business.

She took a deep breath, clasped his hand, and amended her words. "He's my *boyfriend*. And a werewolf." She couldn't bring herself to look at Jun—though out of the corner of her eye, she could see his jaw attempting to deposit itself on the gravel driveway—or any of them. She only pointed her gaze somewhat in their direction as she continued. "They're all werewolves. These are the Lobos. They're a pack, and when they're not hunting together as werewolves, they do construction work. They installed the deck and outdoor kitchen and hot tub back there." Morgen had no idea why she'd included those details other than that they might somehow make the story more believable. Construction-worker werewolves were more plausible than werewolves without jobs, right?

Only when Morgen pointed at the hot tub did she realize that the lid was off and someone was sitting in it. *Two* someones. The jets hadn't been running, so she hadn't realized anyone was back there.

Wendy shrank low and waved uncertainly when everyone looked toward the hot tub.

José Antonio, who must have departed early from the hunt, stood up—utterly naked—and waved at the family. "I did the railings and the steps, and I ordered the six-burner grill for the outdoor kitchen. Come check it out. It's great."

Wendy was wearing a swimsuit, her straps visible, but it didn't matter. Everyone gaped at José Antonio.

Morgen slumped against Amar, at a loss for what else she could say. What could make this seem less bizarre to newcomers?

"I hadn't realized until now how weird my life has become," she whispered.

"No?" Amar wrapped an arm around her shoulders. "Haven't you been living in it?"

His eyes crinkled. At least *someone* was amused, someone besides that dick, Ungar.

Morgen buried her face in his chest, having a feeling it would be a long time before she could look back and laugh at this. Whispers of *orgies* kept floating about the gathering.

When her phone dinged with a text, Morgen pounced on her pocket, yanking it out and hoping for an excuse to leave.

"I'm sorry, everyone," she blurted, waving the phone. "I need to run into town to check on something. There's been another incident at the commercial building I leased, but, uhm, go ahead and go inside. Help yourselves to coffee and whatever you can find to eat. *Zoe* will explain everything."

Zoe had been trundling toward the house, her clothes clutched in one hand, the hide pulled to her chest with the other. "Er?"

"And I'll be back as soon as I can," Morgen promised. "Come with me," she whispered to Amar, not wanting to leave him to endure hostile stares from her family.

"What's wrong at the building now?" he asked.

Morgen showed him the text, which was not from Deputy Franklin but the vegan bakery. *Pumpkin scones ready to pick up.*

"A lack of pastries for the ghost," she whispered.

Bringing up the ghost reminded her of the vision she'd had in the middle of the night. That was another reason she wanted to get Amar alone to talk with as soon as possible. She hoped he remembered something helpful from the night Grandma had banished his ghost.

"A true emergency," he said.

"Yes. Any chance you have your keys and can drive?" She looked down at his lack of pockets. "Never mind." She ran toward the house to grab her purse and keys.

"Morgen," Caden protested. "We came up to see you. We need to talk."

"More than ever," Rhett added.

"Yes, yes. I'll be back as soon as I can." After grabbing her purse, she ran past them, half-afraid one of her brothers would tackle her and pin her to the ground. Caden looked like he wanted to.

Amar had donned boots and jeans and was fastening his leather vest. He pointed her to his truck as he nodded toward her car. Someone had parked behind it, so getting it out would have been difficult.

"Does anyone want to go in the hot tub?" Zoe was offering as Morgen climbed into the passenger side of the truck.

Morgen feared her family wouldn't be any more enlightened when she returned. Maybe it was awful—at the least, it was cowardly—but she hoped she and Amar could have a *long* chat before heading back to the house. She couldn't justify being gone all day, but a big part of her wished she *could*, that she could wait until dark to return—and that all of the Lobos would change forms and show off their wolfness then.

"When we get back, will you change into a wolf to prove to my family that your kind exists?" Morgen hoped he wouldn't be offended that she wanted to use him as a demo werewolf.

Amar only shrugged. "Yes. They seem obnoxious. Do you want me to bite any of them?"

"Maybe just Jun."

"That was your ex-husband?" Amar slanted her an unreadable look.

"Yes. I wasn't expecting him. I wasn't expecting *any* of them until later in the day. Preferably, the part of the day when fewer pairs of underwear would be hanging around the property."

"He seemed uptight," Amar said, not commenting on the rest.

Morgen almost said that it was justifiable, given the circumstances, but it wasn't an unfair assessment of Jun. "Yeah."

"You were wise to leave him for me."

She'd already told him that it had been the other way around, so she didn't correct him. She only smiled and said, "*Obviously.*"

18

"I'VE NEVER HAD SEX IN A CAR," MORGEN ADMITTED, CHEEKS flushed, and one leg slung awkwardly up on the dashboard.

Technically, it was a truck. But she'd never had sex in one of them either.

Amar reached up, removed Morgen's panties from the rearview mirror, and handed them to her with a self-satisfied smirk. Morgen accepted them, her cheeks warming even further as she remembered flinging her clothing wantonly around the cab. And here she'd been judging Zoe an hour earlier for retrieving undergarments in a similar state.

Morgen and Amar were in the parking lot at the bakery. It was the *back* of the parking lot, and there weren't many people there on the foggy Saturday morning, but she felt risqué for having steamed the windows with Amar.

She wasn't sure how it had happened. She'd been distraught as she leaned into him, accepting his comfort—and his kisses—but she hadn't been planning to have *sex*. Not in public. But Amar had been feeling good—and randy—after his long night's hunt.

"Never?" he rumbled. "Because your ex-husband was uptight?"

She swatted him on the chest but admitted, "Yeah. And maybe I was too. Also, neither of our vehicles had a long bench seat. Modern car seats make things more difficult."

"Not to those who are determined."

Since she didn't want to hear about his previous car encounters with lovers, all she said to that was, "And who don't mind getting seat-belt buckles up their butt."

"My truck doesn't have seat belts."

"Funny how you say that like it's a feature, not illegal and a safety hazard."

"Werewolves are bad boys."

She shook her head and kissed him, not able to disagree. His stomach whined, and she leaned back.

"Didn't you get enough elk during the night?" Her stomach was hollow as well, so she shifted to tug on her clothes. She had to pick up her bakery order and planned to have a scone for herself before heading back, at which point she hoped pastries would put her family in a better mood.

"We ran into a moose and took it down. It was quite satisfying, but there were a lot of us, so I'm not as full as I am after hunting solo."

"So, you're in dire need of scones and coffee. And floss to get antler fuzz out of your teeth."

"I didn't eat the antlers, but I'll say yes to the rest."

Amar shifted her off him so he could also dress. Two seagulls landed on the hood of the truck; they were barely visible through the steamed windshield.

"Will you return to your family after resolving this pressing issue at your building?" Amar asked as he stuck his foot in a boot.

"I guess. Whatever Zoe's telling them, it'll probably only make things worse."

"Yes." Amar paused and eyed her. "How and why did she end up wearing my bear hide?"

She remembered the Lobos had arrived *after* Zoe and Ungar had wandered out of the barn and Ungar had left. Amar must have been mystified by Zoe meandering around outside in his bear hide.

"She spent the night in the barn," Morgen said.

"You did not give her a room in the house?"

"Oh, I did, but I didn't encourage her to use it for entertaining."

A moment passed as Amar parsed that vagueness. "You encouraged her to use my *barn* for entertaining? My *apartment*?"

Since Amar still had his tools in the barn and his personal belongings in the apartment, Morgen didn't point out that he was more or less living with her in the house now. "No. No, I did not. When I went to bed, they were sitting on the porch. I'm not sure why they didn't confine their *entertaining* to Ungar's SUV."

"*Ungar?*" Amar's eyebrows flew up.

Had he not guessed which werewolf Zoe had taken to bed? Morgen supposed he hadn't seen the make-out session outside of the Crystal Parlor.

"Ungar was in *my barn*?" Amar roared. The seagulls squawked and flew away. "Did they use my bed?" His top lip reared back from his teeth.

They were normal human teeth currently, but Morgen had no trouble imagining lupine fangs emerging. "I didn't ask. I was too busy being an embarrassment to my entire family."

Amar huffed, grabbed the keys, and jumped out of the truck. More seagulls fled, abandoning the crumbs of a pastry that someone had dropped in the parking lot.

"If they did any damage," Morgen said as they walked to the door, "I'll pay for it. She's my cousin, so I'm responsible for her." She scratched her jaw. "Can you get bear hides dry cleaned?"

Amar gave her a dour look, but he managed to summon enough gentlemanness to open the door for her. As Morgen stepped inside, her phone rang. Sian.

"Hang on. I need to talk to the one family member who isn't dreadfully embarrassed by my new life."

Amar grunted. "I'll get your scones."

"Thank you. Don't sprinkle any fish eggs on them, please."

He squinted back at her.

"Phoebe told me about your recent shopping trip."

"Small towns are riddled with snoops and gossips."

"Members of the coven watch out for each other."

"There's nothing to watch out for. You *eat* fish. You've said so before. I once saw you dip battered cod in tartar sauce and chomp it down."

"I eat the parts of the fish that are delicious drenched in butter and herbs or deep-fried. The eggs don't qualify." Morgen answered the phone before the call could go to voice mail and waved for him to continue inside. The bakery store clerk was watching and listening to them, probably appalled by talk of fish consumption in her vegan shop.

"I'm at the library, and it's closed," Sian said for her greeting.

"Uh. The library here?"

"No, the Seattle Public Library. I understand they have aisles dedicated to historic tanneries in remote tourist towns."

"Well, thank you for driving up," Morgen said, ignoring the sarcasm. She glanced at her watch. It was after nine now, but maybe the library didn't open until ten on the weekend. "Do you want to join us at the bakery for coffee and a scone?"

A seagull flew past with the frosted tip of a long john in its beak. This place had to be paradise for the local fowl.

"It *should* be open," Sian said.

"The library?"

Sian sighed, as if Morgen were being willfully obtuse. "The library, yes. The posted Saturday hours are nine to four."

Morgen blamed any obtuseness on the fact that she hadn't had coffee yet. When Amar walked out with two steaming drinks as well as her bags of pumpkin scones, she hugged him fiercely.

"Maybe the librarian slept in or was late due to having sex with a werewolf," Morgen said. "There's a lot of that going around in Bellrock."

"I am uninterested in the libidinous nature of the local denizens. You promised me a mystery, and since I am now employed full-time, I must solve it within the bounds of the weekend."

"I'll be right there. Maybe there's someone we can call." Morgen waved toward the street. The library was only a block away, so they could leave the truck and walk.

"The head librarian is eighty," Amar said.

"You don't think octogenarians enjoy hot, steamy werewolf sex?"

"I'm certain they do, but I've not seen any of the pack offering their services to women forty or fifty years their senior."

"How uncharitable of them."

They found Sian standing in front of the wood-framed glass library doors with a peeved expression on her face and a coffee cup in her hand. As usual, she wore drab colors, a gray sweater with baggy blue pants, save for pink socks visible between cuff and shoe. Morgen wagered a unicorn was wandering across those socks somewhere.

"Thanks for coming up," she said. "When we're done here, would you mind going to the house and telling our brothers, their wives, and Jun that werewolves are real, that I don't host orgies in the hot tub, and that Grandma was a witch with actual magical power and we're learning to be witches too?"

"Jun came?" Sian asked, not commenting on the rest. "Why?"

"He didn't say. He was too busy gawking at all the nude werewolves."

Sian looked at Amar.

"We were returning from a hunt," he said.

"He probably still cares a bit and was worried about whatever our brothers told him." Morgen winced, imagining that conversation, then leaned forward to try the door handle. It was, as promised, locked.

"I am capable of determining whether or not a door is open," Sian said dryly.

"I wasn't sure if your illness had left you weakened to such an extent that you might not be able to open a heavy door."

"I'm capable of opening doors *and* punching obnoxious siblings."

"In that case, I must direct you and your fists toward our brothers posthaste."

Sian snorted softly. "You have someone you can call?" She waved at the doors. "The librarian? Or would the mayor have the key?"

Morgen couldn't keep from making a choking sound. "I've seen quite enough of the mayor, lately, thank you." She pulled out her phone, but she didn't know the librarian's name and ended up raising her eyebrows toward Amar. "I don't suppose you know her number?"

"As I told you, I don't service her."

"Ha ha."

"Service?" Sian asked.

"Never mind." Morgen called Valderas. He'd been the vet here for years and seemed to know everyone, at least everyone with a pet. Surely, an eighty-year-old librarian would have a cat. That was a rule, wasn't it?

"*I* could have called him," Sian said when she saw the contact on Morgen's phone.

"You should have. He's been pining for you."

Sian eyed her. "He didn't say that."

"No." Morgen almost told her about Valderas's gift shopping, but he might prefer that his present be a surprise. "He asked how you're doing though."

Valderas answered before Sian could reply. "Good morning, Ms. Keller."

"Hi, Doc. Do you, by chance, know the librarian? I thought she might have cats."

"She has four indoor cats and more outdoor cats than she can count."

"I *knew* it. Though I'm surprised at how many people in this town have a large number of cats, especially *outdoor* cats. You know, given how many predators are about."

Amar's eyebrows rose. "You're not suggesting werewolves would stoop to eating people's pets, are you?"

"No, of course not. I just noticed how aggressive the seagulls in that parking lot were."

"As far as I know, she's the only one with that many cats," Valderas said. "Her son has commented frequently on the subject."

"Her son?" Morgen's stomach turned.

"Yes. Mayor Ungar."

Morgen slumped, crossing her fingers that *he* wouldn't be sent with the keys. "Can you give me her number, by chance? We need to do a little research in the library, and it's supposed to be open but isn't."

"It's against my policy to give out the personal information of my clients."

"Sian is here."

"I'll call Linda and find out what's up."

"Thanks." Morgen smirked at her sister, amused that her name had swayed Valderas.

Sian merely twitched an eyebrow.

"Is Sian well?" Valderas asked.

"She's peeved and perturbed this morning, so... about like usual."

"Ha ha," Sian said in her flattest tone.

"I have something to lighten her mood," Valderas said. "I'll come join you at the library."

Sian leaned close to the phone. "The *key* is the only thing I need to lighten my mood."

Valderas had already hung up.

Sighing again, Sian leaned back. She lifted her hands and peered through the glass doors. With the lights off inside, and the foggy gloom outside, Morgen doubted she could see much.

"I love old libraries," Sian said, "but I'm not sure this one is large enough to have much in the way of archives."

"Maybe there's a basement," Morgen said.

"I do hope so. I brought my inhaler in case I ended up inundated with must and dust." Sian patted one of her pockets.

"Armed with such defenses, you're sure to prevail in your quest."

"*Your* quest." Sian turned. "Why did you lease such a building?"

"It was spacious and inexpensive, and I know a talented handyman who can fix anything." Morgen beamed a smile at Amar.

He sipped from his coffee. "Yes."

"I can wait here for the librarian and do the research on my own, if you wish to return to your house." Sian eyed the bags of scones—Morgen should have stopped to put them in the truck. "Shouldn't you be up there if our brothers are there?"

"Them being there is why I'm here. I wasn't kidding, Sian. I'd really appreciate it if you went up and vouched for me."

"You'd rather I attempt to explain your life instead of solving the mystery of your supposedly haunted building?"

"If you could do both things, I'd be forever in your debt."

"Why didn't you *show* them some of your magic?" Sian asked. "You can make fire out of nothing, zap enemies with your staff, and turn invisible. Even skeptics should be swayed by witnessing such acts."

"*Invisible*. I forgot about that one." Morgen wished she'd made herself disappear the instant they drove up.

Sian pursed her lips in disapproval.

"Yes, I guess you're right," Morgen admitted. "But my magic isn't as impressive as other things that happen in this town. I was hoping to get some werewolves to change in front of them. That was, if you'll recall, what swayed *you*."

"I recall well." Sian looked in the direction of Dr. Valderas's Victorian house and office, and he happened to be walking into view.

Unfortunately, Mayor Ungar was walking with him. Morgen groaned. Didn't that man have any *work* to do?

Sian, who hadn't been around for any of Morgen's encounters with the mayor, merely raised her eyebrows before lifting a hand toward Valderas in a chaste wave. It wasn't the most ebullient greeting, but Valderas smiled warmly and held up a bag from the chocolate factory Morgen had mentioned.

When they reached the doors, Valderas drew Sian aside to give her his gift. That left Morgen and Amar standing in front of Ungar, a man that she had seen entirely too much of lately. At least he was wearing clothes now.

"You're not planning to make trouble, are you?" Ungar growled, glancing toward the glass doors.

"In the library?" Morgen asked. "Of course not." What did he imagine? Her inviting the Lobos and Loups in for a showdown between Acquisitions and Periodicals? "My sister will be spearheading the research, and she would be incapable of so much as returning a book to the shelf in the wrong order, even if someone were holding a gun to her head."

Morgen silently admitted that her skin also crawled at the thought of intentionally doing such a thing.

"The order of the books on the shelves isn't what I'm concerned about," Ungar said. "I don't need any more witch activities resulting in damage to public property."

"That's not going to happen. We have no plans to let anyone raise a demon among the stacks."

Ungar eyed her coffee, as if he was debating forbidding her from taking a drink inside—maybe he was—but his phone beeped with a text and distracted him. He looked at the display, rolled his eyes, and stuck it back in his pocket.

"The librarian isn't feeling well today, and her assistant is out of town." Ungar fished out a keychain. "I'll let you in, but don't let anyone else in until I can find someone to man the desk. And if *anything* is damaged, I'll know who was responsible." He gave Morgen a cool smile. "Maybe we'll add the cost of damages to your taxes."

"Goodie."

Since he was unlocking the door, she restrained herself from making a more sarcastic comment.

But his phone rang before he finished. Sighing with the melodrama of a teenage girl forbidden from going out on a school night, he answered.

"I got your text, Mom," he said. "You didn't need to call."

Morgen looked at Amar. He merely shrugged back. Meanwhile, Sian was holding her gift of chocolate-covered caramels fondly while espousing to Valderas the benefits of chocolate for increasing serotonin levels.

"Yes, yes," Ungar said. "I told you, I'll put in an order."

A lengthy chain of sentences from *Mom* followed as Ungar shifted impatiently from foot to foot and did more eye rolling. Morgen thought she picked out the words *cat condo* among them.

Amar, with his keener hearing, snorted softly.

"No, I don't think they have a *catalog*," Ungar said, glowering at his phone.

Morgen nudged Amar with her elbow. "We should prioritize that. How are you at taking pictures? Maybe Wendy with her art skills has a knack for that. I can put everything we offer in a database so we can get it online and start taking orders over the internet."

Originally, Amar hadn't been delighted by the idea of making pet furniture, but since he'd started sharing the house with her, and agreed to assist with the taxes and paying the utilities, he'd been more agreeable when it came to making extra money.

"Yes, yes, Mom. I'll get something ordered today. *Goodbye.*" Ungar looked at Amar. "She wants a deluxe model like you made for the witch."

"Which witch?" Amar asked.

"The one you made a giant cat *thing* for." Ungar spread his arms, then raised one hand to head height.

Sakura, Morgen thought but didn't supply.

"I've made pet furnishings for a number of witches. There's nothing they won't spend to ensure the happiness of their familiars. You're familiar with my rates?" The corners of Amar's mouth were threatening to quirk up in a smile. He must not have had any love for Ungar, either, for he appeared delighted to torment the man.

"No, but I'm sure the words *highway robbery* apply," Ungar grumbled.

"Amar does high-quality work and must be properly compensated," Morgen said. "I'll make sure he uses the special carpet scraps to ensure happiness from your mother's cats."

"Fine, fine." Ungar turned the key in the lock and pulled open the door. "Just make it large enough for *all* of them." He lowered his voice to grumble, "Maybe they'll sleep on it so I don't have to hear daily complaints about how poorly my mother slept because the cats had all her pillows."

Morgen, who understood perfectly how pets liked comfort and could *expand* once they claimed a spot in an owner's bed, almost felt sorry for Ungar. At the least, she could sympathize with his mother.

His phone rang again. "What does the sheriff want now?" Grumbling more, he waved for them to go in, then headed off down the street.

Morgen paused, holding the door open for Sian, who was finishing up with Valderas, and caught part of Ungar's conversation before he walked out of earshot.

"What do you want *me* to do? *You're* the law enforcer. Just because I hunt with them sometimes doesn't mean I can be held accountable for everything they do."

"Did you hear about the Loups getting up to any trouble last night?" Morgen asked Amar.

He hesitated, and concern crawled into her gut.

"You didn't run *into* them on your hunt, did you?" She looked him up and down, afraid he might have suffered fresh wounds. That morning, she'd been too distracted by her family's arrival to wonder why the Lobos had gotten back so late from their hunt, but maybe she should have.

"At one point, some of them picked a fight with us." Amar shrugged as if it happened all the time and wasn't a big deal. "I don't know if they're scheming up something, but they're no match for us when it comes to brawling."

Words that did not set her mind at ease. "Are they still mad about the *rougarou*? And blaming you for what he did?"

"That's the gist of it, at least from what they've said. As I mentioned before, I think it's more that they feel ganged up on now that your coven and the Lobos are getting along to some extent. They think we'll work together to drive them out of the area." His expression grew a little wistful as he shrugged again. "They'll just have to learn to deal with how things are now. If they don't, *we'll* deal with *them*. You don't need to worry."

Morgen smiled bleakly, certain she *would* worry. As she'd been thinking the day before, the idea of losing Amar was even more disturbing now that she carried his baby. The idea of their child never getting to meet his or her father filled her with dread.

19

Sneezes drifted up from the stairwell leading to the archives in the basement.

"Everything okay down there?" Morgen called from the table she'd claimed to peruse a handwritten journal containing entries about the citizens who'd founded Bellrock.

She hoped Sian's inhaler was sufficiently protecting her lungs from dust and mold and who knew what other pollutants lurked downstairs. As far as Morgen had observed, there weren't many old basements in the perennially damp Pacific Northwest that hadn't suffered from water damage over the years.

"Delightful," came Sian's sarcastic and not particularly heartening response.

Hopefully, she would soon find what she sought and come back upstairs.

Morgen had already perused books on the local logging industry and the timber barons who'd gotten rich running it. She'd also skimmed through one on the maritime fur trade and found references to Pierre Toussaint, the guy whose name was on the street perpendicular to Main Street and next to the tannery. It sounded like he'd owned the building and had run the tannery at its inception. What she hadn't found was anything about the subsequent owners or murders that might have taken place there.

"Just the *animal* murders," she muttered, affronted by the thought of thousands and thousands of beavers and other critters being hunted down for their fur. At least Amar and the Lobos thoroughly consumed all parts of the animals they killed and didn't let anything go to waste. "Even the female organs," she muttered with a shudder, surprised she hadn't had dreams about Amar and Pedro trying to force feed her such horrendous delicacies. Maybe if she acquiesced to the fish eggs, that would make Amar happy, and he wouldn't try to push other things on her.

"Are you finding anything helpful?" Amar asked from the other end of the table.

"Not about ghosts. I—" Morgen halted, reminded of the vision her amulet had given her.

When they'd been driving into town, she'd meant to ask Amar about that night, but he'd reached over and fondled her leg, and that had led to the parking-lot sex. At which point, thoughts of ghosts had stampeded out of her mind.

"I had a dream last night. A *vision*." Morgen pulled her amulet out from under her shirt to show him, the new moon-shaped charm coming with it. "You were with Grandma at a cabin in the woods, and she went inside to get your tooth for you."

Amar nodded. "That was about two years ago. I told you about the bounty hunter who came to kill werewolves."

"You did tell me about that, but you neglected to mention that after he was killed, his ghost stuck around to haunt that cabin."

Amar leaned back in his chair. "I do not know if that's exactly what happened, but there were some strange things that happened after his death."

"Such as supernatural phenomena?"

"I guess. His death was... garish. But he also brought it on himself." Amar touched a scar on his shoulder. A spot where a silver bullet had grazed him?

"Something that I'm sure didn't keep his ghost from being bitter. If ghosts exist. Do you believe they do?"

"Maybe. Since moving to Bellrock, I've seen a lot of strange things, but most were a result of witches fiddling with magic."

"Let's assume that ghosts *do* exist. Grandma did something to take care of it while you... smashed your shoulders against the door and windows."

Amar grimaced. "*Magic* kept me from getting in to help her."

"I believe you."

"Normally, my strength would take down a door and window. *Easily.*"

"I know."

"I could have torn that cabin apart log by log if not for magic."

Morgen reached over and patted his arm. "I'm not doubting your virility. I was just wondering if Grandma later told you what she did to get rid of the ghost. It looked like she banished it, but the vision didn't show everything. Knowing what she did might be helpful to me in getting rid of *my* ghost."

Or *helping* her ghost, she amended silently, remembering the words she'd heard when it appeared.

"She didn't speak of it again," Amar said. "She was always reclusive when it came to her magic and what she did in her root cellar. And werewolves aren't interested in witch magic, so we don't pry."

Morgen propped her elbow on the table and slumped her chin onto her hand in disappointment.

"If you intend to confront a ghost," Amar said, "take me with you. I do not like to feel useless or for people to risk themselves while I'm stuck outside and can't help."

"I can understand that."

His voice grew softer as he admitted, "I could have gone in

with her. I didn't expect the doors and windows to magically lock, or I would have. But I was... uneasy about the place."

He'd been afraid. After her experience in the tannery—funny how *those* doors had also magically locked—she couldn't blame him. It had been creepy as hell.

"I get it. And I'll happily take you with me when I go in to confront the ghost."

"When? Not if?"

"Well, we have a two-year lease. I think we'll have to get the ghost out of there somehow. Statistics say that ninety percent of small businesses fail in the first five years, and that's *without* paranormal pitfalls. We need to do our best to tilt the odds in our favor."

"Yes. It is good that I'm talented at woodworking, and you are talented at making charms." His gaze drifted to the moon pendant that she'd left dangling outside her shirt. "You have a new talisman?"

"I made it in Phoebe's shop last night while you and the Lobos were having dinner." Reminded of what it supposedly did, Morgen lifted it to show it off. "It's a *child charm*. Its magic is supposed to ensure the health of my baby, at least while it's inside me. I assume it can't protect kids once they're old enough to ride bicycles off on their own." Though she would see if there was something else she could make to give to her child at that point.

"The magic will make the baby healthy?" Amar sounded a little dubious as he considered it.

"It will," Morgen said firmly, though all she knew was that she'd followed the formula and succeeded in infusing the pendant with magic. "Phoebe gave the recipe to me, and she's an experienced witch, so she knows all about things like this. This means there's no need for me to eat nasty food."

His eyelids lowered as he kept eyeing it—and her—through his lashes. Did he think she was making this up merely to get him off her back about his food beliefs? She wanted to feel affronted, but she *had* lied to her family that morning in front of him.

"You can ask Phoebe if you don't believe me," Morgen said. "I left the formula on her workbench when I was distracted by, uh, something else. I'm sure she can show it to you."

Amar peered into her eyes as he considered her thoughtfully. "No. If you say it is true, it is true."

She gazed back at him, touched that he believed her.

"It is a good idea to use such magic," he added, "since you will only eat inferior foods."

"Does that mean you'll stop trying to foist your supposedly superior foods on me?"

"Do you not believe it would be good to employ *both* methods? In case the charm is only partially effective? I wish for both you and the baby to be healthy."

"I know, but you're..." Morgen stopped herself before finishing with *nagging*. She didn't want to fight about this with him.

"Perhaps you could dump my foods into the blender when you make your smoothies," Amar suggested. "As you do with your pea-protein powder. Then you would not taste or notice them."

Morgen shuddered as she envisioned fish eggs and organ bits floating around in her blueberry antioxidant blend.

Sneezes from the stairs kept her from having to continue the conversation, one in which she was sure the word *nagging* would have eventually slipped out. Sian was climbing up with old newspapers in hand. She paused on the landing to use her inhaler, a tear trickling from one of her watering eyes.

Morgen pushed herself to her feet. "Do you need help? I'm sorry. I didn't know it would be that bad down there."

Sian shook her head. "I've been more susceptible to... *every-thing* since I caught the Dengue Fever again. Even though I've recovered from the sickness, my body has been more reactive to allergens."

"Maybe Amar can make you a blueberry organ-meat smoothie. I'm sure such a superior food would fix you right up."

Amar lifted his brows hopefully, probably imagining both of them guzzling down such a concoction.

"Uh." Sian returned her inhaler to the pocket and finished the climb. "Can you *taste* the organ meats in it?"

As Morgen recalled, Sian had praised Amar's snout-to-tail diet. Somewhat hilariously so, since Sian was even less likely to eat something *healthy* than Morgen. At least Morgen consumed a lot of vegetables. Her sister favored bacon cheeseburgers and chocolates.

"My limited encounters with such foods suggest you can *always* taste them. Did you find anything good?" Morgen waved to the newspapers. "So far, all I've learned about is Pierre Toussaint's adventures in becoming a fur baron in the early days of Seattle, Bellingham, and Bellrock."

"I found murder." Sian spread a newspaper on the table, a photograph of the tannery on display as a Model T drove past out front.

"How *old* of a murder?" Morgen waved at the car. There were also horseback riders visible in the background.

Sian pointed to a date near the headline that read: *Local Woman's Dead Body Found in Bicycle Repair Shop.*

"Bicycle repair shop?" Morgen asked.

Neither the real-estate agent nor anyone else who'd given her information on the building had mentioned that use. Unless the tinkerer who'd built the robot statue had fixed bikes.

"The words *body* and *dead* were what my brain fixated on," Sian said.

"I know, I know. Local woman, huh?" Morgen remembered that the voice she'd heard had been accented. Russian, she'd thought, but it had been hard to be certain after only a few words.

"From the article, it sounds like a lot of violence was reported before the actual death of the woman. The repairman reputedly abused her and others, but the authorities didn't do anything about it since he'd purchased them. Even after the body was found, he wasn't prosecuted."

"*Purchased* them? The *women*? What year was this?" Morgen checked the date again. 1918.

"Maybe Bellrock was late to learn that slavery had been abolished in the United States."

"That's *really* late."

"This isn't exactly a progressive town."

Morgen thought of the bloodstains. Could they have been the result of people being abused? Poor slave women? She'd assumed the bloodstains had been a result of the garish work that originally went on in the building, but if the tinkerer had owned it by World War I, then it hadn't been a tannery for a long time. And what about that hidden stain on the wall that Amar had said smelled of human blood?

Morgen shook her head. Could the bloodstains truly date back more than a hundred years? It seemed like *someone* would have attempted to sand them out or paint over them in that time. On the other hand, other than the tinkerer and the quirky artist who might have installed the meat hooks dangling from the ceiling, how many people had leased the building over the years? Judging by its decrepit state, it had been abandoned more often than occupied.

"Why wasn't the tinkerer prosecuted?" Morgen waved at the article. "Was there another suspect?"

"He said he didn't do it." Sian shrugged. "He was the one who reported finding her one morning when he came in to work, and said someone had broken in during the night."

Morgen's phone rang. Wincing, she pulled it out. Her brothers probably wanted to know when she was coming back.

Zoe's name popped up.

"Hey, Zoe. Everything going okay up there?"

"Everything is *not* going okay," Zoe replied. "Your brothers are too much to handle. They called me an unreliable witness. *Me.* As if I have anything to do with your witchcraft shenanigans. I'm a respected real-estate agent, Morgen. I'm the treasurer for my neighborhood's HOA. They don't let just anyone do that, you know."

Morgen suspected her brothers deeming Zoe *unreliable* had more to do with her nude walk from the barn rather than her HOA credentials. "I'm sorry for leaving you with them."

She took a deep breath. Sian was right. Morgen needed to go up there, explain things to her family, and perform some feat that would convince them that witches and magic were real. The thought gave her performance anxiety, but she'd battled werewolves, witches, and Amar's dreadful enemy. She could handle her family.

"You should be," Zoe said. "But you should be even sorrier that you're not where you said you would be. The stench rolling out of this place is *awful.*"

"Uh, stench?" Morgen looked toward a window, surprised to find the day had grown darker instead of brighter as the morning advanced. The fog was denser than it had been an hour ago. "Where are you?"

"The tannery where *you're* supposed to be. And it smells like rotten animal carcasses."

"It's not far from the water. Maybe a sea lion died on the beach, and the breeze is wafting toward town." Given the dense fog and lack of air stirring outside, Morgen doubted the words as soon as they came out of her mouth.

"I don't think so, Morgen. You better get over here."

"I'll make a copy of this." Sian took the newspaper article and headed for a copy machine that had been state-of-the-art about the time Amar's truck had rolled out of the factory.

"We'll be right over," Morgen said. "Don't go inside."

"And marinate myself in that stench? I wasn't planning to."

"We repaired all the broken windows," Amar said after Morgen hung up.

"Meaning that anything coming from inside and strong enough for her to smell outside is... *really* strong?"

"Likely so."

"Wonderful."

20

As Morgen, Sian, and Amar drove down Main Street toward the tannery, Morgen sniffed gingerly toward Amar's open window. If her hypothesis about something dead on the beach causing an unpleasant odor had been true, she should have caught a whiff in town.

"I smell it," Amar said grimly.

"A dead sea lion?"

"No. I've never been to a real tannery, but it smells like how I imagine one would smell."

"Dead animal carcasses?"

"*Long*-dead animal carcasses and lye soap."

"A delightful combination," Sian murmured, looking like she would have preferred to stay at the library, even if it meant gluing her inhaler to her lips to survive.

"Maybe some of the Loups found carcasses to throw through the windows last night," Morgen said.

"They were busy harassing us in Wolf Wood last night," Amar said.

"All of them?" Morgen wrinkled her nose as the odor Amar

had described grew noticeable to her olfactory senses. Her stomach roiled. She hadn't thrown up in a couple of hours, but that might be about to change.

"No. Ungar wasn't with them."

"Uh, he has an alibi."

Amar eyed her darkly, perhaps thinking of his defiled bed and bear hide, then parked in front of the building instead of the empty parking lot to the side. Zoe's car was there, but Morgen didn't see her.

Afraid she'd gone inside and that something might have happened to her, Morgen nearly climbed over Amar to get out of the truck. As she ran to the closed door, Zoe stepped around the back corner of the building and into view.

A lacy, thin scarf tied around her head covered her nose and mouth, but it was hard to imagine the flimsy fabric doing anything to block the smell. It looked like the kind of thing she might drop in front of a sexy guy to entice him to bend over and give her a view of his backside.

"I'm aggrieved that you lied to your brothers about where you were going," Zoe said.

"Will you be less aggrieved if I give you a pumpkin scone?" Morgen waved toward the truck, though she wished her baked goods were in an odor-proof bag. What if the scones picked up some of the stink tainting the air?

"When I'm done trying my hardest not to puke, I'll have one and let you know."

Amar eyed the front door, not noticeably affected by the smell. That was surprising, given that his sense of smell was so much stronger than theirs, but maybe carcass scents didn't bother a werewolf.

"Let's check inside." Morgen pulled out the keys.

"You check inside," Zoe said. "I'll wait here while hoping a stiff wind picks up and blows that stench out to Puget Sound."

"Right." Morgen stuck the key in the lock.

"Oh, and I brought this for you." Zoe drew a folded paper out of her pocket. "It's a list of all the owners of this place dating back to the seventies. I thought you might find it helpful in your research."

"Thanks, but if that's the *nineteen*-seventies, it doesn't go back far enough."

"That's the earliest decade in the online GIS system. You might be able to get records going back further if you go to the county clerk's office."

Morgen took the list to Sian, who was waiting in the truck with the windows up and her sweater pulled over her nose. Before handing it over, Morgen glanced at it, curious who the owner had been back in the seventies.

Toussaint Trust. Huh. That sounded like the original owner's family. The building currently belonged to another trust, one based out of Florida. It had changed hands in the eighties and again in the nineties. She supposed it would be a long shot if the Toussaint Trust still existed and anyone affiliated with it today knew the history of the building—and why they'd sold it. Her introvert self shied away from the idea of looking up the contact information and calling a stranger to ask.

"A gift." Morgen handed the paper to Sian, though she knew her sister was even less likely to make phone calls. Maybe she could dig up something online.

"I'm getting a lot of those today." Sian accepted it.

"This won't be as mouthwatering as chocolates."

"You never know. Research material is often interesting."

"Sumptuous, even?"

"Sometimes."

Leaving her in the truck, Morgen returned to the building and opened the door. Amar lifted a hand, then walked in ahead of her.

If there was a pile of carcasses on the floor, Morgen was more than willing to let him find them first. She would also be willing to let him find bleach, buckets, and scrub brushes to clean all evidence of them, but that was a lot to ask.

Nose up, Amar prowled into the building and sniffed liberally about.

"Thanks for the list," Morgen told Zoe, who lingered outside. "It might be helpful with our research."

"You're welcome. I thought I would try to do something useful on my little weekend trip."

"I appreciate it." Morgen kept herself from saying she was surprised that Zoe had found the time—or anything else snide. As her cousin had pointed out, she was an adult, and there was nothing wrong with her coming up to get her itches scratched. And Ungar... well, Morgen would simply hope Zoe grew tired of him before he did anything unpleasant.

"There is nothing in here," Amar called from the back room. "I'll check the loft, but I can't detect the source of the stench."

"Really?" That shocked Morgen. Even when he was in his human form, his nose was so much better than hers. "Should I have brought Lucky?"

That earned her a dark look.

"Kidding." She held up an apologetic hand and peered around, finding it hard to believe that the tannery was exactly as they'd left it. "Be careful in the loft. It's a deathtrap."

The Lobos had reinforced the posts supporting the stairs and the beams, but they hadn't yet touched the original floorboards up there.

Amar paused at the bottom of the stairs and gazed toward the top. With all the junk up there, it would have been easy for someone to hide a carcass, but Amar should have smelled it.

He looked toward a window, then removed his vest. "It's dark enough out that I can shift. Maybe my lupine nose will be better at finding the source."

"Just be mindful that we're not alone." Morgen pointed to Zoe and waved to the street out front. Now that the windows were repaired and clean, anyone driving by might look in and see a naked man standing on the stairs.

"I thought your cousin *liked* werewolf nudity." Amar took off his boots and jeans.

"Not enough to stick my head in there." Zoe's voice sounded odd. Ah, the scarf must have been insufficient—now, she was holding her nose as well.

"Are you sure? Amar is pretty hunky."

Amar shifted into a wolf, his gray and black fur changing him from hunky to majestic, at least to a human's eyes. He padded up the stairs. Maybe because his weight was distributed between four legs instead of two, the boards didn't creak as uproariously as they had when Morgen had climbed up.

At the top, he sprang onto a drop-cloth-covered desk and peered around as his lupine nostrils twitched.

"If the fog is dense enough for shapeshifting," Morgen called up, "maybe you can show off your furry self to my family later."

Her brothers shouldn't have been her priority at that moment, but it would be *much* easier to explain werewolves with an actual wolf standing next to her.

Amar peered through the rickety railing at her before returning to sniffing and surveying the contents of the loft.

"What did he say?" Zoe asked.

Morgen shrugged. "He can't communicate with me tele-pathically."

"I thought you might be able to read his thoughts by the way he twitches his ears."

"He didn't growl and bare his fangs. That usually means he's not contemplating mauling and mutilation."

"Given that you're dating, that's promising."

"I find it so."

Amar swished his tail, more like a cat than a wolf, and sprang onto another covered piece of furniture.

"Maybe you could convince him to pee on Caden's car," Zoe said.

"Amar doesn't usually lower himself to juvenile pranks." Morgen recalled that he'd brushed off her suggestion that he mark his territory all around the barn to keep Zorro from invading it to hunt.

"After you left, Caden's wife was the one voicing concerns of orgies the loudest."

Morgen didn't point out that the orgy talk hadn't truly taken off until Zoe and Ungar had wandered naked out of the barn. "He *has* ripped the spare tire off a car before. A van, technically."

She stepped back into the doorway and turned her nose toward fresher air, wishing the odor would abate. She was starting to feel queasy.

"I love these werewolves," Zoe purred. "I'm thinking of moving up here."

Morgen nearly pitched over. "What?"

"It's quaint, there are lots of hot available men, and there's no competition to speak of when it comes to real-estate agents. I could do well for myself."

"What do you mean there's no competition? I just worked with a real-estate agent a few days ago."

Zoe gave her a pitying look. "Morgen, she leased you a haunted butcher shop with bloodstains on the floor. That is *not* competition. I could outsell her blindfolded while buffing my nails. Besides, I'm sure I have far superior assets than she does." Zoe propped a fist on her hip and turned to make her chest more prominent.

"I'm sure the mayor appreciates those assets."

"Oh, he does."

A loud creak came from the loft, followed by a thump-thud-crash.

Morgen surged inside, holding her breath and trying not to inhale the foul odor. "Amar?"

He'd moved farther from the railing, and she couldn't see him anymore.

A growl and a snapping of jaws floated down. Morgen took three steps toward the stairs, but something dark and furry flew over the railing, startling her. It landed with a thud on the floor and didn't move. A white stripe ran down its back and tail.

"Is that... the source of the stench?" Zoe asked from the doorway.

"I've smelled skunks before." Morgen rested a hand on her belly, willing her stomach to settle. "They don't smell like carcasses and lye soap. Though I guess I'm glad Amar got it before it could add its stink to the building."

That said, she looked away from the poor dead skunk. She understood that Amar had hunting instincts—especially when he was in his wolf form—but she hated seeing anything killed.

Amar trotted down the stairs with his head held high. Maybe he was proud that he'd gotten the skunk before it could spray him with its scent. Morgen had to admit that her brothers might be more willing to meet a werewolf if he didn't reek.

"Good work," she told him. "Any idea about the already existing odor? It's..." Her stomach churned, her scone threatening to come up. Damn it.

Amar shifted into his human form, fur disappearing, replaced with human muscle and naked flesh.

Her stomach writhed again, the combination of the stench and the dead animal too much for her delicate state. She darted outside, ran around the corner of the building, and vomited. The lack of fresh air, even outside, made it worse, and tears ran down her cheeks. She wanted to climb in Amar's truck and drive until they escaped the stench of the tannery.

Legs weak, she wiped her mouth and wobbled back around the corner. Deputy Franklin had joined Zoe outside, his SUV parked out front. He was frowning as he eyed the building.

Amar stepped out, his boots and clothes back on. Morgen shambled over to lean against him.

"It's distressing when my nudity inspires women to throw up." Amar wrapped an arm around her shoulders.

"It wasn't you. Though, for the record, throwing dead animals at my feet can activate my upchuck reflex."

"It wasn't *at your feet*. You were outside."

"I thought you were in danger, so I ran in."

"The skunk was the only thing up there. I know your preference is that animals—even pest animals that like to taunt wolves with their rigid upright tails—not be killed, but when he ran out with his fur up, I reacted on instinct."

"I don't blame you," Morgen said. "I might throw up on you, but I don't blame you."

"I will dispose of the skunk."

"Ms. Keller." Franklin had a kerchief pressed to his nose. "I've received a number of complaints about the reek coming from your building, including one from a very wealthy landowner who makes frequent donations to Bellrock's non-profit organizations."

"What did they want?" Zoe asked.

"And was this wealthy landowner a Loup?" Morgen asked.

"Ah, yes, I believe he occasionally runs with the pack and howls at the moon," Franklin said. "He suggested that if the building continues to be an eye sore—and now a *nose* sore—in our town, a town which relies on tourism, that it be condemned and demolished."

Morgen blinked. "But I just signed a lease. We already fixed a bunch of stuff and *cleaned* it."

Franklin made a gagging noise into his kerchief. "I don't believe the cleaning worked."

"This is a psychic stink."

"Well, wave a wand, and get rid of it."

"We'll figure something out." Morgen pulled out her phone to consult her database. If there were incantations to get rid of foul stenches, she would never need fear visiting a vault toilet at a trailhead again. "This rich Loup can't really get the building condemned, can he? It's been here for over a century. Why care about it now?"

Franklin offered a sad smile as he extended a hand toward her. "It's in your care now."

"And they hate me. Right." Morgen slumped against Amar, frustration mingling with weariness toward the entire Loup pack. *She* wasn't the one who'd brought the *rougarou* here or told them to fall prey to his magical manipulation. Why did they blame her?

She didn't want them to blame Amar, either, but she'd had nothing to do with it. Maybe she'd worked to get the witches and Lobos on the same side instead of sniping at each other, but how could the Loups blame her for that? If they weren't such jerks, she would be happy to try to mend the fences between them and the witches too.

Franklin lifted his phone to make a call. Not to whatever authority approved building condemnations, she hoped. It was the weekend. She ought to have *some* time to figure things out. Maybe if she flipped through *Incantations of Power,* the grimoire in Grandma's safe, Morgen would find answers to her problems.

"The mayor isn't answering his phone." Franklin lowered it. "That's my third time trying to call him. You guys haven't seen him lately, have you?"

He looked at Zoe. Word traveled fast in a small town.

"He opened the library for us a little over an hour ago," Morgen said. "I doubt anything has happened to him."

Though he *had* been muttering about the Loups as he'd walked away.

"How loyal is he to the Loups?" Morgen wondered if Franklin knew. "And vice versa."

Franklin shrugged. "He and the leader butt heads a lot. Lucien wants his loyalty and obedience. Ungar wants Lucien to kiss his ass."

Morgen didn't know if that made her feel better or not. Just because Ungar wasn't their loyal minion didn't mean he didn't consider Morgen an enemy. He'd gone out of his way to be a pest and remind her about her taxes often.

"They should do it," Zoe said. "He has a nice one."

Franklin arched his eyebrows.

"Ass," Zoe clarified.

Franklin cleared his throat. "I hadn't noticed."

"They don't teach law enforcement officers to be observant?" Zoe asked.

"I think my work here is done." Franklin stuck his phone in his pocket and headed for his SUV.

"His work?" Zoe asked. "All he did was walk up and deliver a threat."

Morgen opened her mouth to reply, but a strange sensation swept over her. It brought dizziness instead of nausea, and she not only leaned more heavily against Amar but felt the need to press her hand to the side of the building for further support. This didn't feel like a vision from Lucky or Zorro, nor was Grandma's amulet warming against her chest. Besides, the amulet had thus far only shared visions with her while she slept.

Help me, a whisper sounded in her mind. It was the same female voice that she'd heard when she'd seen the ghost.

Wobbly, Morgen started for the door, but Amar still had his arm around her shoulders, and he tightened it to keep her in place.

"I need to look inside," she rasped, certain she would see the ghost floating in there again.

"I haven't disposed of the skunk yet."

Too dizzy to comment on that, she leaned away from him and reached toward the door. Though he seemed reluctant, he walked beside her.

Morgen peered in to find that a dense fog had formed once again. It was even thicker than what blanketed the town. Thicker and less natural. A hint of a white glow came from the back room.

"You see it, right?" Morgen pointed, surprised Amar wasn't reacting.

"The skunk? Yes."

"No, the fog and the glow."

He frowned at her with concern.

Morgen's heart sank. Was she *seeing* things? Or worse, *imagining* things?

No, the meat hook had been real. It had fallen, and the others had seen it lying on the floor. And they *all* smelled the odor wafting out of the place. This might be another vision, something that wasn't being shared with the others, but she was sure it wasn't all in her imagination.

Help me, the voice sounded again. *It is the only way to end the curse.*

"How?" Morgen croaked. "And what curse? Who put it there?"

Only when you end the curse can we all find peace.

"I do want that," Morgen whispered.

"Is she all right?" Zoe asked Amar.

"I don't know," he said grimly.

21

MORGEN SAT IN THE TRUCK BETWEEN AMAR AND SIAN AS HE DROVE them back toward Wolf Wood, fog still blanketing the roads. Zoe was following in her car. Though Morgen couldn't say she was eager to face her brothers again, her experience at the tannery—and Franklin's words that someone might try to get the building condemned—made her want to solve the ghost problem more than ever.

Or was it a *curse* problem? She didn't know how much stock to put in the words she'd heard. She didn't even know who had been communicating with her. The dead woman mentioned in the article? Would a slave have had a Russian accent? She'd read about mail-order brides being convinced to travel out West in the past, but would the newspaper reporter have referred to one of them as a slave? Or a local woman? That didn't seem likely.

"I cannot shift into a wolf without taking off my clothes," Amar announced into the silence.

Morgen and Sian looked over at him.

"I *can*," he amended, "but it destroys my clothes, so I prefer not to."

"That's understandable," Morgen said, not sure why he'd made the announcement.

"You asked me to turn into a wolf for your family." Amar peered out the windshield, perhaps assessing the fog thickness and the light level. "But earlier, you also asked me to be on good behavior and wear clothes."

"Ah." Morgen squeezed his arm. "Yes, that's true, but that was before they arrived this morning and saw you and all of the Lobos naked." She glanced toward his crotch before she caught herself. "The cat's out of the bag."

"I'm glad I went straight to the library this morning," Sian murmured, looking out the window and pointedly not at any of Amar's anatomy.

"This means you do not care now if I wear clothing in front of them?" Amar sounded puzzled.

"Well, I'd prefer we all wear clothing as much as possible—" too bad Zoe wasn't in the truck so Morgen could look pointedly at *her*, "—but I'd also like them to see you wolf up so they don't think I'm crazy, and I know you need to get naked for that."

"You think proving you're living with a werewolf will cause them *not* to believe you're crazy?" Sian asked with amusement.

"Well, at least they'll know werewolves are real."

Though Sian had a point. What if they came to believe magic and werewolves were real but *still* believed Morgen was in some cult—some orgy-hosting cult—and continued to attempt to stage an intervention?

As Amar turned the truck off the main road and onto the long pothole-laced driveway, Morgen fantasized about avoiding her family again. This time, she could lock herself in the library to study Grandma's grimoire. But no, she had to talk to them. Maybe it wouldn't alleviate their concerns or keep them from trying to drag her back to Seattle, but at least it would be... the mature thing to do.

Amar rolled down the window and sniffed.

"That stench isn't following us, is it?" Morgen asked with dread.

She'd smelled it all the way through town. It hadn't been until they'd headed into the woods on the far side that it had faded, at least to her nose. The thought of Ungar showing up with heavy machinery to demolish the building at the behest of a rich uptight Loup came to mind. Maybe she should have called Phoebe or Belinda and asked for help putting some wards around the tannery.

"No." Amar inhaled deeply. "I smell José Antonio's famous elk balls. Also hamburgers and sausages."

Morgen groaned. "Not the French intestine things."

"I believe they're bratwursts."

"I like bratwurst," Sian said.

"As all meat-consuming humans do," Amar said.

Morgen wouldn't admit it out loud, but she missed such things on occasion too. Even more than bratwurst, *bacon* could still set her mouth to watering. Alas, she hadn't yet found an equally delicious version made out of mushrooms or kale.

"And apparently wolves," she said.

"Naturally," Amar said.

At the top of the hill, the fog was thinner, and Morgen could see the outline of the sun through it. Thoughts of having Amar turn into a werewolf for her family dwindled. That might have to wait until nightfall.

Despite the foggy gloom, her brothers were out on the back deck with Wendy, José Antonio, and a number of the Lobos. Amar's pack seemed to have declared her property their second home. She wasn't sure whether it was the proximity of their favorite hunting grounds, or if extroverted werewolves were simply drawn to introverts, the way cats always snuggled up to and left hair on the slacks of those allergic to them.

"I guess I'll find it promising that Gavin is waiting beside the grill with a plate," Morgen said as Amar parked his truck. "They can't be too distraught about my life choices if they're willing to join a barbecue hosted by strangers."

"They're probably relieved everyone is wearing clothes," Sian said.

Morgen had mentioned the morning's events to her during their research session and only nodded. She drew a bracing breath before easing out of the truck, tempted to grab Amar's hand for support. And maybe Sian's too.

Why was losing the good opinion of one's family scarier than facing murderous witches and werewolves? Her brothers had always thought Morgen and Sian a little odd, but before, Morgen had held a good-paying and respectable job, and she'd been married. *Normal* things. She hadn't been the black sheep of the family. But now...

As she walked up, she spotted Lucky working the crowd on the deck, leaning on people and wagging to ensure they petted him as he waved his nose toward their plates, hoping for food to fall. Canines also adored bratwurst. As did ferrets, apparently. Napoleon was running back and forth along the deck railing, his nose in the air as he sought ways to get close to plates.

"Hey, Caden, everyone." Morgen lifted a hand when her siblings turned toward her. The sound of clinking glasses came through the open door that led to the laundry room and the kitchen, suggesting that her brothers' wives were inside and had felt the need to break out alcohol. "Sorry I had to leave so abruptly and was gone so long."

Unfortunately, the concerned and judgmental expressions that turned toward her suggested little had changed in the hours she'd been in town.

"No problem." José Antonio was the one to speak, waving a

spatula from the grill. He bent over a plate, quickly preparing something, then sauntered over.

When Morgen saw the chargrilled burger open-faced on a bun with some sort of reddish-orange relish on top, she assumed José Antonio was bringing food for Amar or Sian. But he extended it to Morgen.

"Uh?" Reflexively, Morgen gripped the plate, but she was *positive* that wasn't a vegetarian burger. Since José Antonio knew about her diet—he'd even grilled portobello caps for her before—she looked at him in confusion.

But he sidled up to Amar and elbowed him in the ribs. "I made her a special dish for the special occasion. Used the fish eggs you got. She'll be glowing with good health after eating them."

Morgen groaned and offered the plate to her sister.

Sian lifted her hands, refusing to take it. She must have realized the garnish on top wasn't *relish*. Though Sian enjoyed meat, she didn't like anything with an odd taste or texture. Fish eggs likely qualified.

Amar shook his head and pointed to the burger. "She doesn't eat meat, remember? You'll have to put the fish eggs on toast if we're going to entice her. Like a slice of avocado."

"Oh right." José Antonio took the plate and headed into the kitchen.

"Fish-egg toast, the next artisanal snack food that's sure to take off." Sian hopped the steps and beelined toward the pile of bratwursts fresh off the grill, but Caden waylaid her, and Rhett and Gavin sprang in with an embrace.

"Sian, we haven't seen you since you got back into the country," Gavin blurted.

Sian, who enjoyed hugs the way a cat enjoys baths, endured the familial smothering for almost two seconds before ducking low and squirming out from under their arms.

"I have been very busy with a new job," she said by way of

excuse, though Morgen knew her sister didn't visit her brothers any more often than she did.

Not only were they not introverts, but their favorite discussion topics were sports and home beer brewing, subjects that Sian had no interest in opining on. If anything, she was more likely to study those who congregated for such activities. Morgen still remembered ten-year-old Sian making graphs and flow charts in an attempt to better understand appropriate greetings and interactions at social gatherings.

"A new job two miles from where I work," Rhett said. "Let's have lunch next week. There's a great sushi place in the U-District. They have sake tastings!"

Sian threw Morgen a beleaguered look, as if their brothers being reminded that she existed—and wanting to afflict her with raw fish—was *Morgen's* fault.

"I do consume lunch on a daily basis," Sian said—was that an acceptance of the invitation?—before offering a curt wave and continuing to the grill.

"I'm not sure she's going to be able to help as much with my problem as I was hoping," Morgen muttered to Amar, who was standing beside her with his bare arms crossed, looking intimidating to strangers and supportive to her. She appreciated that. "The sibling problem anyway. She was helpful in the library. That's more her milieu than gatherings."

It was more Morgen's milieu too. She looked longingly toward a second-story window, wanting to lock herself in Grandma's library to check the grimoire for ghost-banishing ideas.

But all three of her brothers were walking toward her, shoulder to shoulder. They stopped farther away than they might otherwise have if Amar hadn't been there. They eyed him warily, and he eyed them back, not saying anything. Admittedly, Morgen didn't know what to say, either, and this was *her* family. She'd already introduced him.

"Nice to see you all," she made herself say. "I mentioned that Amar is a woodworker, didn't I? Would you like to see some of his pieces?" She extended an arm toward the barn while not letting herself fantasize about locking her brothers in and escaping to the library.

"Not right now," Caden said.

Gavin and Rhett both nudged him and nodded significantly toward Morgen. Electing Caden to do the talking?

He sighed and stepped forward. "Morgen, may I speak to you for a minute?" He eyed Amar again. "*Privately*?"

"To tell me about breakthroughs you've made in new beer-brewing recipes?"

"No." Caden took her arm, as if she were a toddler who'd wandered off at the grocery store.

Amar watched the movement but didn't stop it. He would be supportive, but he also wouldn't get in the way of her family talking to her. She supposed that was good and that she also shouldn't fantasize about him turning into a wolf and nipping at their heels, herding them to their cars like a gray-and-black sheepdog.

Reluctantly, Morgen let Caden lead her down the steps and out to the driveway. Lucky had realized she was there and bounded after them. He butted Morgen's hand, then rose up and put his paws on her shoulders, wagging his tail and showing his delight at the situation. How had she, an introvert to the core, ended up with such an extroverted dog?

"You know you're not supposed to jump on people," Morgen said, turning so that he had to drop to all fours. "Especially when you have bratwurst breath."

Caden arched his eyebrows. "Are you *sure* he knows that? Because he greeted Suze by jumping on her and knocking her down."

Since that was one of the wives who'd been most vociferous

with the orgy comments, Morgen was tempted to give Lucky a treat. All she said was, "I'm still working on manners with him."

"Isn't he three or four years old by now?"

"You say that as if that's the age of maturity for vizslas."

"What *is* the age of maturity?"

"I met a nine-year-old one with white fur on his snout and feet. He was moderately mature until a squirrel chittered at him, and then he took off like a gunshot."

"We need to talk, Morgen," Caden said, ruining any hope she might have had that they would merely discuss dogs. "Zoe mentioned that there's some weird stuff going on up here, and that you're in the middle of it."

Zoe had joined Wendy on the deck and was shoveling food onto a plate. Since she'd been helpful with finding information on Wolf Wood and Grandma's house—and also the tannery building—Morgen couldn't find it within herself to bare her teeth in Zoe's direction, but she wished her cousin hadn't said anything. If she hadn't, *years* might have passed before her brothers came up for a visit.

"Bellrock is a bit of an odd town," Morgen said. "I'm just doing everything in my power to make sure Grandma's house and the land around it—did you know that all of Wolf Wood was hers?—don't get slurped up by the county or some real-estate developer because I can't pay the taxes. They're going up a lot this year, now that it's in my name. Did you know Grandma had a lot of exemptions?"

"The land and the house aren't what we're concerned about."

"*I'm* concerned about them."

His brow furrowed. He didn't know anything about the magic in the woods or the real-estate developers who had their eyes on the land.

"I don't know why. It's a decent house, but why not sell it and go back to Seattle? You were a computer-science major and worked in the field for almost twenty years. This isn't your life." Caden curled a lip as he looked toward the garden and the trees.

"It *is* my life now." Morgen looked at Amar, who was watching from afar, not to eavesdrop, she knew, but to keep an eye on her and make sure she didn't need help. "I..." She didn't want to bring up her pregnancy now—it was bad enough the Lobos all knew about it already—and chose her words carefully. "I'd much rather raise a family someday out in the country than in the densely populated city where you have to worry about crime and weirdos."

Not that she didn't have plenty to worry about here—both werewolf packs, the coven, and half of the citizens of Bellrock had to count as *weirdos*—but she'd made progress when it came to gaining acceptance and dealing with the enemies she had inadvertently acquired. She lived in hope that things would improve further.

"A *family*?" Caden looked incredulously at her, then thrust a finger toward Amar. "With *him*? Is that what *he* wants? Morgen, you've never spoke of wanting a family in your whole life. You and Jun were married for more than ten years, and I never heard you so much as *talk* about wanting kids."

"We discussed it now and then, but it wasn't until I turned forty that I started to realize I was running out of time and maybe I *did* want them." At least one. One would do, right? She thought of how often she'd fantasized about being an only child. Her brothers hadn't been bullies, but they'd been loud, obnoxious, and rambunctious, and she and Sian had spent a lot of time trying to avoid them.

"Not with that guy." Caden shook his head firmly.

"Amar's a good man." And sexy and exciting in bed, she thought but did not say out loud.

"He looks like the drummer of a Latino rock band."

"He's a woodworker and an artist." And a werewolf. She

decided to wait to bring that up again until it was dark enough that she could prove it.

"I've known you your whole life. He's not your type." Caden looked toward the deck again and pointed. Jun had come out and was watching curiously, a soda in hand. "Your type wears polo shirts with pocket protectors."

Morgen rolled her eyes. "Nobody wears pocket protectors anymore. Today's sign of geekiness is a phone case with a spaceship on it." She knew because Jun had three of those from three different science-fiction franchises. There was also one with a wormhole gate on it. "As to types, haven't you heard that opposites attract? And that people's tastes change?"

Caden sighed, gripped her shoulder, and looked deep into her eyes. "People don't change, Morgen. They have midlife crises. You were fired, and Jun divorced you. Having those things happen back-to-back would affect anyone. It's not your fault. We want to help you. Come home."

"This is my home now. Lucky loves it here." Morgen waved to where he was snuffling at the tall clumps of grass growing along the wall of the barn.

"Lucky loves it anywhere there are people and table scraps."

"He gets to run free here, the way he can't in the city unless we go to a special off-leash park. And I..." Morgen stepped back, so her brother's hands would fall away. "I like it here too. I'm learning about my heritage." She took a deep breath. "Grandma was a witch. If you have any doubts, look in the root cellar. And I'm learning to be one too. It's in my blood. It's in *all* of our blood." She pointed at him, though she hadn't come across many mentions of male witches—or warlocks—and wondered if it was something more pronounced in women. "Honestly, it's really cool."

Caden winced and looked toward the deck for help. Rhett and Gavin headed down the steps, and even though it was an irrational fear—probably—Morgen couldn't keep from envisioning them throwing her into a straitjacket and locking her in the back of a car for a ride to an asylum.

Amar lowered his arms, looking like he was debating if he needed to swoop in and help. Morgen told herself that he wouldn't let them take her against her wishes, and that even her sturdy brothers wouldn't be a match for him. Besides, there were other Lobos here who would help. Nobody was going to take her anywhere, but she worried her brothers would have other bullets in the chamber if their first plan didn't work.

Sian came with their brothers and stepped up to Morgen's side. "Perhaps now would be the moment to prove that magic exists and you're capable of casting spells."

"Do you think that will convince them of anything?" Morgen pulled out Grandma's amulet and gripped it.

"It convinced *me* that you're not crazy. Though I suppose the jury is still out on whether all this is a midlife crisis."

"Ha ha."

"You don't believe the witch garbage, do you, Sian?" Caden asked. "You can't possibly. You're a scientist."

"I've seen evidence to bring my beliefs on such matters into question," Sian said.

"That means *yes*, she believes," Morgen said. "She casts spells now too. When werewolves attacked the house last month, she cast fireballs. Well, more like tiny spurts of flame, but they were very dangerous to people with substantial eyebrows."

Sian gave her a flat look.

"I saw it in a vision," Morgen said.

Caden groaned and rubbed the back of his neck while holding Rhett's and Gavin's gazes for significant lengths of time.

"Just do something," Sian told Morgen. "Everyone's here, and I'm sure they have open minds."

Morgen was sure from the expressions on her brothers' faces

that they did *not* have open minds, but as Sian said, maybe it would make a difference. Seeing was believing, right?

The amulet was surprisingly cool in Morgen's hand. Her palm was sweating anyway. This whole setup had her ridiculously nervous, and she licked her lips a few times as she struggled to call to mind an incantation that would show them that magic existed. The invisibility spell. That ought to be perfect. And once she made herself invisible, maybe she would *stay* invisible until they went home.

She lifted her chin. "Under the moon's magic, avoid cruel and obscene by turning the caster unseen."

Three sets of eyebrows went up. The amulet, which usually warmed in her grip, remained cool, and Morgen was positive nothing was happening.

She swallowed, willing the magic to come from within her and from within the amulet, and repeated the words. Meanwhile, the skepticism on her brothers' faces only deepened. Damn it, nothing was happening.

"That one's hard," Morgen said, though it had worked the first time she'd tried it. "Let me do something else."

Sweat broke out not only on her palms but all over her body, and panic welled up in her chest. Flames burned behind her cheeks, turning them bright red with embarrassment. With *shame.*

Why wasn't this working? She'd called up her magic to fight numerous enemies. This was just her family.

Maybe something simpler.

She held her amulet up and said, "Witch light glow!"

It should have brightened with magical illumination, but if anything, it grew cooler in her grip.

Sian frowned at her in puzzlement.

With the panic growing, Morgen tried the invisibility incantation one more time.

"Are you sure better poems aren't required for witchcraft?" Rhett asked.

"Morgen..." Once more, Caden reached for her shoulder.

It was probably meant to be a friendly, if condescending gesture, but the image of him throwing her in a straitjacket returned.

"I have to go," Morgen blurted, spinning to dart away.

Her first instinct was to run into the house and lock herself in the library, but numerous people on the deck blocked the way and —damn it—the wives had come out on the front porch. Not only were they standing in front of the door, but they'd seen Morgen's failure to conjure so much as a wart on a frog.

She veered toward the woods and the path behind the barn.

"Do we go after her?" Rhett asked.

"Maybe she's going to get a wand," Caden said.

"We have to do something."

"Morgen," Caden called as she kept running. "Come back!"

She didn't.

22

As Morgen ran down the trail through Wolf Wood, feeling like a child but not sure what else to do or where else to go, she grew aware of someone following her, fallen leaves rustling and foliage rattling. She glanced back, expecting her brothers or—far more preferable—Amar, but Lucky was the one bounding after her.

With his mouth open and his tongue lolling, he ran past her, then off into the woods, springing over logs and ferns. He seemed to think it was time for their daily exercise session. Wonderful.

She glanced back again but didn't see anyone else. At least her brothers weren't chasing her down.

With her breathing growing heavy, Morgen slowed down. Reminded that she was pregnant, she slowed even further, resting an apologetic hand on her abdomen. She doubted *running* would do anything harmful to a baby, especially at this early stage, but she still felt guilty for her thoughtless actions.

And cowardly. But she couldn't bring herself to go back and be calm and rational in the face of all those pitying stares. A part of her wondered if she was starting to experience mood swings, but she wagered anyone's mood would be dreadful in these circumstances.

The spring came into view, a few mushrooms under the granite bench glowing in the fog. She veered toward the spot, deciding she'd run far enough. It wouldn't be hard for anyone to find her here, but maybe the magic of the place would soothe her. And maybe it would recharge her *own* depleted magic stores. As soon as she sat down, she pushed her hands through her hair, wondering what had happened.

In the past, she hadn't gotten every incantation to work perfectly the first time, but they'd worked *eventually*. Even when she'd been in harrowing situations. This new awareness that her magic could fail her if she was under too much pressure worried her. Now, every time going forward, she might doubt herself.

A squirrel chittered from a branch on the opposite side of the spring. Lucky charged through the water, planted both paws on the tree, and barked up at it.

"People *really* aren't going to have a hard time finding me," Morgen told him, but she couldn't bring herself to drag him away and order him to stop.

At least *someone* was having a good day.

Before the sweat cooled fully on her body, she spotted someone coming up the trail. Amar. She peered behind him, hoping he wasn't leading the whole family to her, but he was alone. She sighed in relief.

He joined her on the bench, and she leaned her shoulder against his.

"It's perfectly normal and acceptable to hide out until one's judgmental brothers go away, right? It's not cowardly and pitiful, is it?" Morgen looked plaintively at him.

She didn't *think* he would judge her for this, but she wasn't positive. He'd praised her often for courageously standing at his side in battle. This behavior might disappoint him.

"I assumed you were stressed out and needed to escape for a time," he said.

"That seems logical. And hardly cowardly at all."

"Yes. If you wish to have passionate sex on this bench, I'm available for your needs." He wrapped his arm around her.

"You think that'll help? Such as by providing a physical and emotional release?"

"Absolutely." He kissed her on the forehead.

She was too distraught over the betrayal by her magic to contemplate tearing his clothes off, but she slid her arms around him for a hug. "Thanks for coming after me."

"You are welcome."

"Is there any chance that as you left, my brothers and their wives were getting in their cars to drive away?"

"They were staring into the woods and at each other."

"Darn."

She and Amar stayed like that, his arm around her shoulders and her arms around him, for several long minutes. The spring gurgled softly, a falcon screeched somewhere above the trees, and Lucky snuffled around, looking for prey that he had a hope of reaching.

"There is something I'd like to ask you about," Amar said, "but maybe it should wait until you've resolved things with your family."

"I'm not sure if I'll be able to resolve anything with them. The best I can hope for is that they give up on me and go away."

Would they? Considering how seldom Morgen interacted with her brothers, they'd seemed rather concerned about her well-being. Maybe she should have appreciated that, but she mostly felt smothered and remembered why she'd stopped going to family gatherings.

"Go ahead and ask your question, though, as long as it's not about which nasty foods you can inflict on me for the health of our baby." She smiled at him, meaning it as a joke, but his face grew troubled.

"I do not want to *inflict* anything on you. I just want the baby to be healthy. Your diet troubles me."

"My doctor recommended it. It's a *good* diet. I mean, maybe not the part where I eat scones and pumpkin cheesecake, but I don't eat those all the time. They're special treats." She pulled her arms back, not wanting to talk about this any more than listening to her brothers telling her to leave Wolf Wood. "The reason I made this charm," she said, pulling out the moon pendant, "is because I also want our baby to be healthy. And I was hoping it would stop you from... foisting things I've made it clear I won't eat on me."

He gazed at the charm, then lifted his fingers to touch it. When Morgen handled it, she could sense the magic in it, the same as she could in her amulet, but she didn't know if a werewolf could. Before she'd started working with magic, she hadn't been able to sense anything. Admittedly, she hadn't encountered a lot of ensorcelled charms in her old life. They weren't in the toolkit of the average database programmer.

"I understand." Amar lowered his hand. "I don't want to cause you stress. *More* stress."

"Thank you. And look, if José Antonio puts fish eggs on toast, I'll give it a try. Once in a while. Maybe I can... take a bite of it and then take a bite of something good to wash it down. Like chocolate. That's a logical pairing, right?"

"You'd have to ask José Antonio. I'm not the culinary expert that he is."

She smiled, imagining José Antonio's appalled expression at the combination, and hugged Amar again.

He stroked her hair, his touch soothing, and she closed her eyes. Her body finally unwound enough that she could enjoy being here with him.

"Sorry," she murmured. "I didn't let you ask your question. What is it?"

"I was talking with the pack about... proper behavior."

"Proper behavior? Like not peeing on the tires of Phoebe's car?"

"No, that's appropriate for a wolf."

"Is it? She seemed distraught."

"The witches have given us a lot of grief over the years. They deserve to be distraught now and then." Amar cleared his throat.

She realized he was hemming. Was he nervous about something? That wasn't like him. She peered curiously into his eyes.

"What I mean by proper behavior," he said slowly, "or maybe it's etiquette... societal expectations... *women's* expectations..."

She nodded encouragingly, though she had no idea where he was going.

"I didn't want to blindside you or assume..." Amar took a deep breath. "I wondered if you would like me to propose."

"*Oh.*" Morgen leaned back in his arms, glad it wasn't something dreadful. "Oh. Hm."

Since she hadn't considered it herself yet, she didn't have an answer prepared. *Did* she want that? It hadn't been that long since her divorce, and even though she loved Amar and was now, through the existence of their baby, linked to him in a way that she hadn't been a couple of weeks ago, she didn't know if she felt compelled to get married. Yes, people did it all the time when a baby came along, but it wasn't as if these were the Middle Ages or she was worried about her *reputation.*

She almost laughed. Even if she had been, how much worse could her reputation get after her failure in front of everyone?

"Pedro and Maria thought it would be proper," Amar said. "Fernando agreed and suggested I wear a button-down shirt to propose. One with sleeves and cuffs and everything."

Was it her imagination, or did a shudder course through him?

"Wouldn't you find that awful?"

"Yes," he said without hesitation. "But if you agree that it's proper that I propose and we get married, I would do it. While taking you to dinner at a fancy restaurant in Bellingham. Or maybe up to a cliff with a view of Rosario Strait, with a picnic basket and a bottle of wine."

That sounded more his style than a fancy restaurant.

"What would be *in* the basket?" she asked, amused that he'd been debating this.

"Delicacies that you would adore."

"So soysages and meatless balls?"

That time he *did* shudder. "You can't consider those delicacies."

"They're not bad. I like mushroom pâté on toast points too."

"Perhaps we could have spaghetti and... balls. A variety of balls to please both palates."

She wasn't sure a meal of *balls* sounded more appealing than soysages, but she squeezed his hand, glad he was thinking of compromise. "Yes."

Amar raised his eyebrows. "Does that mean you *want* me to propose?"

"I..." She'd been joking, but his grave, intent face promised he wanted a real answer, and she went back to considering the matter more seriously. "I'm not sure I'm ready so soon. I mean, I'm definitely over Jun—" More than that, she wished he hadn't come along with her brothers to witness her embarrassment. "But I'm not sure I'm ready to be married again. Not right away. And not just because I got pregnant. I wouldn't want you to feel obligated. Do you even want to be married, or is this a result of peer pressure? *Pack* pressure?"

He snorted softly. "It crossed my mind first, and that's why I brought it up to them, but I already consider you my witch and me your wolf. I do not need rings and papers to make this official, but if you wish them, I would not object." He brushed a lock of hair behind her ear. "I admit that the baby is the reason this all came to my mind so soon. I do not wish to rush you."

"Thank you. I'm glad, and I'm pleased that you don't object to the idea of marrying me someday." She bit her lip, *more* than pleased.

"I object only to the buttons."

"They do sound dreadful." She patted his bare arm. "What do you wear in the winter? Your bear hide?"

"Rarely more than this. It never gets very cold in the Pacific Northwest. That is one reason the Lobos chose this side of the mountains. Even though we are thickly furred as wolves, when we are men, our southern blood doesn't crave snow."

"Clearly, that's why we should send the *Loups* over there. They're from Canada, so their blood should want them to snuggle up to glaciers."

"Clearly." Amar took her hand. "When you *are* ready to get married, will you let me know? I'm not good at interpreting the feelings and desires of women. Especially witch women."

"Because we're all so quirky?"

"Yes." He tilted his head. "I also wished to be certain... you would not object to marrying someone like me? Someone who is not your *type*?"

Morgen wasn't surprised he'd heard that conversation. She was fairly certain *everyone* had.

She squeezed his hand again. "You're way better than my type."

"So, I don't need to get a—what was it?—pocket protector?"

"Which pocket would you protect?" She poked his leather vest. The two zip pockets didn't look like they were meant for pens, pencils, compasses, and the other tools that engineers and scientists had traditionally needed to protect their shirts from.

"I've got a leather smock for when I paint and varnish. It has many pockets."

"A smock? How come I haven't seen this sexy garment?" She hadn't even known that leather smocks existed.

"I don't wear it outside of the barn."

"Maybe you could show it to me later. Do you wear anything *under* the smock when you do these activities?" She smirked at him.

"Depends on how warm the weather is. I get hot easily."

"I bet you do." She kissed him, wondering if he was still up for sex on the bench. It wasn't a very *large* bench. Too bad she hadn't grabbed a blanket before storming into the woods.

But he drew back and tilted his head in the direction of the house. "The fog has deepened again. If you wish to return with me as a wolf beside you, I can do that now."

She did *not* wish to return, but she knew she should. Not only because she was being cowardly but because she still needed to check her grandmother's book. She had no idea how quickly a well-to-do Loup could have a court order issued for the demolition of a building, but she didn't want to dawdle. Given that stench, it was possible the town wouldn't wait for a court order.

"All right." Morgen stood up. "I would appreciate that. And if you want to pee on the tires of their cars on the way past, I wouldn't object."

"As you shouldn't." His blue eyes glinted. "It is, as we discussed, appropriate behavior for a wolf."

23

MORGEN COULDN'T BRING HERSELF TO WALK QUICKLY BACK TO THE house. She ambled, holding hands with Amar, though as soon as Lucky ran ahead—no doubt to check if anything new was on the grill—she sighed, knowing people would expect her to be with her dog.

As she and Amar neared the edge of the woods, she mentally braced herself. The Lobos' trucks were gone, but her brothers' vehicles remained.

Amar stopped, removed his vest, and handed it to her. "Do you know why your magic didn't work in front of them?"

"Performance anxiety, I assume."

"You've performed without trouble during life-and-death battle situations." His boots came next.

"Family is more harrowing."

He cocked an eyebrow as he reached for his jeans. Morgen peered around a tree, hoping nobody on the deck could see them and was wondering why her boyfriend was stripping in the woods. Everyone was still outside—what *was* the fascination with that deck?—and gathered by one of the railings, where a number of candles had been set. Sian and Wendy stood in front of them, Wendy gripping her chin and nodding while Sian pointed a stick at them. No, that was the bone wand that had been among Grandma's belongings. Were they... demonstrating magic?

Morgen would be disappointed if *Sian,* Sian who had only studied magic for one weekend, could perform in front of their brothers when she'd failed. But she would also be relieved if Sian did something that prompted everyone to believe that magic and witches were real. If not her, maybe Wendy could do something.

"You think it's nerves then?" Amar handed her his jeans. "Not some kind of hex?"

Morgen blinked. She hadn't considered that. Was that *possible*?

Grandma's books were ridiculously full of hexes, everything from making warts sprout on people's toes to ensuring an enemy had weeks of bad luck to causing someone to be afflicted by toenail fungus. Since most were long-acting and a bit silly, Morgen had dismissed them, but they *did* exist. What if there was something that could override a witch's power and render her magically impotent?

"I can't know for certain," she said slowly, "but if it was possible for another witch to hex me, I think they would have already done so. Calista would have hexed me left and right and all the way to the moon."

"Maybe so." Amar stepped away from her and threw back his head, but he managed to keep from howling as he sprouted fur and shifted into his wolf form. Since the sun hadn't yet set behind the fog, maybe he wasn't as compelled to howl as he would be when the moon came out.

When he stood at her side, a mighty black-and-gray wolf, she rested a hand on his back and nodded that she was ready. Even if she wasn't, she had to deal with her problems.

"Like a mature adult," she murmured.

Amar cocked his head.

"And a mature wolf. We won't tinkle on anyone's tires on the way to the deck." She doubted Amar had seriously been considering that. It had been *her* fantasy.

As they walked out of the woods together, Sian chanted softly, and Morgen recognized an incantation to create fire. A tiny flame appeared in the air above one of the candles.

"Good," Wendy said. "Now guide it down to the wick."

"What incantation *guides* flames?" Sian asked.

Their brothers and Jun stood behind them, appearing more skeptical than amazed. They exchanged the kinds of looks people did when they suspected a street performer was trying to fleece them. They hadn't yet noticed Morgen walking up with a wolf. Would they think furry Amar was a hoax, as well?

"The one you already said is fine. Just will it lower." Wendy pointed at the wand.

Sian squinted at the flame for several seconds before it descended. It missed the wick and balanced on the edge of the candle, melting the wax.

"I see your aim with magic is as good as it is in sports that require hitting or throwing balls," Morgen said.

"Activities I've spent an equal amount of time mastering," Sian replied without taking her focus from the flame. She finally *willed* it to the wick and lit the candle.

"Is that a wolf?" Jun whispered.

"This is Amar." Morgen dropped her hand onto his back again, fingers finding comfort and support in his thick, cool fur. "You met him earlier."

"Morgen..." Caden sighed and shook his head, as if all this proved was that she truly was a nut.

"What do you guys want? I'm not crazy. Magic exists, including witches and werewolves. If you don't want to believe it, that's fine, but please leave me alone."

"We care about you." Caden stepped forward, hands lifted imploringly. "You're throwing away your life up here doing... whatever it is you think you're doing. Come back to the city, get another job, and get on with your life. A *real* life." He glanced at Amar and, once again, didn't step as close as he might otherwise have. "If you and Lucky like it so much, you can come up and visit, though I'm sure you'll be in a much better position financially if you sell the house."

"My finances are fine," Morgen snapped, trying not to think about Ungar and his tax-assessor buddy. "I've started a new business with Amar's help, and we're doing great."

Her brothers exchanged more she's-crazy-but-what-do-we-do looks. Frustration welled up inside of Morgen, and she started toward the steps, intending to chant an incantation and show them what she could do. This time, she wouldn't fail. She wasn't hexed, damn it.

But a howl came from the woods in the direction of the train tracks and the Strait. Amar's head swiveled in that direction, pointed ears perking.

"Someone else taking advantage of the fog to hunt early?" Morgen asked, though it wasn't as if he could communicate with her unless he shifted forms. She almost suggested that, even if it would leave her standing next to a nude man, for seeing the actual shifting would do more to convince her family than anything.

More howls sounded, and a shiver went down her spine. Lucky heard them, whined, and ran under the deck to hide.

"It's not the Lobos, is it?" Morgen didn't think Lucky was afraid of them anymore.

Amar looked up at her, his head shifting from left to right. No. He lifted his snout and howled.

Even though he was *her* wolf, Morgen shivered again, wincing at the eerie sound so close to her ears. Her brothers scooted farther back on the deck. Lucky whined again.

Amar trotted toward the lawn, though he paused, patting a front paw on a particular spot and looking back at her. He'd touched one of the wards. He wanted her to activate them again.

Because trouble was coming? A showdown between the Loups and the Lobos? What else could it be?

Uneasy, she nodded to let him know that she understood. He loped off, not toward the howls but toward the driveway and the road beyond. Maybe he was going to get the rest of his pack.

"Let's move the party inside," Morgen said, though she could hardly call it a party. She was tempted to shoo her brothers to their cars instead. Whatever was happening, her family would be safer back in Seattle.

"It does look like rain," Minh offered.

Morgen didn't think it would rain, but she waved in agreement, hoping everyone would go inside. She would activate the wards and be ready if something happened and Amar needed her help. A part of her wished she'd grabbed her staff and run off with him, but she couldn't leave her family to fend for themselves. As she knew from past experience, the wards weren't perfect. Someone with enough power could get past them.

Jun lingered on the deck after the others went inside. Morgen turned her back to him as she pulled out her amulet and mumbled the words to activate the wards, then also issued formal invitations, letting the magic know that it shouldn't zap her family members. No matter how tempting it might be.

She felt her magic flow into the wards and a little zing as they flared to life, a chain of them surrounding the house. She *wasn't* hexed. That was proof. But it disturbed her to have learned that if she was nervous enough, she could fail at casting incantations.

"Is everything really okay?" Jun asked when she turned back toward him.

"I'm not sure about all the howling, but overall, things are fine." Feeling compelled to be civil, Morgen added, "How have you been doing?"

"Uhm." Jun glanced at her amulet, probably wondering if he should comment on her mumbling of incantations. He also glanced at the candle burning on the railing and settled for, "I'm good. I have to admit I didn't think you'd be the one dating before me."

"Because I'm so homely and incapable of attracting a man?" Morgen hadn't meant the words to come out bitter but realized she hadn't quite forgiven Jun yet. It wasn't so much that he'd wanted a divorce but that he'd blindsided her and hadn't discussed it with her before having the papers drawn up.

"No, no." He lifted his hands.

More howls sounded in the woods, and Morgen, once again, longed to run upstairs to the library. It was possible this had nothing to do with the building and the ghost, but... she wasn't sure. Everything had escalated since she'd leased it. Maybe whatever curse was afflicting that place had even stirred up the Loups and made them surlier than usual.

"You're just such an introvert. I couldn't imagine you going out to singles bars or wherever one finds..." Jun's gaze drifted in the direction Amar had been standing, and his forehead furrowed. He had to be trying to parse a lot more than the fact that she had a boyfriend.

"He came with the house."

The forehead furrow deepened.

Morgen didn't want to explain, not when she had so much else on her mind. "Can we go inside?"

The others already had, and someone had closed the door, as if to give them the space they needed for a private conversation.

Maybe her brothers thought Jun would succeed in talking sense into her when they'd failed.

"Just a minute." He held up a finger, though he lowered it when more howls sounded. They weren't as far in the distance as they had been before. "I never did say I'm sorry. I wanted to do that."

"Sure." She almost said it was fine, but was it? She'd resented him at the time. A lot.

"I should have talked things through with you before, uhm... It's just that I thought about it in my head for a long time, but it was hard to actually bring it up. We were both busy and not seeing each other that much so..."

"It was easy to avoid mentioning that you weren't happy?" Morgen asked.

"It was easier to avoid everything. Feelings and stuff. But I should have been less of a wuss and not let the lawyer do the talking for me."

"No kidding. He wasn't even a good talker. You'd think someone who bills by the hour would be less terse." Morgen remembered staring in puzzlement at the papers, then being left alone with little explanation.

Jun winced. "Sorry. I don't know why I couldn't say something. I was afraid you'd explode and be hurt and make me feel guilty and like a jerk for... Oh, I don't know, Morgen. I know you're not the histrionic type."

What an accolade. Maybe someone would put it on her tomb-stone someday. *Morgen Keller: kind of odd but wasn't too histrionic most of the time.*

"It was really my issue, not yours," Jun said. "I... bought a Ferrari afterward. Your brothers think *you're* having a midlife crisis up here, but I'm probably the poster child for that."

"Are you hitting on hot blonde college girls too?"

"I attempted to pick one up. She wasn't as impressed with my Ferrari as I'd hoped."

"You didn't show her your Star Trek phone case, did you?" Morgen asked.

"Do you think that would have helped?"

"No."

"*You* liked it."

"As I recall, I said it wasn't as hideous as the green-camo Stargate one."

"I remember. It was big praise." He smiled, the boyish smile little changed after all these years.

"Look, Jun, if you need closure or something, that's fine. I forgive you, and I'm sorry if I wasn't that great at reading you and didn't realize that you were going through things. I know I wasn't the perfect wife either." She kept herself from pointing out that *Amar* didn't seem to mind her. They'd been through a lot together in a short time. Multiple life-or-death situations. That had caused them to bond in a way that ten years of marriage hadn't for her and Jun. It was funny, but she almost felt like she knew Amar better. At the least, she had proof that he had her back. Jun and Morgen's relationship had never been tested in the same crucible.

"Thanks, Morgen. Is there anything I can do for you?" More howls filtered through the trees. "Are you okay here? Do you need a place to stay? You can move back into the house for a while if you don't want to stay with your brothers."

"I'm fine here, and I have a house. A *good* house." Now that it had been remodeled, it was downright lovely. And if werewolves howled at night... Well, such things happened when one's house was in the middle of the woods.

He pressed his lips together. "I heard there were witches in the woods too."

"The witches live in town. And, uhm, here." Morgen waved to the house. "Did Sian's demonstration not convince you?"

"I don't know what that demonstration was. Were she known for having a sense of humor, I'd assume a practical joke."

Ugh, what would it take to convince them that magic was real? A portal opening above the house and a dragon flying out?

"She's learning witchcraft," Morgen said. "As am I."

Jun sighed and stretched a hand toward her. "Morgen, I'm worried about you. Have you started some new medication? I don't want to hear about you running up and down Main Street with a broom between your legs."

"It's an antler staff, and it would hardly be the strangest thing that's happened in Bellrock." As Morgen thought of her stench-emitting building, she decided it wouldn't even be the strangest thing that had happened that week.

Another howl drifted up from the woods. It sounded agitated.

Morgen stepped back to avoid Jun's touch. "I need to do some research. Zoe can find you a room if you want to stay here tonight, though the family might be more comfortable at the Wild Trout. Witches rarely frequent it, unless they feel the urge to rummage through your suitcase and leave your panties hanging on a lamp."

Jun opened his mouth, but nothing came out. Well, if her magic didn't return, she'd still have the power to render people speechless.

Morgen walked inside, not wanting to deal with anyone else, but caught Jun's voice again before she closed the door. At first, she thought he was talking to her, but he must have called someone.

"No, sir. It's as bad as we heard—maybe worse—and nobody's able to convince her to leave. You may want to come back and see if you can do something."

Morgen slumped against the door jamb. Jun had called *her father*? Her father in Singapore, who barely communicated with Morgen or her sister? Her father, who she had nothing in common with and who was far more likely to side with her brothers in an argument?

She told herself that it would be fine, that her father couldn't force her to leave any more than her brothers could, but she wasn't actually certain of that. What if her family tried to have her declared *non compos mentis* and dragged her back to Seattle? What if they took Wolf Wood, and Grandma's house, and even Amar from her?

24

MORGEN CLOSED THE BACK DOOR, NOT WANTING TO HEAR ANYTHING else Jun might say to her father. She headed for the stairs, hoping to escape into the library before anyone spotted her. Ferret chitters drifted down the hall from the living room.

"Has that thing had a rabies shot?" Suze asked. "I can't believe she's letting wild animals in here."

"He's not a wild animal," Wendy said. "He's my familiar."

Morgen groaned as she climbed the stairs. As well intentioned as Wendy and even Sian were, they only seemed to be making matters worse.

Clacks sounded behind her—Lucky's claws on the wood treads as he trotted up after her.

She paused at the library door. "What happened? Did someone want to give you a rabies shot too?"

He shook his head, ears flapping, and the tags on his collar jangling. He was either reminding her that he'd *had* his rabies shot and had proof, or someone had dumped a drink on his head.

"Your fur *is* damp," Morgen muttered, rubbing his head. "You'd better hide in the library with me."

Lucky looked toward her bedroom at the end of the hall. Maybe the long day of socializing had worn him out. He took a few steps in that direction, then gazed back at her and wagged his tail hopefully.

"It's five p.m. I'm not going to bed."

He peered in the library, then looked pointedly at the bedroom again.

"I know there's not any comfy furniture in the library, or even a dog bed, but there's a nice wool rug under the table."

Lucky tilted his head.

"*Some* dogs find lying on a rug to be sufficient. They even plop down on cement sidewalks and such outdoors."

He sat, wagged his tail, and gazed up at her as if she were saying crazy words.

"Everyone's looking at me like that these days." Morgen pushed open the library door.

Lucky followed her in, padded around the table once, peered out the window, then headed to the bedroom.

"He's not a good research assistant anyway." Morgen closed the door and was tempted to lock it. Once her family solidified plans regarding what to do about her questionable mental health, they might send someone up to get her.

The gargoyle on the bookcase in front of the secret vault gazed at her without judgment as she manipulated it, then used Grandma's amulet to open the locked door. *Incantations of Power* lay in its usual spot. Morgen tugged out the large handwritten book and carried it to the table. Per Grandma's request, she'd never published any of the information for others, so none of it was contained in her app. The knowledge was too dangerous.

"Let's just hope there's something about ghosts that can convince them to leave this world."

Morgen skimmed the table of contents, shuddering at the memory of the demon in the graveyard. The imp-banishing spell hadn't worked on it, and she doubted it would work on a ghost either. Ghosts weren't mentioned anywhere in the table of contents. Disappointed, she flipped through the pages, hoping something inspiring would leap out.

"Here's something to make an enemy's armor fall off. That's useful in this day and age." She tapped the incantation into her phone in case she ran into an enemy in a bulletproof vest. Maybe if she used it on Mayor Ungar, his pants would fall off. "Zoe would appreciate that."

Morgen shook her head and continued her perusal. The word *curse* in a header caught her eye. Ah, she hadn't been looking for that in the table of contents, but she didn't think it had been mentioned. The book didn't have an index—few of the aged tomes on witchcraft did.

"Put a curse on a rival's home, an enemy's lair, an ex-lover's virility, a warlock's tools... How about something for *removing* curses?" She read through the page about cursing an enemy's home, hoping the entry might mention *removing* a curse that had been put on one's own home. Or one's tannery. "Wait, is this it? 'Once you no longer need the curse, stand in front of the affected person or place and repeat the incantation.' Hm, but you'd probably need to know the incantation that was used in the first place, right? To cancel it out? Otherwise, I could end up double cursing the place." Just what she needed.

Still, she tapped the incantation for the curse into her notes app, then read through it a couple of times to memorize it. Maybe it didn't need to be the same incantation to work. A line at the bottom of the page said that one needed to be naked and cast the curse at night for maximum effectiveness.

"What is with all the witch nudity?" Morgen envisioned pulling off her clothes while furniture flew around the tannery, fog crept around her legs, and a floating white form watched from the doorway. "Let's hope it isn't required for removing curses."

Morgen closed the book and leaned back. It would be worth trying to remove the curse, especially if that had something to do with why the ghost was trapped in the tannery, but what she really needed was to see a vision of what Grandma had done inside that cabin in the woods. There might be a simple incantation to banish ghosts, and if there was, Morgen wanted to know it. Given how strange her life had become of late, who knew how often that would come in handy?

In the past, the amulet had sent visions in pairs. Maybe tonight, she would get the second part.

A howl in the woods sounded loudly enough to be audible through the window. Unfortunately, she didn't know if she could wait until tonight.

She leaned her head back, closed her eyes, and willed whatever spirits or deities helped witches to help her. She was tired of feeling impotent, both with her family and with that damn building.

The amulet around her neck grew warm through the fabric of her shirt. It pulsed a few times, as if sending out a beacon.

"Oh sure." Morgen touched it. "*Now* you activate."

She was about to put the grimoire away when a soft knock sounded on the door. Chittering sounds followed it, as well as dog claws clattering on the hall floor.

"Come in," Morgen called softly, hoping Wendy hadn't brought the whole family up.

The door opened, and Lucky trotted past Wendy and entered first. Napoleon scolded him from Wendy's shoulder.

"What," Morgen said to the dog, "you got tired of sleeping alone?"

He yawned, leaned against her leg, and wagged his tail. Outside, the fog had deepened into twilight.

Wendy stepped inside and closed the door. "Your brothers are close-minded."

"They're open-minded in some areas. Like trying new flavors of home-brewed beer or wandering into a tasting room located in someone's garage."

"I floated a vase for them, turned myself invisible, and made one of the women's pants unbuckle."

"Is that the armor-removing incantation?"

"They thought it was all a hoax, that you hired me to help convince them that witchcraft is real. I told them you hired me to design buttons and logos for your apps, but they didn't want to hear about that either."

"Any chance they left in a huff for a hotel?" Morgen looked hopefully toward the window, but she hadn't heard any cars start up.

"Not yet."

"Has Sian given up on lighting candles for them?"

"She said she couldn't endure the claustrophobia of so many people in one house and was going to her room to read."

"Maybe *we* should go to a hotel," Morgen said.

Napoleon sprang from Wendy's shoulders and landed on the table, his slinky body undulating as he bounded to the book and sniffed the pages.

"I prefer my van," Wendy said. "The hotels in town don't allow ferrets."

"Not even the Wild Trout? They allowed Lucky."

"The owner says ferrets stink."

Morgen sniffed Napoleon. "He seems okay."

Napoleon nosed the book open.

"Any chance he's giving me a clue about how to solve my problems?" Morgen asked.

"Maybe. He's a smart and useful familiar."

"When he's not playing dead?"

"Yes."

Once the book was open, Napoleon rolled onto his back with his legs in the air.

"Look here. I'm sure my grandmother wouldn't have appreciated you getting oil from your fur all over her ancient book." Morgen reached for the ferret but paused.

He'd nosed the book open to one of the pages on curses. Specifically, it covered the one about cursing an enemy's lair.

As Napoleon wriggled about, Morgen lowered her hand. There were hundreds of pages in the book. It would be quite a coincidence if he'd randomly chosen one she'd been looking at. One she'd dismissed in favor of the curse for homes. But how could he have known what she'd been looking at? And was it a sign that *this* was the curse Morgen should try to remove from the tannery?

The ferret *had* been in the building. Maybe he'd been able to sense what kind of curse was upon it, what had scared him out of the loft.

"*Napoleon,*" Wendy scolded and plucked him up.

"Has he ever shown clairvoyance or... some ability to know what you're thinking and how to assist you?" Morgen asked, adding the curse to her notes.

"He's very helpful, and sometimes, he knows what I'm thinking, but... clairvoyance is like telling the future, isn't it?"

"More or less. Glimpses into it anyway. I believe there's a curse on the tannery and that it may have to do with the ghost. Though it may not. I've read that ghosts can be trapped if they died horribly, and witchcraft might not need to be involved at all, but..." Morgen shrugged.

Wendy peered at the page. "Sometimes he—and I've heard other witches say this about their familiars too—does things that are kind of inexplicable. Like he'll know things you wouldn't think a little animal could know."

"Maybe I should go down there tonight and try dissolving the curse with this incantation."

There was nothing that said she couldn't take the book and try *all* of the possibly relevant incantations. Except for the concern that she might layer on more curses. Still, how much more cursed could that building get?

A scratch at the window startled Morgen, and she jumped to her feet, almost knocking her chair over. Wendy spun, Napoleon in her arms, and pointed him toward the window like a gun. A gun that promptly went limp in her arms, head dangling upside down.

Slightly more ferocious, Lucky ran to the window, propped his paws on it, and barked. Something battered at the glass before disappearing. Had those been wings?

"Zorro?" As Morgen hurried to the window and pushed Lucky aside, she realized it could also be another avian familiar. Witches had used their birds to spy on her in the library before, and she hesitated before opening it. But a *hoo hoo* came from the roof. It *was* Zorro.

"Sh," Morgen told Lucky and opened the window. "It's your buddy."

Lucky growled dubiously.

Morgen didn't know if Zorro would fly in, but she opened the window wide enough that he could if he wanted. More wolf howls floated up, and was that the distant sound of fighting? Snapping and growling?

Worried once again for Amar, she wondered if she should grab her staff and go out into the woods. He might need help.

Zorro appeared, flying toward the window, and she backed up. But he merely landed on the sill and peered in.

Lucky recognized him and wagged. Napoleon went limper. Did owls in the wild eat ferrets? Napoleon seemed far too large to be devoured and hacked up later as an owl pellet.

"It's interesting that all of the familiars were drawn here," Wendy mused.

"Napoleon was drawn?" Morgen blinked and thought of her amulet pulsing. Was it possible she'd somehow *done* something when she'd implored the spirits and deities for help?

Wendy nodded. "He ran down the hall and led me to the stairs and the library. I didn't mind, since I wanted an excuse to get away from the muggles."

"Interesting."

"They're not very, no." Wendy wrinkled her nose. "Sorry, I know they're your family, but... family can be a huge pain in the ass sometimes."

Remembering Wendy's sisters, Morgen could only nod. "Tell me about it."

She turned to Zorro, who was waiting patiently for a command. Patiently and alertly. He wasn't preening under a wing or hawking up the remains of his dinner—breakfast—on the floor.

"Zorro, can you check out the tannery for me?" Morgen asked. "See if anything odd is going on? Odder than the smell? And if it's okay, will you check on those howling wolves and make sure Amar isn't in trouble? Actually, can you do that first?"

She cared far more about Amar than the building.

He hooted, then sprang from the windowsill, flapping off in the direction of the howls.

"Hopefully, he'll send a vision soon," Morgen said.

Napoleon lifted his head and squeaked a few times, looking toward the window.

"Yes, it's safe now." Wendy stroked his back.

"Wasn't it safe before too?"

Wendy lifted a shoulder and set Napoleon back on the table. "He's wary around large predator birds. We saw an eagle make off with someone's poodle once."

"I'll assume a toy poodle, not a full-sized one."

"It was a big eagle." Wendy pointed toward the door. "I'm going out to my van to try to level up, unless there's anything I can help you with?"

"Not unless there turns out to be trouble with the Loups."

Judging by Wendy's grimace, she didn't want anything to do with the Loups.

"If Amar and your hot tub buddy are in danger, they might need us."

"José Antonio?"

"He's the only one I keep finding naked in the hot tub with you."

Pink colored Wendy's cheeks. "I didn't *ask* him to get naked. He said the bubbles were filling up his shorts, and it was annoying, so did I mind if he took them off."

"Did you?" Morgen raised her eyebrows. "Mind?"

"I'm not *dating* him, if that's what you're asking. My sister would kill me. She already thinks I'm betraying the family and all things witchy by parking my van on your property and helping you."

"I was asking if you minded him getting naked in front of you. I'll tell Amar to thump him if he's being crude."

The pink color in Wendy's cheeks brightened. "I didn't mind. He kept himself under the bubbles. And he's..."

"Sexy?"

"*No.*"

Morgen raised her eyebrows higher, wondering if this was similar to the situation with Phoebe and Ungar, where a witch didn't want to admit she liked a werewolf. "So, I won't see your van shaking once you two hook up?"

Napoleon chittered, then shoved his head under the cover of the book.

"Or did you already hook up, and that was what your familiar did during the event?" Morgen pointed at him.

"I can't believe I came up here to help you." Wendy scooped up Napoleon again, who squeaked in protest.

"I appreciate that you did. And that you're enjoying the company of such a fine chef." Morgen meant the words when they came out, though she wanted to retract them when she remembered the fish-egg burger.

"Good." Wendy flipped her hair over her shoulder and walked out with Napoleon in her arms.

Morgen put Grandma's book away. "What now, boy?"

Lucky was still at the open window, nostrils twitching as he sampled the breeze.

"Wait until Zorro reports in?" She wrapped her fingers around her amulet, thinking about going down to the building to try the curse removal right away. But what if Amar needed her?

Lucky left the window and trotted into the hall. He looked back expectantly.

"Do you want to lead me somewhere?" Morgen followed him out, but Lucky only trotted to the bedroom. She snorted. "You're a little one-note there, Lucky."

He hopped onto the bed, curling up against the pillows.

Worried voices drifted up the stairs from below. Since Morgen had no desire to join her siblings, she walked into the bedroom and closed the door. Once before, the amulet had given her a vision while she'd been napping. If she could manage to fall asleep, might it do so again?

"Too bad I'm not tired." With everything going on, her mind was racing. There was no way she would doze off. She would have a hard time even sleeping later that night.

Eyes closed, Lucky didn't respond. Morgen stretched out on the bottom half of the bed—since he'd managed to hog *all* of the pillows.

"Wait, there's an incantation in here to prompt a good night's sleep, isn't there?" Morgen opened the app on her phone, and a message from a user came up before she could enter a search.

Thank you for this wonderful program. The Mayberry Coven in Mount Airy is finding it very useful. We've sent a twenty-five-dollar donation as well as scans from a few of our texts that don't appear to be in your app thus far. Perhaps you can enter them and add even more helpful information for the witches of the world to access. We've also heard that you're talented at making charms for witches and familiars. Do you have a catalog or website so we can see your offerings and place orders?

"Huh."

Morgen opened the attached files and found nothing on ghosts but a lot on potion-making and wild-crafting. She made a note to enter everything into the database once things settled down. In the meantime, the praise warmed her. Her family might not understand her new life and that she was doing something useful, but others did. And for the first time, it occurred to her that her app might be a way to pull in more orders for the charm business. A few weeks earlier, she'd taken the software out of the beta-testing stage, and the last she'd seen, tens of thousands of witches —or people who fancied themselves witches—were using it. Even though she hadn't put it into any app stores—something the coven had forbidden—people were forwarding it to their colleagues, and the usage statistics were improving every week.

"If nothing else, I don't think paying the taxes will be too hard. If we can get the building issue fixed, and I can keep my family from throwing me in an insane asylum, or the modern-day equivalent, Amar and I should be set."

Lucky snored loudly, as if to inform her that he'd led her back here for a reason.

"Yes, yes, the nap."

Morgen found the sleep incantation and whispered it, then set the phone aside and attempted to snuggle into the covers while gripping her amulet and willing it to send her a vision. It was hard to think about anything except plans for the business, trying the curse incantation on the building, and whether Zorro would send a vision or not, but sleep sprang like a cougar from a cliff and captured her.

25

THE VISION APPEARED IN ITS USUAL CORNER OF THE BEDROOM. Morgen shifted around to peer at it, pushing aside a dog paw that was pronging her in the back of the neck.

The chinked logs of a cabin interior formed, and she lifted her head in hope. Wavering silver light spread over the single room where blankets lay rumpled on a bed, pots dangled over a cooktop on a wood stove, and kindling from an upturned basket was strewn across the floorboards. In the center of it all, a large blood-stain marred the floor.

If the werewolves had killed the bounty hunter in this cabin, the presence of a bloodstain made sense. Fortunately, Morgen didn't see a decomposing body.

She didn't see Grandma, either, and that filled her with disappointment. She'd hoped to watch the fight from the previous vision, this time from *inside* the cabin.

A pot flew across the room, striking a log wall. A woman cursed. Grandma?

She *was* in the cabin, her back to the door. Usually, when

Morgen had these visions, they showed Grandma and Amar from behind.

"Get down," Grandma barked.

Who was she talking to? Morgen didn't see anyone else, though the door shuddered, and she remembered Amar had been outside, throwing himself against it.

Her point of view changed—lowered—as if she were obeying the order to get down. Morgen gaped in confusion. Could the Grandma in the vision somehow see *her*?

Grandma raised her antler staff, the tips already glowing with green light. Another pot flew across the room toward her—it tumbled past over Morgen's head—and the green light coalesced into a beam. It lanced out and struck the pot, deflecting it onto the bed.

Light swirled inside the cabin, and an apparition formed near the stove. The ghost of the dead bounty hunter?

An eerie keening sounded, reminding Morgen of a similar keen she'd heard in the tannery.

As Grandma lifted her staff and started to say something, another thump came from the door. It shuddered but didn't budge.

"Damn wolf," Grandma growled. "He should have come in from the beginning if he wanted to be a part of this."

A piece of wood lifted from the floor and flew straight at her.

Grandma didn't have time to do anything to deflect it and could only duck. It struck the log wall behind her and shattered into pieces, bark flying. A shard of wood struck her in the back, and she grunted, then snarled, lifted her staff again, and spoke:

"Unsettled spirit of yore,
You'll walk this realm no more,
To the world after you must go,
Forever depart, even your shadow."

Morgen didn't recognize the incantation, but she hurried to

repeat it to herself, making sure to memorize it. This was what she'd wanted. The amulet had helped her once more. *Grandma* had helped her.

The keening sounded again but much weaker now. The apparition and the silver light slowly faded, and Grandma lowered her staff. She shocked Morgen by turning to look at her.

"You can get up now," Grandma said dryly.

"You can see me?" Morgen heard her own voice ask, though she hadn't opened her mouth. Just as with Grandma's voice, hers seemed to come from the vision in the corner of the bedroom.

"Apparently."

"But we're not... I wasn't there when this happened. And you're..."

"Dead. Yes, I know. I'm glad you took care of the bitch who arranged my death. I would have haunted *her* if I could have."

"Couldn't you have?" Morgen wondered.

If a bounty hunter killed by werewolves and whoever was stuck in the tannery could haunt people, why couldn't her grandmother? Her death hadn't been peaceful either.

"Ghosts can only haunt the area where they died. For me, that would have meant the canyon where I crashed. There was nothing down there except for trees and ferns. From what I've gathered, vegetation is unconcerned by ghosts."

"Strange."

"Indeed." Grandma looked her up and down.

Though Morgen didn't seem to have much control of herself in the vision—she couldn't tell what she was wearing or what she looked like to Grandma—she willed herself to appear confident and competent. Someone who had her shit together and wasn't worrying about her family's opinion of her.

Grandma snorted. "They all thought I was nuts too."

Morgen blinked. "They knew about your witch hobby? My brothers?"

It had been a shock to her when she'd found the root cellar, the pentagram, and all of Grandma's witch paraphernalia.

"Those kids? No. But my daughters—your mother and aunt— knew. I wish I could have convinced them to come up and learn from me. Maybe they could have found a way to stave off the cancer and live longer—you know about the spring, right? And its rejuvenating powers?"

"Yes, though my sister refuses to drink coffee made from the water. Due to the possibility of bacterial contamination, and, uhm, coyote pee."

Grandma quirked her thin white eyebrows. "What do you think offers the rejuvenating powers?"

"I'd assumed magic."

"That too. The girls were positive I was crazy, and the husbands they married steered them even further away from me." Grandma shook her head. "It was easier to say I didn't want to see the family than have to endure their concern and pity."

After the day with her brothers, Morgen could understand that perfectly well.

"I'm glad you came up," Grandma added. "I chose right in leaving Wolf Wood to you. I figured you were the one most likely to need an escape from your mundane life and be willing to open your mind instead of judging me right away."

Morgen wondered if Grandma had known about her divorce and job loss. If those things hadn't happened to Morgen, would she truly have had an open mind and been willing to stay in Bellrock long enough to figure everything out? She liked to think she would have, but she didn't know.

"I wish I'd come up before you passed," Morgen said. "It would have been handy to have you teach me some of this in person, and I'm sorry I didn't get to know you when you were alive."

"Yeah, I'm a real delight." Another thump sounded—Amar

still trying to get in—and Grandma shouted. "Hold your horses, you big brute of a wolf."

"Well, Amar liked you."

"Grumpy loners like other grumpy loners who leave them alone."

"Poetical."

"Yup." Grandma started to fade, the log walls growing visible behind her.

Realizing the vision was also fading, Morgen lifted a hand. "Wait. I need to get rid of a ghost of my own. Do I just say that incantation? It wasn't in any of your witch books, even the grimoire in the library."

"That's because it wasn't a witch incantation," Grandma said. "You can't magic a ghost out of existence. You have to perform an exorcism. Don't they teach kids anything in college these days?"

"I don't think the exorcism class was an elective I could take under my programming degree."

"Talk about a narrow curriculum. Sprinkle holy water around the premises, then say the chant." Grandma held up an empty vial. "Your witch power *should* help. You need to be stronger than the apparition's will to stick around. When people die horribly and want revenge on those who did it, their ghosts can be hard to send away from the mortal plane."

"Where do I get holy water? The church in town?"

But Grandma had faded completely and didn't answer. The rest of the vision also disappeared, leaving Morgen staring at the dark corner of the bedroom.

She rubbed her face. All of her problems remained, but Grandma had given her the chant she needed. *And* Grandma had believed in her, known that she above all her siblings had been the one she could trust her heritage to.

"I'll find a way to deal with the rest of the family," Morgen whispered. "Even if I have to become an aloof hermit in the woods like she did."

Lucky lifted his head from the pillows.

"I don't suppose you know where to find holy water?" she asked him.

It was hard for her to imagine that little church in town having a fountain inside, one that had been consecrated or whatever by a priest.

Lucky tilted his head.

"Never mind." Morgen sat up. "I—"

Nausea swept over her. Nighttime morning sickness? No, she realized as a view of the forest came to her. Zorro was sending the vision she'd requested.

Two gray wolves sat on their haunches below the trees, with the Strait and the railroad tracks visible off to one side. They weren't fighting, as Morgen had thought when she'd heard growls and snaps earlier, but sitting and howling. In between howls, they looked expectantly up the hill from the water, in the direction of the house. They howled again. It was as if they were trying to be heard by someone. By the Loups? By *her*? Did they want to lure her down to investigate their noise?

One wolf had a gash in its shoulder that wept blood. They didn't seem to be worried about enemies, but something must have happened earlier.

Zorro flew past them, following the tracks toward town. Morgen glimpsed another wolf below, this one running north in the same direction that he was flying. Like the others, it had gray fur, and she couldn't tell which pack it belonged to. All the gray wolves looked the same to her.

The trees grew thinner as Zorro continued north, and he soon flew over the two-lane highway that would turn into Main Street. As the first buildings came into his view, Morgen's phone rang.

Locked into the vision, her stomach twisting with nausea, she barely managed to pat around. She'd left the phone on the bed, hadn't she?

Vehicles came into view, parked along the street at the north end of town, and there was the tannery. Numerous cars, including sheriff's department SUVs, were there, filling the lot. What was that large flatbed truck doing out front? A flatbed truck with... was that a *crane*?

"What the hell?" she rasped as her hand landed on her phone.

Numerous wolves stood between the big truck and the building—two packs facing each other. The Lobos and the Loups. A brunette in a white dress—*Olivia*—stood behind the Loups, arm in arm with a well-dressed man in a beret. Was that their leader? Lucien?

The wolves snarled as they faced off, most focused on each other. But a large gray-and-black wolf—Amar—looked toward the driver of the truck, lips rippling back to show his fangs as he growled.

As Zorro banked to give her another look, Morgen realized that was more than a crane on the back of the truck. A huge wrecking ball hung from it.

"What the hell?" she rasped, stunned.

Yes, the place was cursed and stank, but they couldn't just demolish somebody's building. Had they even had time to contact the out-of-state owner?

The phone rang again.

I'll be down as soon as I can, Morgen thought to Zorro, hoping he would let the vision go and realizing that the wolves howling by the tracks had likely been trying to keep her focused on Wolf Wood instead of where the true danger was—at least to her building. Those Loup bastards were going to try to demolish it tonight.

26

"Hello?" Morgen asked on the last ring before the call would have gone to voice mail. As Zorro's vision faded, she managed to scoot out of bed.

"Ms. Keller?"

"Dr. Valderas?"

"Yes. I don't know if you've heard, but I thought I should warn you: something's going on at the building you leased."

"I know. Thanks."

Morgen hung up and grabbed her shoes. "I need to get down there and stop them. Somehow."

What incantations did she know that could keep a wrecking ball from crashing into the side of a building?

Lucky sprang out of bed and beat her to the door.

"I think you should stay here." Morgen grabbed her staff while wishing she had more weapons. Maybe some grenades to lob at the tires of that wrecker. Or at the Loup guy who'd arranged its appearance. Or at *Olivia*. Morgen hadn't spoken to her in months, but she couldn't be surprised that she was involved. It did, however, shock her that she was working with the Loups to get her revenge. "The enemy of my enemy, I guess."

When she let Lucky out of the bedroom, he ran down the hallway, only to stop in front of Zoe who was stepping off the stairs.

"I need to go," Morgen said. "Can you keep everyone busy?"

Zoe shook her head as she stopped in front of the door to Sian's guest room. "Ungar just called."

"He can't be looking for a date now." Morgen eyed her cousin.

Zoe wore a jacket and had her purse looped over her shoulder, as if she were on her way out.

"He just canceled our date and said to stay out of town because it's dangerous." Zoe squinted at her. "He also said for you to get your butt down to your building."

Morgen snorted at this concern for *Zoe's* well-being and utter disregard for *her* well-being. "Where he no doubt hopes I'll be pummeled by a wrecking ball."

Maybe it meant something that Ungar wanted to keep Zoe safe.

"I came up to deliver his message," Zoe said, "but I'm coming with you."

"Into danger? No."

"I can handle myself. I'm packing heat."

"You're what?"

Zoe patted her purse, unzipped a compartment, and pulled out a compact firearm. Or what *looked* like a firearm at first glance but had an orange lining in the barrel.

"Is that a starter's pistol?" Morgen asked.

"Yes, but it's fooled would-be muggers in downtown Seattle."

"Into what? Springing into foot races?"

"Funny. Look, I'm not defenseless. I have to show houses by myself after dark sometimes, you know." Zoe rummaged in her purse, dropping ketchup and salt packets purloined from a restaurant before pulling out a hot pink container of pepper spray and a keychain with a personal alarm that promised 140 decibels of noise.

"I guess that'll make the keen-eared werewolves cringe." Morgen grabbed the fallen packets and thrust them back at her, noticing more condiments taken from restaurants in that purse pocket and wondering what Zoe's fridge at home looked like.

"Exactly. And, knowing I was coming up here to the woods, I even brought this." Zoe pulled out a can of bear spray. "I wasn't sure if the Mace would be enough."

The door to Sian's room opened, and she scowled out at them. "What is going on, and why must it occur immediately outside my room?"

"Zoe is showing off her personal arsenal, and I'm going into town to stop a showdown between the Loups and Lobos, a witch holding a grudge due to her sister's death, and an unknown complainer with access to a wrecking ball."

Not at all a daunting number of people to be up against. Morgen grimaced.

"Do you want assistance?" Sian surprised her by asking.

Morgen hesitated, inclined to tell them both to stay put, but unlike Zoe, Sian had magic in her blood and had helped in battle before. What if Morgen wasn't strong enough to put an end to the curse, the ghost, and the wrecker alone? She trusted the Lobos to handle the Loups, but even they might need help if the Loups had been plotting and setting this up for a while. And if a powerful witch was on their side. Amar might be in over his head.

The thought sent fresh fear flowing through her veins, and Morgen moved past Zoe. She couldn't dawdle.

"Sure, come if you're willing, Sian," Morgen called, heading down the stairs.

"How come she's invited, and I'm not?" Zoe demanded. "What's she going to do? Throw a book at your enemies?"

Shaking her head, Morgen didn't answer. She headed for the

back door, not wanting to pass through the living room and deal with her family. She tried to slip away without letting Lucky out, but he bumped her hip and surged past her. He ran off the deck, circled the barn twice as he wagged and sniffed, and reached the car before Morgen did. Before Morgen, Sian, and *Zoe* did.

Exasperated, Morgen pointed back at the house. "Zoe, you're not coming. Why do you even *want* to come? Ungar said your date is off, right?"

"Yeah, but he sounded stressed and irritated."

"He *always* sounds like that."

"I thought he might need my help." Zoe patted her purse.

"Trust me; he doesn't." Morgen opened the driver-side door and jammed the antler staff awkwardly inside while wondering how to get away without Zoe *or* Lucky. She would rather not worry about them in a fight. "He's a werewolf, and you're a real-estate agent with a starter's pistol."

"Don't forget my rock-star boobs," Zoe said. "I can distract his enemies with them."

"Finally," Sian said, climbing into the passenger seat, "Cousin Zoe's superpower is revealed."

"You're not helping," Morgen told her.

Before she could get her seat belt on and drive off, her cousin popped into the back, letting Lucky in with her.

Morgen groaned, but she didn't want to delay any longer. "Just promise to stay in the car when we get there."

"How will she use her superpower from back there?" Sian's eyes glinted with humor. *She* hadn't received a vision from an owl and didn't know how big a fight was breaking out in town—had likely *already* broken out.

"I'm sure she's used them in back seats before," Morgen grumbled and headed down the driveway.

In the rearview mirror, she glimpsed someone opening the front door of the house to peer out. Caden?

Feeling guilty for leaving without a word, Morgen vowed to get things straightened out with her brothers in the morning. After she got everything straightened out in town. Which would—she hoped—be doable.

Her phone rang. Pedro.

Busy navigating the winding driveway, Morgen thrust her phone at Sian. "Will you answer that? It's got to be about the fight."

"Yes, introverts adore speaking to strangers." Sian frowned but answered.

"Pedro isn't a stranger. He's the alpha of the Lobos, and it's important."

Sian tapped on the speaker option and lifted the phone to her mouth. "This is Morgen's phone."

"This is Pedro's phone," someone who wasn't Pedro said— was that José Antonio? "Amar asked me to let you know your building is in danger but not to come to town until we deal with the ugly mother lovers *putting* it in danger." Growls, yips, and the snapping of jaws sounded in the background. "Normally, we'd like a witch on our side to help, especially one who's charmed and dangerous—" he sniggered, and Morgen was positive he'd come up with that joke himself, "—but Amar doesn't want you endangered, on account of your delicate condition."

"My condition is fine," Sian said.

"Says the woman who needed an inhaler to do research in a library." Morgen turned onto the paved road and took her phone back.

"See how hale you are after contracting the Dengue Fever twice."

"*Morgen's* delicate condition," José Antonio clarified.

"Delicate condition?" Zoe gaped from the back seat. "Morgen, are you *pregnant*?"

"Not now, Zoe," Morgen said. "José Antonio, is everyone all right? We're coming down."

"Amar and Pedro said not to. It's real tense right now."

"I won't get between you and the Loups, but I need to make sure the ghost is gone and the building stops stinking, so the guy who wants to demolish the place doesn't have a leg to stand on."

After a puzzled pause, José Antonio said, "He has four legs to stand on."

"Not for long."

"The building *is* a problem," he said. "That stench is what made the mayor sign off on demoing it, and now there's an awful wailing noise coming from inside too."

"That bastard was ready to sign off on demoing it as soon as *I* leased it." Exasperated, Morgen hung up, put both hands on the wheel, and accelerated beyond the speed limit. As much as Ungar disliked her, she couldn't believe he had agreed to something illegal. Unless... was it possible Olivia was using a were-wolf-control incantation to coerce him? Hell, maybe she was even coercing the Loup leader. "Zoe, we're going to need your rock-star boobs."

"Obviously."

"I need you to use them on the mayor, not his enemies. Get him to leave my building alone."

"Are you sure you wouldn't be better off without it?" Zoe asked. "It seems problematic."

"I don't care. I didn't sign a two-year lease to set up my charm displays on a pile of rubble."

As they drove down Main Street, the flashing lights of the sheriff's department SUVs came into view. Even more ominous were the yellow lights of the flatbed truck that had brought the crane with the wrecking ball. Since Zorro had shared the vision with her, the big piece of equipment had been unloaded. Now, it loomed close enough to the building to take down its walls. A guy in overalls was approaching its cab while a uniformed man guarded him, a rifle in his hands. It was one of the deputies.

Morgen's heart wrenched at this betrayal. The sheriff's department was working against her too? She'd helped the town, damn it.

"Ungar ordered it," Morgen whispered with certainty, her fingers tightening on the wheel. Whether of his own accord or under Olivia's influence, she didn't know, but Ungar doubtless had the power to order the law-enforcement officers around.

The Lobos—bless their furry flanks—were trying to impede the wrecking-ball operator and keep him from reaching the cab. But the Loups were fighting them. A confusing snarl of twenty or thirty wolves were snapping for each other's throats.

A couple of dark furry lumps on the ground weren't moving, and fear made Morgen's palms so sweaty that she almost lost her grip on the wheel. With all the fighting going on, she couldn't tell much about the wolves that were down.

She had to fight the urge to floor the accelerator, force her way between the fighting packs, and ram into the wrecker in the hope of damaging it so thoroughly that it couldn't be used. Her car was tiny next to the towering crane. It would be flattened like a bug hitting a windshield, and Morgen and her passengers would end up in the hospital—or worse.

As soon as they passed the putt-putt course, she turned left. As much as she wanted to charge in, sneaking in the back might be a better choice. It wasn't as if she could stop the madness with a firmly spoken word—or incantation.

"Aren't you going to park up front?" Zoe pointed at the chaos.

"I suggest *not* parking the car next to a wrecking ball." Sian waved for Morgen to continue in the direction she was going. "Advice that seems prudent in all situations."

"I'm going one block over." Morgen turned again, nearly taking off a hubcap on the curb. Worry for Amar and the Lobos made her driving shaky. She hadn't seen Amar's gray-and-black form out front. What if he'd been among the wolves down on the ground, too injured to continue the fight? "We'll park behind the building."

Sian made a gagging noise. "I can still smell it. The windows aren't even down. No wonder they want to destroy it."

"They won't after we get rid of the ghost and the curse." Morgen just hoped there was time to try. If the sheriff's department was siding with the Loups against the Lobos, they might gain the upper hand quickly.

Was there something she could do to stop the fight? To buy time?

Morgen parked behind the building, and Lucky barked excitedly, destroying any hope she'd had of a sneak attack. "Stay here, everyone."

As she grabbed her staff and opened the door, Lucky barked again.

"*Especially* you."

The last thing she wanted was for him to run into the deadly werewolves and have one of them tear his throat out.

"Zoe, stay with him," Morgen ordered.

"But I've got—"

"No weapons that can help here." Morgen got out, hoping her cousin would listen, but there wasn't time to make sure she did.

At least nobody seemed to have noticed Lucky's barking. With the fighting out front and one of the sheriff's department SUVs running its siren, they probably hadn't heard him.

Morgen thought about using the invisibility incantation, so she could sneak in close and figure out how to help before anyone saw her, but two uniformed figures crouching next to the back wall of the building startled her. What the hell? All the action was going on out front. Why were they hiding back there?

Wait, they weren't hiding. They were putting something next to the back wall. Were those *explosives*?

They were going to blow up the building before she could remove the curse and set the ghost free.

What if destroying the structure did nothing? Or only irked the ghost? It could end up haunting all of Bellrock, and getting her business off the ground would be the least of her problems.

27

Fury stole Morgen's fear, and she ran toward the men planting explosives. "Stop that!"

They spun, reaching for their firearms, and she halted with her staff up. They wouldn't *shoot* her, would they?

Her amulet warmed through her shirt, and unbidden, a green glow blossomed inside the antler tips of her staff. Grandma had directed it to deflect a pot in that cabin, but asking it to deflect bullets seemed a stretch.

Fortunately, when the men saw her, they didn't draw their weapons. But they also didn't back away from the explosives.

"I'm sorry, ma'am, but we have orders to help with demolishing this building. The stench has made it a menace to Bellrock."

"Those Loups out front are a menace to Bellrock, and you aren't demolishing *them*."

The men looked at each other, then turned back to what they'd been doing. Morgen took a step closer, her fingers tightening around her staff as she envisioned cracking them on their heads, but if she attacked law officers, she would end up kicked out of Bellrock—or in *jail*—even if she did pay her taxes on time.

"Stop it, or I'll hex you, damn it." The words sounded ridiculous as soon as they came out of her mouth, but the men paused.

One eyed her warily over his shoulder. "The mayor said—"

"*I'll* talk to the mayor." Morgen clenched her jaw. "And I'll get rid of the smell. You two stay there, and don't blow anything up."

The men exchanged long looks, then one stood up to face her while the other went back to what he was doing. Arming the explosive? The standing man eyed her staff, her fingers around her amulet, and murmured something into a radio.

Morgen leveled her staff at the explosive he'd left unguarded on the ground and dredged incantations from her mind. Wendy knew one to levitate objects, and that would have been perfect, but Morgen hadn't memorized it and feared she didn't have time to search in her app. The other officer had finished arming his device, and he backed away with a detonator in hand.

"Back away from the area, everyone. You especially, ma'am."

Morgen switched her grip from Grandma's amulet to the child charm. "My baby is in danger," she whispered, envisioning the explosive going off and hurling her across the street. "Use your magic to protect it."

Nothing about the child-charm formula had promised sentience, but she willed it to understand and tried to funnel her power into it, the power to get rid of the threat. Surprisingly, it *and* her amulet grew warm against her chest. Energy hummed, flowing between the two magical pieces of jewelry.

"Ma'am," the man with the detonator said. "Move back. Ralph, get her out of the way."

Ralph hesitated but firmed his jaw and strode toward Morgen.

"Now," she implored the charm.

A breeze whispered through, and both explosives flew upward

and away from the building. They arced over the trees, sailing into the dark sky toward Rosario Strait.

"There's little point in detonating them now," Morgen told the men, though they had been looking at her and hadn't noticed their explosives flying away.

Booms and flashes of light came from the water, and the men jumped, their eyes bulging. Nobody had pressed the detonator. Maybe her charm had decided to completely get rid of the threat.

"One does like to be thorough," she muttered.

The men gaped at the sky, then spun back toward the building. Lucky barked, and Morgen glanced back. Sian had stepped out of the car, but Zoe was still in the back with Lucky. She had the window down and looked to be taking pictures with her phone.

Well, whatever kept her in the car and out of the way.

"What's going on back here?" a familiar voice shouted.

Morgen winced and turned back toward the building as Mayor Ungar charged into view. She'd *known* he would be here, personally handing out explosives to Franklin's men like holiday bonuses.

"*You*," he snarled, pinning Morgen with his hard gaze.

He ran straight toward her. She leveled her staff, tempted to blast him with its power, but hurting him would be even worse than hurting the sheriff's men. Of all people, he had the most power to drive her out of his town—or throw her in jail. But she had to defend herself.

She gripped the charm again, wondering if its magic could hurl *him* over the trees and into Rosario Strait, but before she could try, a shadow swept down from above. Zorro.

He flapped down, talons extended toward the top of Ungar's head. Ungar must have heard the wingbeats—amazing that he could pick them out with all the noise coming from the fight—for he spun and raised his arms. Zorro still managed to batter him and rake at him with his talons.

Ungar roared in fury and pain. Morgen winced again, knowing Ungar would blame her for the familiar's attack, but she couldn't fault Zorro for defending her.

Worried Ungar would hurt the owl, she groped for an incantation that she could use. She didn't want to risk hitting Zorro with a blast of power.

Ungar swatted at him several times before roaring again and shifting into his werewolf form. His clothing ripped, since he didn't have time to change, as his human body sprouted fur, and his face elongated into a snout. A snout full of fangs. As soon as he landed on all fours, he sprang up, snapping at Zorro.

Lucky's barking grew more intense. He managed to spring past Zoe and out the window. Overcoming his fear of werewolves, he ran toward Ungar, determined to help protect Morgen.

Afraid Ungar would kill her familiars, Morgen banished her hesitation. As soon as Zorro wasn't in the way, and before Lucky reached Ungar, she chanted, "Under the moon's magic, bad behavior correct and this witch protect!"

Green energy crackled among the antler tips of her staff, and a powerful beam struck Ungar. He flew through the air, hitting the pavement ten feet away and snarling in pain as he rolled into the street.

"Don't hurt him!" Zoe cried.

She'd gotten out of the car and was waving her phone in distress. She took a few steps toward Ungar.

"Get back in the car," Morgen snapped. "He's dangerous. To *both* of us."

A growling Ungar rose to his feet, his hackles up. He focused on Lucky and roared, more like a lion than a wolf. It was too much for Lucky, whose momentary bravery faltered, and he backed up to hide behind Morgen.

She couldn't blame him. In his wolf form, Ungar was as large as Amar. And as powerful and deadly.

He turned his lupine gaze on Zoe, who halted before taking another step. Fear flashed across her face as she perhaps realized for the first time just what kind of being she wanted to date.

But Morgen was the one Ungar snarled at. Fangs bared, he stalked toward her and eyed her staff, as if envisioning snapping it in two.

He could *try*. Morgen dropped into a crouch and pointed it at him. As powerful a werewolf as Ungar might be, he wasn't the *rougarou*, and her magic had thrown him a lot farther. If he pushed her, she would blast him again.

Another lupine snarl came from the side of the building. The officers, who'd been staring as Morgen and Ungar faced off, cursed and scattered. A gray-and-black wolf charged into view and sprang, coming down between Morgen and Ungar.

Amar.

He faced the mayor with his hackles up and his fangs on full display. Ungar's gaze shifted from Morgen to Amar. With another lion-like roar, Ungar charged.

Fearless, Amar charged as well. They crashed together, rising up on their hind legs, chests butting as they snapped their jaws at each other's throats.

"Morgen!" Zoe cried. "Stop them. Do something!"

If Morgen hadn't been worried about Amar, she might have taken the opportunity to run into the unguarded building and attempt to nullify the curse. She couldn't help but think that if she could do that, and the stench and keening went away, the mayor would have to see reason and stop the destruction. Though if Olivia was controlling him, maybe that was a vain hope.

Besides, Morgen had never seen Amar and Ungar fight before and couldn't tear her gaze away. It was mesmerizing and terrifying. Which of them was the strongest? Who would end up on top? And did Ungar hate Amar enough to *kill* him if he got the opportunity?

The wolves dropped to all fours, alternately circling and

crashing together, jaws snapping for vital targets. They *were* trying to kill each other.

Morgen pointed her staff at Ungar, but she had to wait for an opening, lest she hurt Amar. Sweat ran down the side of her face, and she grimaced as the rumble of machinery came from the front of the building. Had that man made it to the cab and started the wrecker?

"Bradley Ungar," came a new call from the side street. Phoebe was running up, her pumps slapping on the pavement and a wand in her hand. "Stop that at once. What are you *doing*?"

Morgen would have guessed him too locked in battle to hear her, but Ungar glanced toward Phoebe. Amar took advantage and bowled him off his feet. With a surge of his great muscles, he sprang and landed atop Ungar.

He might have locked his jaws around the mayor's neck, but Zoe and Phoebe cried, "No!" in unison.

Morgen could tell Amar hadn't planned to finish Ungar off anyway—he was likely as worried about potential ramifications as she—but at their yell, Amar backed away. Again, he placed himself protectively in front of Morgen.

Snarling, Ungar rolled to his feet. Blood dripped from a gash in the side of his neck and onto the pavement. He backed into a position where he could keep Amar and Morgen and Phoebe in his line of sight.

Phoebe strode fearlessly up to him. "What are you doing siding with them?" She thrust her wand toward the battle that continued to rage in front of the building. "You're your own man. The Loups don't own you. You've told me that yourself."

Ungar backed farther from everyone, then lowered his head with another snarl and shifted back into his human form. Naked and bleeding, he opened his mouth to respond, but a whistle came from the front of the building.

It sounded like someone calling a dog, and Morgen spun,

afraid Lucky might respond to it. But he'd disappeared. She swore and looked toward the car, hoping he'd jumped back inside. But Zoe had left the door open, so Morgen could tell that it was empty.

"Where'd Lucky go?" she called, hoping Sian had seen his departure.

Sian had a wand out and her phone open—looking for a helpful incantation within the app?—and could only shake her head.

"Come back here!" Phoebe yelled. "Brad, where are you going?"

The naked Ungar was running toward the front of the building. To help the Loups? Or was he responding to that whistle? *Olivia's* whistle?

"I think he's under the influence of a werewolf-control spell," Morgen said.

Confusion wrinkled Phoebe's brow as she turned. "What? The Loups can't cast that."

"Olivia is up there with the Loup leader."

"Olivia? Damn it, we kicked her out of the coven."

"But not Bellrock, right?"

"We don't have that kind of power." Phoebe stamped her foot. "You're right. She must be manipulating Ungar. *Controlling* him."

"What do you mean *controlling*?" Zoe asked. "Like with magic?"

"Werewolf-control spell," Morgen repeated, glancing down as Amar shifted into his human form. "Witches can cast them to make werewolves do their bidding."

"It's a bitch." Amar straightened, as naked as the mayor was, and bared his teeth.

"Being controlled is a bitch, or the witch who does it to you is?" Zoe asked.

"Yes."

Aware of the rumble of machinery, Morgen pointed to the

building. "I have to go inside and figure out how to end the curse and set the ghost free."

Before she could take a step, Amar gripped her arm. "You can't go in there. That wrecking ball is about to slam into the front of the building."

"That's why I need you to stop it." She hugged him and kissed him on the cheek. "Thanks."

"I came to protect you," Amar blurted.

"What better way than by ensuring a five-ton wrecking ball doesn't land on my head?"

Maybe he agreed with that logic, for when she pulled away, Amar allowed it.

"Sian, Zoe," Morgen called back. "Please find Lucky." She didn't know where Zorro had gone, either, but she trusted the owl to be able to fly out of danger. If Lucky had run in the wrong direction, he could end up as collateral damage in the werewolf fight.

Phoebe ran after her. Morgen was tempted to send her away, too, not wanting her to be flattened if the wrecking ball got through, but her mentor knew a lot more about magic than she did and might be able to help.

Help me, came a now-familiar call as Morgen raced toward the door on the side of the building. Numerous werewolves remained on the sidewalk and in the street out front as the rumble of the wrecker grew louder. Amar, back in his wolf form, sprinted past Morgen and Phoebe. Hopefully, to tackle whoever was in the cab.

"Did you hear that?" Morgen asked Phoebe.

"What?"

Set me free, the voice pleaded. *I've been trapped here for so long.*

"That," Morgen said as silvery light flared from within the building, spilling though the windows and out to the street.

"All I hear is the fighting and that machine firing up," Phoebe said.

Great. Morgen had been chosen as the ghost's conduit.

She opened the door, and the stench of rotting carcasses rolled out, even stronger inside. Her stomach heaved, and she bent over on the threshold, afraid she would end up vomiting instead of helping.

"Stop right there," someone yelled. Damn it, that was Ungar again.

Morgen couldn't stand up to face him, couldn't do anything except grip her stomach and gasp in air, trying not to throw up. But the air was foul, not refreshing, and breathing it only made things worse.

"Brad," Phoebe said, fear in her voice. "This isn't you. You don't want to do this."

"Don't you dare point your wand at me," Ungar snarled.

Morgen managed to jerk to the side so she puked on the pavement instead of the floor, but she couldn't keep from throwing up. Neither Phoebe nor Ungar noticed. Their gazes were locked on each other.

Even as she vomited, Morgen glanced up and saw a gun in Ungar's hand. He was pointing it at them.

28

"You don't want to shoot us, Brad." Phoebe almost managed to sound calm, but a quaver made her voice tremble.

"Say the wolf incantation," Morgen rasped, gagging and struggling to make her stomach stop heaving.

If Phoebe didn't understand what she meant, Morgen would have to do it herself. *Before* Ungar shot them.

"Under the moon's magic, turn the snarling hound from angry foe to witch bound!" Phoebe cried, her wand pointed at Ungar's chest as he kept his gun pointed at hers.

Unfortunately, her magic didn't seem to do anything. Ungar's gun remained trained on her. No, wait. The magic *was* affecting him. His hand shook, making the gun tremble, but he couldn't shift it away, couldn't take his finger from the trigger. Someone was definitely controlling him.

"Brad," Zoe called softly from the side. Why hadn't she gotten back in the car?

Sian wasn't in the car either. She was creeping past them toward the front of the building, gripping her wand with a determined expression on her face. If Morgen hadn't been gagging, she would have shouted at her sister to get out of there. But maybe Sian had found an incantation to throw a magical wrench in the workings of the wrecker. If so, Morgen would kiss her later, whether she wanted to be touched or not.

"Phoebe," Ungar said hoarsely, his hand still shaking as he clenched the gun. "Get out of here. I... I don't want to... shoot you."

"Stand with me, Brad," Phoebe said. "Not against us. Is that Olivia controlling you?"

"She's... strong," he bit out. "I can't—" Ungar clenched his jaw, the tendons in his neck standing out.

Morgen's stomach finally stopped heaving, and she straightened and faced him.

"Under the moon's magic, turn the snarling hound from angry foe to witch bound!" she cried, throwing all of her will into it.

Ungar's body and gaze jerked toward her. Had she done it? Overridden Olivia's incantation? Maybe her and Phoebe's power had combined to do it.

"Put the gun down and help us, please," Morgen told Ungar.

His arm snapped to his side.

Morgen didn't want his help, just for him to leave them alone, but when she stepped into the building, Ungar walked robotically in behind her. Well, better with her than against her. She hoped he didn't later resent her—resent her *more*—for taking control of him.

"Watch him," Morgen whispered to Phoebe as the three of them walked warily into the building. No, the *four* of them. Zoe came in after Ungar.

Afraid anyone inside was in danger, Morgen almost snapped at her to go back out, but two snarling and biting wolves rolled across the pavement not five feet from the doorway. It wasn't any safer out there.

A woman's scream of frustration came from the front of the

building. It sounded like Olivia was pissed that she'd lost control of Ungar. Too bad.

"Look!" Phoebe pointed at the large windows.

Thanks to the Lobos' repairs and the magical silver light streaming out of the building, they had no trouble seeing the wrecker looming out front. The crane arm was drawn back, poised to sling the massive steel ball into the front wall. They also had no trouble seeing Amar fighting a great black wolf on the roof of the cab. The operator was inside, but he crouched down with his arms over his head, afraid of the wolves battling above.

"Hopefully, we've got a minute," Morgen whispered and ran toward the back room. It might not matter where she chanted the words to—she hoped—end the curse, but the chalk outline and the bloodstained wall seemed like the center of the horrors this place had seen.

A clang sounded, the front door slamming shut. The faint click of a lock turning was audible over the noise outside.

"Uh," Phoebe said.

"Maybe we'll just do this here." Morgen halted and couldn't keep from glancing up, but the Lobos had thankfully removed all the meat hooks.

Had the ghost locked the doors, or was the curse responsible? Morgen didn't know, but there hadn't been time to go hunting for holy water, so she didn't have the option to exorcise the ghost.

"Curse first, ghost second," she whispered.

Phoebe looked warily at her. "Curse?"

Ungar only looked blankly at her, making Morgen feel guilty. She'd turned him into an automaton. If she hadn't worried that Olivia would regain control over him, she would have released him from her spell.

"Later," she whispered and pulled up the incantation on her notes app to make certain she'd memorized it correctly. Staff in hand, she raised her arms and her voice. "Under the moon's magic, if to witches you are averse, your foul lair I—"

Before she could finish the incantation, the floorboards heaved, causing her to stumble. She flailed, almost cracking Phoebe in the head with her staff.

"I don't think the curse wants to be removed," Phoebe said as the floor heaved again, wood snapping and groaning.

The loft shuddered, vats and machinery thudding and clanking against each other. Morgen skittered back, making sure she wouldn't be underneath it if the whole thing came down. The Lobos had reinforced it, but what did that mean in the face of a curse and a ghost?

Outside, light flashed, and a yowl of pain pierced the night. Morgen spun in time to see Amar fly off the top of the wrecker. What had struck him? The wolf he'd been fighting was on the ground.

Light flashed again from behind the wrecker. Morgen couldn't see the source, but she wagered it was Olivia. She couldn't see Sian either and prayed she hadn't gotten herself hurt.

"I'll go help," Phoebe said grimly, turning toward the door.

"You can't," Morgen said, just as grim.

As the floor shuddered again, Zoe turned and tried to open the door. "We're locked in."

"Ungar," Morgen said.

His glazed eyes focused on her.

"Can you break down that door?" Morgen pointed, waving for Zoe to get out of the way. "Please?"

Forcing the door open hadn't worked when *Morgen* had tried it, but Ungar had a lot more mass to throw behind his efforts.

Fists clenching, Ungar strode toward it with intent. Morgen hoped that fist clenching wasn't because he was furious with her for commanding him. As she knew from experience with Amar, Ungar would remember all of this.

Legs spread for balance, Morgen started to speak the words for the curse again. The fact that the building was trying to stop her made her think she was on to something. Made her *hope* she was on to something.

Ungar threw his shoulder against the door. It didn't budge.

"Under the moon's magic, if to witches you are averse—"

Glass shattered behind Morgen, interrupting her again.

She flung her arm up in anticipation of the wrecking ball coming through the window. Then, realizing her *arm* wouldn't do anything, she ran and dove toward the door.

Glass tinkled to the floorboards but not as much as if the wrecking ball had blasted through. A single pane near the top had shattered. Either one of the men outside had thrown something at it, or it had broken of its own accord.

"There's dark angry magic in this place," Phoebe whispered.

"No kidding." Morgen pushed herself to her feet.

Zoe had her back to the wall as Ungar hurled himself ineffectively at the door, and was recording what was going on with her phone. Morgen shook her head, but it wasn't as if there was something more helpful her cousin could be doing. Her *boobs* would be no help against curses or ghosts.

"Help me help you," Morgen called to the back room, envisioning the floating white apparition she'd seen. Could it hear and understand her?

"Try the incantation again." Phoebe glanced toward the loft as the floorboards creaked and more machinery thudded together. Something toppled and fell through the railing. An old kerosene lantern. Its glass shattered when it hit the floor, more shards flying.

"Right." Morgen wrapped her hand around her amulet and charm and pointed her staff toward the ceiling. "Under the moon's magic, if to witches you are averse, your foul lair I now curse!"

This time, she got all the words out. She held her breath, waiting to see if anything would happen.

"Did you uncurse it or curse it?" Phoebe asked.

"The book said to repeat the curse in order to remove it."

Phoebe looked dubiously at her, but the floor stopped quaking. The silver light dimmed, and the keening faded.

"Get that owl!" someone outside shouted. "He's attacking the operator."

Thank you, Zorro, Morgen thought, but she also worried about him. A lot of the men out there were armed.

"Did the door unlock?" Morgen held a hand out toward Ungar to keep him from battering it again.

Zoe tried the knob and shook her head. "We're still locked in."

Two loud clanks came from the back room. Morgen whirled toward the doorway, half-expecting the ghost to be floating there. There was no sign of it. Ominous thuds floated out of the room.

"What *now*?" Morgen whispered, then spoke the incantation again, wondering if it had only partially worked.

The thuds grew quicker until something hulking loomed in the doorway.

"What is *that*?" Phoebe asked.

Morgen groaned. "It's that statue from the closet."

"It looks more like a giant robot than a statue," Zoe said.

"More pertinent," Phoebe said, as the construct bent in the middle to fit through the doorway, then strode forward, flakes of rust falling from its metal body, "where did it get that huge axe?"

Morgen shook her head and stepped forward, leveling her staff at what she feared was their new enemy. "Ungar, help me disarm that thing."

Before he could get in the way, she chanted her attack incantation. "Under the moon's magic, bad behavior correct and this witch protect."

Green energy gathered between the antler tips, then shot

out in a beam. It struck the construct in its cylindrical chest piece with the same power that she'd hurled at Ungar earlier, power that had knocked him ten feet. It didn't do anything to the robot. It didn't even make it pause in its steps.

Remembering one of the witches telling her that her wards would be ineffective on machines, Morgen feared the same applied to the metal construct, that it was impervious to magic.

It lifted the axe in both arms as it strode closer.

Swearing, Morgen and the others scattered. Only Ungar, compelled by her command, ran at the ambulatory statue.

Afraid that whatever magic powered it would allow the creation to defeat him, Morgen ran in from the side to help, but she had no idea what to do beyond smacking it with her staff. Maybe she could knock the axe out of its metal grip.

Some consciousness must have existed within the robot, for it saw Ungar coming and responded. As he ran in low, crouching like a wrestler in a match, it swept the axe toward his chest.

"Look out!" Phoebe and Zoe cried together.

Agile for his size, Ungar ducked under the swing and kept closing. He jumped around behind the construct and leaped on its back, wrapping his arms around its metal head—it didn't have a neck to target. He wrenched and twisted, but like the locked door, some magic reinforced it, and even his muscular arms weren't sufficient to tear it to pieces.

As the robot lifted the axe again, Morgen jumped in and swung her staff. It connected with the arm, clanging hollowly. The contact hurt her far more than the construct, sending a jolt through her elbows and shoulder joints.

She backed away as it focused on her, ignoring Ungar trying to rip off its head. Probably because he wasn't having any luck doing that.

Once more, Morgen pointed her staff at the robot and spoke

the attack incantation, but it did no good. And Ungar, close enough to catch the nimbus from the beam, cried out.

"Sorry, sorry," Morgen yelled, wincing in sympathy.

A thud sounded at the exterior door. Amar? Someone else?

Whoever it was couldn't get in, and Morgen thought of the vision she'd had of her Grandma battling the ghost in the cabin while Amar was helpless to break down the window or the door.

The robot stomped toward Morgen, raising its axe again. Ungar lunged over its shoulder and grabbed the haft. For a moment, the construct couldn't lift it higher, its power not enough to overcome his raw strength, but then it whirled. It spun so quickly that Ungar flew free, hitting the floor hard and tumbling away.

Morgen backed toward the loft as she eyed one of the support posts. Would bringing down the ceiling and all that machinery on their enemy be enough to stop it? She cringed at the idea of having to fix that mess, but that would be better than being killed.

The construct didn't follow her. Instead, it turned to stomp after Ungar.

"No," Morgen blurted. "Over here, you ugly tin can."

It didn't listen.

Silver light pulsed, and fog crept into the room. Phoebe pointed her wand at the construct and cast an incantation that Morgen didn't recognize. Whatever it was, the attack did no more than hers had against their metal foe. The construct kept stomping toward Ungar. Fortunately, he'd regained his feet, and he managed to back away from it.

But he was backing toward the windows, and lights flashed out there. Lights that seemed to come from the crane. Was the man in the cab about to hurl the wrecking ball through the windows?

"Careful, Ungar," Morgen called. "Get away from there."

"And go *where*?" he demanded.

"Come this way. We'll try dropping the loft on it." Her magic might not work on the robot, but it would work on those support posts.

With a lurch, she realized it might also work on the axe. It appeared to be an ordinary weapon.

The walking statue is what slew me, the female voice whispered into Morgen's mind as she ran to the side to target the axe. *The tinkerer built it to keep out the law and the coven, those who objected to the way he treated the women he enslaved.*

How do I stop it and get rid of the curse?

I placed the curse to stop him. And it did. It is his body that was outlined by chalk in this room, his blood that stains the wall. His creation got me in the end, but it was worth it.

I'm glad, but we have other problems.

If you free me, the curse will be no more, but his construct will remain. He made it to protect this place, and it will never stop.

We'll deal with that if the rest of this building is normal.

The ghost—the former witch?—offered no more commentary.

Morgen chanted the attack incantation once more and targeted the axe. When the beam struck, the wooden handle shattered to pieces. The metal axe-head flew free, nearly slamming into Ungar.

He rolled to the side, just avoiding losing an ear. Though disarmed, the construct continued after him, its metal arms raised.

As Morgen had urged, Ungar raced toward the loft. She ran to the side, finding a spot where she could target one of the support posts. If her magic had taken out the axe, it ought to have no problem with them.

"Lure it under there," Morgen said, "and then get out from under the loft yourself."

"You think?" Ungar gave her a scathing look as he backed to the far wall.

"Your control spell may have worn off," Phoebe said.

"I think so. His normal wit has returned." As the construct

stomped closer to the loft, Morgen pointed her staff at one of the support posts and tilted her chin toward the other. "Can you knock that one out, Phoebe? With a spell?"

"I'll try."

"Also, any chance you know how to make holy water? We need to exorcise the ghost before the curse will disappear."

Phoebe frowned at her. "How did you learn that?"

"It's been chatting me up."

"The ghost?"

"Yes."

The construct slowed as it neared the overhang of the loft. Its head hadn't been designed to tilt back, to allow it to look up—Morgen didn't even know if it could see like humans did—but somehow it sensed that it was in danger, that they were setting a trap.

Ungar waved his fists. "Come on, you coward. Not so brave without your axe, eh?"

"Father Cutty is the priest at the church in town," Phoebe said. "You'd have to get him to make holy water. It's not a witch thing."

"So I've learned." Morgen glanced at the locked door, wishing she could open it and send Zoe to the church.

Before, she hadn't tried anything beyond the lock-opening incantation on it. Perhaps something more powerful would work.

While the robot debated whether to continue under the loft, Morgen shifted her staff toward the door. Once more, she chanted the attack incantation, imagining every ounce of magic within her blood and her amulet assisting her.

A blast of green energy struck the door, and wood snapped. The door remained intact, but the jamb and wall around it blew outward with a great whoosh. The door stood still for a moment, then wobbled, tilted, and fell backward.

A whine came from outside, and a copper-colored snout poked around the edge.

"Lucky," Morgen blurted.

The rest of his head came into view.

"Go to the church and see if Father Cutty is there," she said, forming a generic image of a priest in her mind—she'd never met the man and had no idea what he looked like. "We need holy water."

She didn't know why she added that. It wasn't as if Lucky could convey that message.

His head cocked, and Morgen didn't know if he'd grasped her meaning or not. Since he'd become her familiar, he'd gained more intelligence and understood her better, but since he didn't know the priest...

"Just get anyone who's in the church," Morgen ordered.

Lucky barked and ran off in the right direction, but Morgen realized it might not do any good. This late in the day, it was unlikely anyone would be at the church.

"Zoe," Morgen started, thinking to send her cousin.

But Zoe flung a hand toward the loft. "Look out."

Morgen spun back with her staff in time to see the construct kick one of the very supports she'd wanted to target. But their enemy wasn't *under* the loft; Ungar was.

"Get out of there, Bradley!" Phoebe yelled.

He'd figured that out for himself and was running out from under the loft. But when one of the support posts snapped, the ceiling above him shuddered once and gave out. He dove, but he wasn't fast enough. The ceiling and hundreds of pounds of junk crashed down, burying him.

29

"No!" Zoe ran toward the rubble that had buried Ungar.

The entire loft hadn't collapsed, but most of it had, with all the junk up there tumbling down. Morgen couldn't see Ungar and didn't know if he'd survived. The robot, clearly intending to finish him off, stomped toward the rubble pile.

"Here, you bastard." Morgen blasted it again with her staff, aiming at its head. Even though her magic couldn't hurt it, she hoped it would distract the thing.

Zoe ran faster than the construct did, darting around it. As she reached the rubble, a beam shifted, and a hand thrust out from under an upturned vat.

"Zoe, get out of there," Morgen barked.

"I'm not going to let him *die*."

Phoebe also cast an incantation at the robot. As with Morgen's magic, it did nothing, and the construct lumbered closer to Zoe and the buried Ungar.

He heaved the vat off the top of the pile, and the top half of his body came into view. Zoe grabbed him under the armpits and pulled, but his legs were trapped by something else. The robot was almost to them, its uncaring arms outstretched. Ungar wouldn't be able to squirm free in time.

"You're going to get trampled," Morgen told Zoe, as she waved her staff, trying to lure the robot toward her.

She chanted her incantation again, blasting it in the side with magical energy. As before, it did nothing to harm the construct, but it *did* draw its attention.

It turned and strode toward her. Morgen skittered back and glanced at the ceiling, wondering if she should try to bring the entire *roof* down on its head.

With Zoe's help, Ungar managed to crawl out from under the rubble. That was good, but who was going to help Morgen?

Thinking of the invisibility spell, and wondering if a robot would be able to see through it, Morgen started to chant, but she was interrupted again.

"Duck down!" Amar yelled from outside.

Morgen glanced back. Through the window, she saw the movement of the crane arm.

"Down, down!" she yelled to everyone and flung herself toward the door.

The construct sensed danger as well, and took a step, but it didn't move quickly enough. The wrecking ball smashed through the window, wood and glass shattering and flying in a thousand directions. Five tons of steel slammed into the back of the robot, lifting it from its feet and carrying it all the way to the back wall, where it struck with an earsplitting wrenching of metal.

Chain clanking, the ball thudded to the floor, cracking the boards. Dented like a can of soup hurled off a building, the robot fell atop the rubble from the destroyed loft.

Amar leaped out of the cab of the wrecker and raced into the building.

Ungar, limping and bleeding, snatched up the axe-head, all that remained of the broken tool. Gripping it with both hands, he hobbled to the robot as fast as he could. He and Amar arrived at the same time. One leg of the construct twitched, as if it still lived and wanted to rise and carry out its mission to slay them all.

Ungar fell upon it, hacking with the axe blade. Amar hadn't battled it, but he seemed to have as many aggressions to take out, for he also tore into it.

Morgen glanced toward the destroyed window, but she didn't see any wolves fighting out front. She didn't see any wolves at all.

"I think it's dead," Amar said, drawing back.

Panting, Ungar kept striking the downed construct with the axe-head. Neither arms nor legs were attached now, and he'd obliterated its torso. None of the circuit boards and wires Morgen would have expected in an actual robot were visible—it was hollow inside.

"Propelled by magic," she said, wondering if the tinkerer had been a warlock or had possessed some other kind of magic entirely. She shivered, imagining the battle that must have once taken place here, resulting in the building being cursed and the witch who'd done it killed. *Murdered.* "I still need to exorcise the ghost, so I can help her find a safe passage to the next realm."

"Will the fog go away then?" Zoe had scooted away from Ungar and the wreckage from the loft, and she had her phone up, recording again. She waved at the misty gray stuff with one hand. "And the *smell*?"

"I hope so," Morgen said.

At least the floor had stopped quaking. A good thing because what remained of the loft could come down at any moment.

Morgen rubbed the back of her neck, wondering if even the construction-handy Lobos would be able to get this place service-able again.

A bark came from the doorway.

"Lucky," she blurted in relief, turning and intending to wrap her arms around him.

But he wasn't alone. Lucky had a man by the hem of his jacket and was pulling him inside. Not only did Morgen not recognize him, but he didn't look anything like the image of the priest she'd shared with Lucky.

The bewildered white-haired man in jeans and a flannel shirt gaped around at everything, his eyes wide, a La Croix can clenched in one hand. Had he been in the middle of dinner when Lucky dragged him away?

"I'm so sorry, sir." Morgen wondered how Lucky had managed without tearing the man's jacket. What had gotten into him? "That's my dog, and I don't know what he's doing. Are you okay? I'm Morgen."

The man blinked watery eyes and peered at her. "The new witch. I've heard."

"Er, and you are?" Morgen grabbed Lucky's collar, afraid she would have to pry his jaws away from the man's jacket, but Lucky released it and sat down. He puffed his chest out proudly and wagged his tail.

"Joe Cutty."

"*Father* Cutty," Phoebe said. "It's who you wanted, Morgen."

"You wanted me?" Cutty pressed a hand to his chest. "Don't take this the wrong way, but I've been trying to avoid you and all of *them*." He thrust his can of carbonated water toward Ungar and Amar, who'd finished their annihilation of the robot, and then toward what had been the huge battle of the packs outside.

"I'm sorry to pester you," Morgen said. "It's just that the building I leased is cursed and haunted. I was told I need holy water to exorcise the ghost. Do you have any by chance? Or can you *make* some?" She eyed the La Croix can, wondering if carbonated grapefruit-flavored water could be used.

"I've been by this building before. It'll take more than holy water to save it." Cutty eyed the wrecking ball lying on the floor, window glass shattered everywhere, then wrinkled his nose. "I've been *smelling* it from the church all day."

"The ghost told me that if we can set her free, the curse will vanish with her," Morgen said. "I know a poem to say—something my grandma used to set a ghost free—but need some holy water to sprinkle around."

Cutty's gaze turned back to her. "Gwen taught you?"

She hesitated, thinking about mentioning that it had been in a dream—in a vision—but that might not hearten him. "Yes, sir."

"Well." He also looked down at his grapefruit water. "I technically *can* make holy water. I know the ritual and have my cross." He tugged out a gold cross on a chain. "But I need salt. Pure salt."

"Zoe." Morgen found her cousin had drifted to Ungar's side but managed to wave her over. "I need the contents of your purse."

"The what?"

"I saw some packets of salt in there."

"Oh. Sure. I save everything when I'm traveling. You never know if a place you're staying at will have the necessities." Zoe opened her purse as she walked over and gave Morgen a significant look. "Like *meat*."

"I hope that's not in your purse."

"Just a pepperoni stick."

"I only need salt and a bowl," Cutty said.

"Here you go." Zoe produced a white packet.

"That's iodized. It needs to be pure."

"Have no fear. I eat at the snooty places that provide sea salt too." Zoe dug deeper and pulled out a higher-end salt packet. "And you said a bowl? Hm, I've got..." She rummaged some more and poked into a makeup kit. "Brushes, sponges, Q-tips, eyeshadow, mascara..."

Sian appeared in the doorway behind the priest, then squeezed in while Zoe kept rummaging, pulling out applicators and brushes and who knew what else as she searched.

"I've seen chemistry sets with fewer components," Sian murmured.

"What were you doing out there?" Morgen asked, relieved to see her sister in one piece.

"Thwarting the bad guy." Sian lifted her chin and looked decidedly smug.

"Which one?" Morgen felt like they'd been battling the whole town.

"Here you go, Father." Zoe unscrewed the lid of a tub of tan powder. "You can use this. Just make sure to get it back to me. I don't want setting powder all over my purse.

"Setting what?" Morgen murmured, wondering what it said about her that her makeup arsenal didn't go beyond lipstick, mascara, and blush.

"Chemistry set," Sian repeated—she didn't deign to use even those items.

Father Cutty eyed the items dubiously but knelt by the wall and seemed willing to attempt to make holy water.

Morgen hoped that because the witch *wanted* to be freed, it wouldn't take a perfectly performed exorcism. She couldn't be *that* tied to this place, could she?

"To answer your question," Sian said, "I employed the were-wolf-control incantation that I saw you so effectively use on the mayor."

"On whom?" Morgen asked, hoping Sian hadn't created any enemies.

"The man in a beret that I believe was leading the Loup were-wolves. The woman beside him kept telling him what to do."

"Olivia."

Sian shrugged. She hadn't been around for Morgen's war with Wendy's older sisters.

"Once I had him under my sway," Sian continued, "I ordered him to attack her. She shrieked and ran off in that direction." Sian pointed inland toward the houses above the commercial part of town. Possibly toward the Loup lodge. "After she left and the man was no longer giving orders, a lot of the Loups also left. I—"

"Who *dared* ensorcel me?" came a male bellow from the parking lot.

Sian glanced back. "Uh oh."

"I'll take care of him." Ungar strode toward the doorway, pausing long enough to point a finger at Morgen. "*You* remove the curse, the ghost, whatever."

"I'll try," Morgen said.

"Here." Father Cutty, having finished murmuring and waving his cross, stood up. He carefully held the makeup lid, water a centimeter deep inside it. "You can use this."

"Is it... suitably holy?" Morgen accepted the lid gingerly, tempted to protest at how little water there was, but her grandma had used a tiny vial on her ghost. Maybe it would be enough.

"We'll find out. I've never used *carbonated* water."

"I guess we can find some tap water somewhere if it doesn't work." Morgen didn't quite know *where,* since the plumbing to the building had never been turned on, but the town wasn't that far away.

Rehearsing the prayer in her mind, Morgen walked to the center of the room, glass crunching under her shoes.

Amar joined her. "Do you need help with anything?"

Shouts came from the parking lot, Ungar telling Lucien that his wolves were out of hand, and the Loup leader reminding Ungar that he was one of them.

"I think *they* may need help," Morgen said, but she leaned against Amar, not wanting to send him away again. "Thank you for keeping the wrecking-ball operator from knocking down the building." She glanced at the huge ball lying on the floor, the chain limp. "Until the end."

"*I* did that," he said dryly. "I saw the robot drop the loft on the mayor and that it was impervious to your magic. It seemed necessary."

"I think it was, but it's a shame that your window repairs were so swiftly destroyed."

"We'll fix the windows again. And the rest of the place. Assuming you can get rid of the stench and the fog."

A keening moan came from the back room.

"And that," Amar said.

"Right." Emulating what Grandma had done, Morgen dipped her fingers in the holy water and flicked it around. She also took some into the back room, directing several droplets toward the chalk outline. The keening continued, raising goosebumps on her arms.

With the water spread, she gripped her amulet and charm, their magic warming her palm. It might be a holy religious prayer and not a witch incantation, but her magic might help.

Willing the words to have power, she chanted them loudly, though she almost faltered when she spotted Zoe recording again. What was she going to do? Post this on the family messaging app?

The words flowed easily out of Morgen's mouth, as if they wanted to be heard—had waited for *decades* to be heard. Her amulet warmed further, and the silver glow returned, brighter than it had ever been.

Morgen winced and squinted her eyes shut, afraid she might have made things worse. Amar clasped her hand, his calloused palm warm and reassuring. The light flashed, and the keening faded.

When Morgen opened her eyes, letting them adjust to the new dimness, the chalk outline was gone. So was the fog.

"I think you did it," Phoebe said from the other room.

Morgen walked out and might have smiled, but the arguing was still going on outside. Zoe had given up recording to peer worriedly out the doorway at the two men.

"Just because you made me a werewolf doesn't mean you *own* me," Ungar shouted. "Take your pack, and get out of my town. By dawn. I don't want to see any Loups again."

"You can't kick us out. We own half the property here." Lucien flung his arm toward his pack, though few remained. Only seven wolves stood behind him in their furry form, and half of them were injured.

Interestingly, the Lobos had chosen to stand behind Ungar. There were fourteen of them, and they were injured, too, but they held their heads and tails up, and Morgen knew they'd won the battle.

"Then *sell* it," Ungar said. "I know you strong-armed the previous owners into selling to you at outrageous prices. And I've never believed that Dr. Strat and Mrs. Deckenbauer died of natural causes."

"You can't prove anything."

"If I could, I would have killed you myself years ago." Ungar flexed his hands in the air, his nudity revealing the power of his shoulder and arm muscles. "But you'll leave my town now. If I see any of you again after dawn, I'll sic the witches on you."

Lucien scoffed. "They don't obey you."

"I might," Phoebe said.

"Me too." Morgen smiled sweetly at Lucien. "If it meant driving you out of town."

Sian didn't say anything, but she was the one Lucien glowered at. She lifted her head and drew out the book-shaped pendant that Wendy had crafted into an amulet for her. Morgen was touched that she'd kept it.

Morgen also gripped *her* amulet and glared at the Loup leader, letting him know that she would jump in if he tried to do anything to her sister. She might even defend *Ungar,* since he was standing up to the guy.

Lucien spat on the pavement at Ungar's feet. "This town has

gotten too crowded anyway. The hunting in Wolf Wood isn't *that* good."

"And here I thought it was those catnip mushrooms that kept all the wolves around," Morgen murmured.

Amar slanted her a sidelong look. She batted her eyelashes at him and slid an arm around his waist.

"We will leave," Lucien said, "but we will take our time and go when we wish."

"You had better wish by dawn," Ungar said.

"Our properties—"

"Can be sold *remotely*."

Zoe lifted a finger. "I can help with that. I'm a real-estate agent."

"I doubt the commissions would be great on Loup properties," Morgen whispered to her. "Or Bellrock properties in general. This isn't Seattle."

"I've seen your taxes," Zoe said. "The property values are fine."

Morgen couldn't object there.

After another snarl, Lucien whirled, his expensive coat flapping in the breeze. A breeze that was—thank all the spirits, sprites, and deities in the world—blowing away the stink of the building.

After Lucien and the Loups disappeared from view, Ungar walked up to Zoe.

"You're going to move up here to sell real estate?" he asked her.

"Move?" Zoe blinked. "Well, there *are* a lot more available hot men here."

"Yes," Ungar agreed, smiling wolfishly.

Zoe eyed his naked chest with a smile of her own.

Morgen barely kept from curling her lip. She didn't want to watch them flirt, if that's what that was. But she did appreciate that Ungar had turned sides and was going to drive out the Loups—that meant a lot. As long as he wasn't too much of a jerk to her going forward, she figured she could get along with him.

"Maybe I should date one of them a few more times before deciding," Zoe said.

"Reasonable." Ungar glanced at Amar and Morgen—Sian had found something on her phone more interesting than watching their byplay—before turning his back to them and clasping Zoe's hand. "Thanks for risking yourself to help dig me out of that mess."

"You're welcome. Do you need to stick around, or can we go find something to eat?"

"I think the sheriff's department can handle things from here."

Zoe and Ungar walked off hand in hand.

Morgen clasped Amar's hand. "I suppose I need to go back to my family instead of running off to get a snack with you."

"You do keep abandoning them."

"The term you're looking for is *fleeing from*." Morgen peered back into the building, where Father Cutty was patting Lucky and crooning to him that he was a good boy. A clear dog lover. He probably would have let any hound drag him off on an adventure. "You said you think your pack would be willing to help with cleanup again?"

Amar considered the wrecking ball, the chain leading out through the demolished window, and the equally demolished loft, its contents heaped all over what remained of the floor. "That *cleanup* is on the extensive side. You may have to bribe them with charms."

"Flea-and-tick charms?"

"Perhaps anti-ghost charms."

"I'll see what's in the literature about that." Morgen dug out the keys, as if she could lock up the building, but with the door lying in the parking lot, that wasn't that feasible. "Lucky, are you ready to go home?"

Now, he was on his back with all four legs crooked in the air as Cutty gave him a belly rub.

"You can visit your new friend again the next time we're in town," Morgen told him. "I should probably start going to church again, anyway."

"Have you been sinning lately?" Amar asked.

"Well, I'm cavorting with witches, demons, ghosts, and were-wolves. Aren't there Bible verses forbidding such things?"

"Father Cutty wouldn't get anyone in the pews if he didn't allow witches and werewolves and those who cavort with them to come to church."

"True."

Cutty walked out with Lucky. "You should absolutely come to church. I allow service animals and keep dog treats in my lectern."

"No wonder Lucky likes you. Do familiars count as service animals?"

His eyes crinkled. "I believe so."

30

AMAR'S KNEES CLUNKED AGAINST THE GLOVE COMPARTMENT, AND Morgen did her best to drive around the potholes instead of through them. His long legs never made her compact car a good choice, but he didn't complain. They'd been victorious, and he appeared relaxed, despite the number of wounds he'd received battling the Loups.

Morgen wished *she* could feel relieved, but her family would be waiting with questions and accusations of craziness. She glanced in the rearview mirror at Sian and Lucky in the back seat, Sian with her hands in her lap and a grimace on her face, likely due to the dog tail flicking her ear. Lucky had his nose out the window, inhaling the nocturnal scents of Wolf Wood.

"I should be researching incantations to make one's family content with one's witch career," Morgen said. "Do you think there is such a thing?"

"Witches would not be the family black sheep if there were," Sian said.

"Maybe you could find a spell to make your siblings forget you exist," Amar said.

"I wish," Morgen murmured.

When they pulled up to the house, her brothers' cars were, alas, still parked in the driveway. Surprisingly, almost everyone was out on the porch with Wendy, looking not at Morgen's car but toward the woods beyond the garden beds.

Morgen parked and got out, and Napoleon chittered from the railing. Lucky ran straight to the garden to sniff who knew what. Wendy waved cheerfully, and Morgen hoped that meant everything was okay. She doubted Wendy had known anything about her sister's involvement in the chaos in town.

"Was there trouble while I was gone?" Morgen spotted Jun in the living room looking out the window. "Trouble *here*, I mean," she amended, classifying everything from the cursed building to the werewolf battle to the wrecking ball as *trouble in town*.

"A couple of Loups came nosing around," Wendy said. "Your family got to see the wards in action. They also got to see me light a wolf's tail on fire. Normally, I wouldn't have done anything so drastic—" she glanced warily at Amar, as if he might judge her for her action, "—but when they couldn't get past the wards and to the house, they got a little rude."

"Rude?" Morgen looked around the property.

"They peed on the barn door and the garden beds. But I drove them off." Wendy smiled and wiggled her fingers.

Amar's eyebrows flew up, and he strode toward the barn. Well, that explained what had Lucky's interest in the garden.

"By lighting them on fire?" Morgen asked Wendy.

"Just their tails."

"You should have incinerated their penises," Morgen said, though she didn't care about the Loups anymore. If their pack was leaving forever, she could forgive them for their rude behavior.

"My aim isn't that good," Wendy said.

Caden came down the porch steps to stand in front of Morgen, and she braced herself.

"I—we—may owe you an apology," he said.

"Oh?" Dare Morgen hope the wolf-tail fires had been enough to prove to her family that magic existed?

"Zoe sent the video of your... battle in that old building. Then we saw men turn into wolves before our eyes and Wendy here do much more than light candles with tricks."

"So, you're ready to believe that magic exists?" Morgen asked. "And witches and werewolves?"

Suze gasped and pointed toward the barn. Amar had removed his clothes and was turning into a wolf before their eyes.

Morgen frowned and peered toward the woods, wondering if the Loups had returned to threaten them. It was likely those two hadn't yet gotten the message that the pack was leaving town.

But once he shifted, all Amar did was stride to the barn door and lift his leg.

Wendy snickered. "That's where the Loup peed. He must be covering its scent with his own."

Morgen sighed and rested her hand on her abdomen. *That,* she thought silently to her unborn baby, *is your father.*

Napoleon chattered in vociferous disapproval from the railing, probably more because Amar had taken his wolf form than about what he was doing. Jun was either so appalled that he'd moved away from the window—or he'd fainted. He wasn't made of the sternest stuff.

"We are, uh, willing to admit that *werewolves* exist. As to the rest..." Caden looked around at their brothers. "We'll try to keep an open mind."

"Does that mean you're not going to try to drag me off to an insane asylum?" Morgen asked.

"We were *never* going to do that. We just wanted you to come back to Seattle and regain your sanity."

"And now?" She lifted her brows.

"I guess you'll have to regain your sanity here."

"That's a big ask. Have you seen this place?"

"Just the videos." Rhett held up his phone, Zoe's footage paused on the screen.

Morgen got a glimpse of herself launching a green beam of energy at the robot. "I'm going to suggest to the mayor that he not let the tourism department use that video."

"Wise," Caden murmured.

"I'm glad you've come around, but I'm a little surprised you didn't accuse Zoe of sending you a doctored video."

"Someone did mention that possibility, but we've seen the real-estate videos that Zoe has put together, and her thumb stars in every other one. *That*—" Caden pointed at the phone, "—would have been quite the advancement in her video-editing skills. Besides, she was still recording at the end when she stuffed her phone in her pocket." He grimaced. "We were treated to the sounds of her kissing someone."

"And that added verisimilitude?"

"Let's just say that we all know Cousin Zoe."

Morgen smiled in agreement.

"Are you all right with us spending the night here," Caden asked, "or are you going to boot us to a hotel in town? It's been a long day."

"Tell me about it." Morgen looked toward Amar, wondering if he would allow one of the couples to use his apartment bedroom.

He'd completed his task, changed back into a man, and was pulling on his jeans.

"He doesn't wear underwear," Suze said. "That's a little uncouth, don't you think?"

"Thirty seconds ago, he was peeing on the door," Caden said, "and you're worried about his commando preferences?"

"So uncouth." Suze shuddered and went into the house.

Morgen wondered when she should tell them about the baby... and the possibility that she and Amar might get married one day.

How would her brothers' wives feel about having a werewolf in the family?

The rest of the group walked inside after Suze, with Sian and Wendy trailing them. Morgen waited for Amar, but he paused to open the door of his truck. Lucky must have thought they were going on another adventure, for he ran over to investigate.

Amar pulled out a basket. A... picnic basket?

As he strolled over with it in hand, Morgen braced herself again. What dreadful thing did he want her to eat *now*?

"I've been thinking about your child charm," Amar said. "Since your other charms are effective, I must assume it will be effective too."

"Yes," Morgen said instead of the less confident *I hope so*. If he believed it would be effective, maybe he would stop trying to foist things on her.

"I've also realized that no matter how much I want our baby to be healthy, I shouldn't try to influence what you eat."

"*Yes.*"

"Even though you try to sneak minced mushroom balls into my meatballs," he said.

"I don't *sneak* them in. They're there to balance out all the meat you eat. And mushrooms are good."

His eyelids lowered. It wasn't quite a *baleful* expression, but it was a frank one that made her aware that she did the same thing to him that she'd been complaining about him doing to her.

Morgen lifted a hand in defeat. "You're right, and I'm sorry. I'll respect your choices about meat."

"Good. And I will not bring you organ sausages or fresh bones chomped in half to offer access to the delicious and nutritious marrow inside."

"You didn't bring me any bones."

Lucky, who'd had his head in the truck while they spoke,

backed out and trotted toward them with a long femur in his mouth.

"I considered it," Amar said.

"I see." Morgen made a mental note not to ride in his truck again until she'd cleaned it out and sprayed disinfectant all over the interior.

Lucky took his treat inside, clunking it on the doorframe along the way.

Morgen might have to clean and disinfect the house too.

Amar extended the picnic basket toward her.

"Do I want to know?" She reached warily for the lid.

"Yes. I got it earlier and have had it safely in a cooler in my truck. You will find it appealing."

Nestled inside the basket was a large box from the vegan bakery. Morgen squeaked and withdrew it, opening the lid with the delight of a six-year-old tearing into Christmas presents.

"Pumpkin cheesecake?" she guessed, catching a whiff of nutmeg.

"Yes."

"Will you have some of it too?"

"I will, but I thought I might give you bites while we're lying contentedly on the bed." His eyes glinted. "Naked."

Morgen grinned, suddenly in the mood to celebrate the night's victories. Naked.

"I'm amenable to that." She extended a hand toward the door.

"My home would be more private." Amar tilted his head toward his barn apartment.

"The entrance to *your* home was recently defiled by wolves. *Twice.*"

"The second time wasn't defilement. It was the stamping out of defilement."

Morgen wrinkled her nose.

"I'll carry you over the threshold," Amar said.

"I guess that's acceptable."

She admitted that she would prefer the privacy of the barn, especially if things got spicy. The guest rooms upstairs were entirely too close to her own bedroom. Her family might be ready to accept that she was a witch, but she doubted they were ready to accept that her werewolf lover inspired her to howl while they made love.

"Don't forget the cheesecake," she said as Amar swooped her up into his arms.

"Naturally not." He carried her *and* the picnic basket to the barn.

EPILOGUE

Ten months later...

Summer sun streamed through the windows of the repaired, reno-vated, and un-cursed workroom in the back of the ex-tannery now known as Charmed: Your store for magical jewelry, deluxe pet furniture, and indestructible toys for the fanged. The toys were a recent addition to the line-up and, judging by the squeaks coming from the showroom, currently being tested by the latest batch of tourists and their dogs.

Three-month-old Alonzo gurgled happily from his crib. The name, which Amar said meant *brave* or *ready for a fight,* might apply more when he got past his fascination with Lucky's tail and his own toes. Morgen hoped their child wouldn't ever *have* to fight, especially now that the Loup pack had moved out of Bellrock and Olivia hadn't been seen since the previous fall, but the town was still full of witches, magic, and haunted buildings, so who knew.

Since removing the curse and exorcising the ghost from the tannery, Morgen had been called in to handle three haunted mansions, a cursed carousel ride, and a possessed parrot. To think, she'd once worried she wouldn't be able to find enough work to pay her taxes.

Between the income from the business—now thriving with the arrival of summer and tourist season—the apps, and other odd jobs the townsfolk believed her uniquely qualified for, she'd paid her taxes and reimbursed her 401K.

"And *these* will fund your college education," Morgen said, holding a fuzzy green toy aloft over Alonzo's crib. He flexed his fingers and giggled with delight.

She'd sewn all the pieces together—a new skill that she hadn't previously imagined herself acquiring—and was ready to sprinkle the necessary spell components on the toy while chanting the incantation that would make it indestructible. That would have to wait until later, though, as that particular ritual required nudity.

On a phone call a couple of weeks earlier, Sian had primly informed her that a business owner wasn't supposed to wander the premises naked while customers were in the other room. Not unless the business was a brothel. Her sister's willingness to advise knew no bounds.

Amar, who was gluing carpet onto cat trees in the machine shop, probably wouldn't have minded. As he informed her regularly—and demonstrated every time the moon called—nudity was a healthy part of adulthood.

His machine shop was where the loft had once been. Instead of rebuilding it, he and the Lobos had removed the rubble and put in a wall dividing the large main room into Amar's space and the showroom. He'd decorated his area with chains, corrugated metal, and wood paneling. Morgen had, with Wendy's assistance, painted murals of cute frogs, dogs, cats, and bunnies all over the showroom. Amar spent as little time in there as possible and rippled a lip toward the bunnies when he passed them.

A knock at the door prompted Morgen to set down her work. When she opened it, her sister stood there.

Morgen grinned and lifted her arms for a hug before catching herself and turning it into a handshake. "Come in, come in. He's over there." She waved to the crib.

Busy with work, Sian hadn't visited since the week Alonzo had been born. Per a phone conversation the day before, she'd come up for "the obligatory cooing and praising that being an aunt requires" and a coffee date with Dr. Valderas.

Too bad she wasn't around more often. Morgen thought about mentioning that Zoe, who'd moved up to Bellrock—supposedly for the real-estate opportunities but really to date Mayor Ungar—had a number of Loup-owned properties she was still trying to sell. Apparently, the Loup lodge was available. Maybe Sian needed a weekend home outside of the city.

Squeaks from the other room trailed Sian inside, along with Wendy raising her voice to explain the merits of the toys. After her first semester at art school in Seattle, she'd returned to work in the shop over the summer—and frequent the hot tub with José Antonio.

"Those don't look like magical charms." Sian waved at the fabric, stuffing, and squeakers waiting to be assembled on the worktable.

"I'm still making those—" Morgen pointed at her jewelry-crafting area, "—but customer demand has been greatest for our newest product line. As a non–dog owner, you probably don't know how impossible it is to find pet toys that are soft, squeaky, and a joy to play with as well as being indestructible. The softer and squeakier, the more dogs like to rip them apart. But I found an incantation to charm my toys so that even *werewolf* fangs can't tear them asunder."

Sian arched her eyebrows. "Did Amar test that for you?"

"He and Lucky both did."

"I'm imagining them playing tug of war with a toy in front of your fireplace."

"It was on the lawn, but you're not far off."

"Such an interesting man you're dating."

"He's wonderful." Morgen couldn't keep from beaming a besotted smile in the direction of Amar's machine shop.

Sian made a gagging noise. One day, she would gaze in besotted rapture at Valderas, and Morgen would catch it and mock her appropriately.

"Babies like my toys too." Morgen held her latest over Alonzo's crib again.

He couldn't do much besides gurgle, giggle, and make grabby hands yet, but he managed to do all three as she put it within his grasp.

"Amazing anyone can be that excited by a lizard," Sian said, coming over to observe.

"It's a *dragon*, Sian. See the little wings?"

"Little is correct. Those wings couldn't possibly lift something of that size and mass into the air."

Morgen rolled her eyes. "Dragons use magic to fly. Didn't they teach you anything in college?"

Alonzo squeaked the toy and giggled again, then put the tail in his mouth.

"I wonder if a special teething line would do well," Morgen said. "It would have to be less fuzzy. I can't imagine felt tastes good on the tongue."

Sian curled a lip and perused the workshop. "It's arts-and-crafts central here. Do you miss database programming and stimulating your mind?"

"I've created a custom inventory-management solution for the business, and Wendy and I have expanded our app lineup to serve more than witches." When Morgen had told her father all about the business, he'd been quite interested. After Jun had called him that eventful weekend that her brothers had shown up at the house, she'd worried that he would lecture her about her weird new life, but as soon as her father had found out she'd become an entrepreneur, he'd wanted to talk about *that* with her. For the first time in her life, they had a common interest. He was even flying in to see her and the baby—and the business—in a couple of weeks.

"I'm quite stimulated, thank you," Morgen said, lifting her chin.

Amar walked in, not nude but with his shirt off and sweat gleaming on his chest.

"I'll bet," Sian muttered.

Amar leaned over the crib, lifted Alonzo into his arms, and showed him off to Sian. "See how *healthy* he is?" His eyes gleamed as he looked at Morgen.

She snorted softly. To make him happy, and because her diet didn't forbid it, she'd eaten a weekly serving of fish eggs during the pregnancy. Fortunately, he'd rewarded her desirable behavior with a weekly serving of sweets from the bakery.

"I'm relieved my nephew isn't furry," Sian said.

"Are you sure?" Morgen asked. "You study furry things for a living and find them fascinating. If Alonzo was covered in a thick pelage, you might visit more often."

"I *would* be interested in studying the offspring of a werewolf," Sian mused, "to compare and contrast it to a human baby."

Amar wrapped Alonzo in his arms and stepped back from her. "Our baby is perfectly normal, as normal as a child born to a *witch* could be."

He shared a smile with Morgen, bringing to mind the conversations they'd had on the subject.

"In other words," Morgen told Sian, "you're not experimenting on our baby."

"A few tests would do no harm," Sian said. "He wouldn't remember them."

"No. If you want to experiment, you'll have to find a willing werewolf and have your own baby." Morgen looked out the window as a familiar vehicle parked by the curb. "Is that Dr. Valderas?"

"He's picking me up for our coffee date."

"That's how it starts," Morgen said. "First coffee, then sex, then babies."

"For us," Amar said, "it started with me leaping on your car and growling at you."

"Yeah, but you're a brute. I don't expect such behavior from our refined vet."

Amar grunted. "He's staid and boring for a werewolf."

"Sian likes that in a guy."

Sian tilted her eyes toward the ceiling before walking out.

"Maybe I was wrong to call *you* the strange one in your family," Amar said.

Morgen leaned against him. "*Obviously.*"

THE END

Printed in Great Britain
by Amazon

79939951R00171